HER OUTBACK HOME

SMALL TOWN ROMANCE

LEANNE LOVEGROVE

To Princess, the best dog a family could ask for, we miss you.

PROLOGUE

November 2001
    Davey is crying in his cot and milk leaks from my breasts dampening my shirt. The sound seems far away, in the distance and like an echo I can't reach.

Bare feet shuffle across the floorboards and I feel the slight shake of the house frames with the movement. Or is that my head throbbing? No, Hannah rushes to Davey.

Daylight penetrates the fine cotton curtains; it must be midday, but I lay in bed. I haven't eaten, I'm not hungry. My head aches, my mouth is dry, and I yearn for a tiny sip of water. The bed coverings are heavy and my arms weak, but I am warm.

I hear singing, a lullaby, ever so soft and sweet. The crying stops as the music starts and then there is a childish giggle before the house is quiet for a moment.

The corner of my lips curl into a smile and I close my eyes for just a few more moments. That will make everything better.

CHAPTER 1

June 2019

       His eyes lowered to watch her tongue sweep across her dry lips. Those eyes darkened with desire and heat engulfed her body at the anticipation of what might follow; of his lips upon hers, of his hands caressing her bare skin.

Hannah stood on her tiptoes, daring those sweet lips to meet hers, to transport her, help her forget. She needed this moment, this man, to remind her she was lovable, was worthy, even if only for a short time; as long as the connection lasted, perhaps until the dawn broke. It didn't matter. Anything to block out the pain, the loss of her own mother, the mother's love she'd never known.

Their mouths moved closer; lips a hair's breadth apart. So, close his hot beery breath fanned her cheek. Okay, it wasn't romantic. But she wasn't after romance. She wanted the sweet bliss of forgetting.

She gently cupped his cheek with one hand, and the other

dropped to his butt. The noise in the rowdy Saturday night venue receded as hope built to a crescendo. Her heartbeat and its speed and rhythm against her chest cavity matched his as he leaned into her.

His head bowed and he whispered. A baritone simmering sound that ricocheted deep down straight to her core. 'You're so pretty.'

She wasn't but it was nice of him to say so. But there was no need for flattery to get what they both wanted.

He wrapped a strand of her wild, curly hair around his finger and pushed it away from her face. A frisson of discomfort spiralled through her tummy. The gesture was intimate, and her body ached for his touch, for his kiss, but not his kindness.

This guy wasn't her usual type; he wore a suit in this small country town in the middle of nowhere. He was good-looking in a city kind of way with his clean and smooth edges. But that's exactly why she liked him; it was obvious he was from out of town. There'd be no tomorrow, no strings attached, only company for tonight.

His mouth touched the corner of hers and pleasure raced up her spine, while her groin throbbed with longing. She pulled him closer, so their bodies became one. He gazed longingly at her and the forgetting commenced.

His phone vibrated in his top shirt pocket between them. He hesitated and pulled back slightly.

'Ignore it,' she said. Nothing could stop this moment. He increased the space between them and retrieved the phone and checked the screen, held up one finger, telling her to wait. He answered and she watched his lips.

The fire burning in her belly simmered and died out.

'Mum! Mum, I can't hear you. I'm at the pub. I'll duck outside.'

Rejected for this guy's mother. That hurt. Regardless of what she thought, his tall and slim frame disappeared into the distance, across the pub and away from her and the crowd and noise.

The moment was escaping. Her chance of oblivion disappearing. She desperately wanted to be held, and her body worshipped. But, oh, she knew, understood, it was so much more than that.

Hannah's breath caught in her throat as her composure slipped. Gone was the bold and brash woman filled with confidence of moments before; his rejection tore open old wounds, raised familiar insecurities and worst of all, made her remember. Maybe she should have picked a local lad. Grabbing her well-worn Akubra hat, her hands shook as she tugged it on, self-disgust and loneliness melded with sadness. The guy had left behind a full schooner of beer. She skulled the remainder and scanned the room unable to bear the thought of heading home alone.

CHAPTER 2

*T*he golden sun penetrated her closed lids and sparkles shone in front of her eyes. Sitting on a rock in the middle of the gently flowing stream, Hannah Wallace leaned her head back and bathed in the warm rays of the June winter sun.

Birds perching on branches in the nearby trees filled the air with their throaty chuckles; the cold water lapped at her ankles and the distant sound of children shouting and giggling to each other drifted over on the light breeze.

Hannah soaked up the familiar noises. She loved this place, her home. Even if it left her dead on her feet most days.

After her late night, it had been a hectic morning at the *Boondaburra Bush Resort*: guests arriving and checking out, families preparing for hikes, others purchasing supplies and her playing catch up with the cleaning roster. Her thoughts turned to food as the unmistakeable whiff of frying bacon and eggs drifted towards her from a nearby tent. Her tummy rumbled.

Damn, she'd forgotten to have breakfast; something else to add to her to-do list.

Should she roast beef for the cook-up this week or stick with pork? Was it the right time to commence another ad campaign? What about introducing a fancy new cocktail at happy hour this afternoon? Should they hold a Christmas-in-July dinner in the upcoming school holidays?

Trying to catch a few minutes reprieve, her mind swirled, business always the priority. The bush resort was her entire existence. A never-ending list of tasks to do and problems to solve. Or more recently, ways to improve, seduce more guests and make more money.

A niggle of guilt twisted her stomach. Dad and Davey were manning the desk while she basked in the sun. But she was entitled to a break, wasn't she? She wasn't indispensable, she understood. Well, maybe she was, sort of. Well, actually, hell yes, she was. She ran this place, and they knew it. But they could manage a little longer without her, surely?

The sun pinched at her bare skin, providing a prickling and warm sensation. Hannah enjoyed it after the overnight cool climes had them all hustling for a spot beside the indoor fires. She lifted her unruly long hair away from her neck, pulled it into a makeshift ponytail and held it on top of her head. She relished the cool escape on her skin.

A car engine rumbled in the distance. Could be on the main road and heading toward the Gorge. It was one of the most spectacular days of winter so far; this weather would attract visitors. The cooler months were the boom season out here in Central Queensland, and for the nearby tourist attraction.

The car sped past and her shoulders slumped.

But then the rumble became louder, and the sound of tyres

on gravel travelled towards her. Opening her eyes, she sat up straight. In the distance a blur of black flashed through the surrounding bush.

A caravan of large, black cars headed down the entry.

She tilted her head to the side, thinking. There weren't any other bookings that she could recall in the diary. Particularly for a group.

Hannah's hands scraped on the abrasive rock as she gripped it, swaying to the right to get a better vantage through the trees. But there was no need, the vehicles were right beside her now and the deep roar of a powerful engine shattered the peace and quiet; it was loud and unpleasant, jarring the serene environment. She grimaced and stood as the first vehicle passed by, a shiny metallic all-wheel drive, the leader of the pack. The darkened windows prevented a view of the occupants.

The second, a Land Rover Discovery, followed not long after and then another nondescript petrol guzzler. Did these people not care about the environment? The downside of too much money and not enough sense? Those cars would keep the fuel industry alive and thriving. Not to mention the polished sheen of the cars revealed they hadn't been anywhere near an outback track recently. They did get all sorts out here. Serious environmentalists and hikers, campers, loads of families for a cheap holiday and occasionally those desperate to see the beauty of the Gorge but from the comfort of a real resort. Comfort *Boondaburra* didn't offer.

Boondaburra was a resort all right. A resort of the bush kind.

Those city-folk with no desire to rough it were usually the toughest customers. They wanted their five-star restaurant and room service and fancy en suite. Not to mention air-conditioning.

So who were *these* people and what did they want?

Hands on her hips, Hannah balanced on the rough edge of the boulder, craning her neck to see more.

One hundred metres down the road the cars squealed to a stop, too fast to avoid rocks and pebbles flying.

Idiots.

The SUV's front door opened. One foot in a polished leather boot was followed by another, and then legs clad in designer deep blue denim. A snug fit reaching up to meet a lighter chambray blue fabric hidden by a sharp, tailored jacket in yet another shade of blue. A blue bonanza. The man was tall and lean.

No hat covered his light locks, worn short with a longer fringe. All this guy needed was an Akubra and he'd be the quintessential Aussie bloke. In looks anyway. Still wouldn't fit into the country, though.

As if she'd sung out a cooee in greeting, his head turned in her direction. If she'd been closer, her reflection would have been crystal clear in the silver aviator sunglasses he wore. She'd seen the movie *Top Gun*; no one she knew wore glasses like that. Particularly not in the bush. Most likely would blind anyone you dared look at and not protect eyes from the deadly UV rays.

But what did it matter?

If he was a paying guest, he could be all the tosser he wanted, and she would welcome him with open arms—him and his entourage and out-of-place clean cars and designer sunnies.

Perhaps their guests would learn to appreciate the environment during their stay? Hannah would happily assist in that regard.

The guy paused, slammed his door shut and reached up

and yanked off those glasses. His glare ran the length of the small path between them. A shiver crawled up her spine and the hair at the back of her now covered neck, stood to attention.

Was he enjoying the surrounding forest or the flow of the rambling creek?

No. No. No.

Realisation hit her like a punch to the gut. It couldn't be. What were the chances?

Did the guy from the pub last night recognise her? Even at this distance she felt the heat of his stare. All of sudden she felt naked. And there was good reason for that.

Damn it, Hannah.

In an effort to stay cool, she'd pulled her old white *Boondaburra* tee off and discarded it at the creek edge before she sat and soaked up the sun. She wore short, and she meant short, ripped pants a lighter shade of denim than his. And less new.

Exposed, all her layers were bare. Her tatty, old, sports top had never bothered her before, but now, she observed its age and the sagging straps and the slight roll of skin that sat at the waist of her shorts. Instinctively, she stood taller trying to balance out her bits.

Another member of the group stood beside the man. They spoke and pub guy reluctantly, it appeared, turned his gaze away from her. Others came to join them. A group of six. Two women and four men. All dressed for a night out to a restaurant in Brisbane. Smart-casual she guessed you'd call it. Overdressed for this place; more office-wear than bush resort.

City-slickers.

Were they two couples and two friends? Why did she care? Pub guy—whom she'd almost kissed, and more —seemed too cool for school as her brother, Davey, would say.

The screen door of the shop and reception opened, and other guests wandered out; children licking icy poles and parents sipping from bottles of fresh water.

The sun suddenly spiked too hot, her eyes squinted against the glare and her feet stumbled from lack of concentration. She swayed and her feet inched over the rounded edge of the rock. Her arms flapped like one of the birds in the trees and she came asunder. One foot landed in the creek bed filled with smaller boulders and she couldn't gain any traction on the mossy, slippery bottom. The other foot slid to meet it and she stumbled as she attempted to right herself.

Hannah blamed the scene she'd just witnessed making her feel all discombobulated. Or was it the handsome stranger? Her previous contentment dissipated like the heat swirling above her. She'd been walking this creek since a child and could manage it in all conditions. Not today. She tumbled and landed on her backside, her hair now saturated and sticking to her clammy skin.

DAVEY ERUPTED INTO LAUGHTER AS SHE ENTERED THROUGH the back door, wringing out her hair at the same time.

'Look what the cat dragged in,' he chuckled.

'Ha, ha, Davey,' Hannah retaliated.

'What in God's name…' her father, Robert, said taking in the scene in front of him. 'Hannah, you're dripping on the floor and making a puddle. Someone might slip.'

She'd pulled on her dry tee but hadn't bothered to dry off after her accidental dunking in the creek. The light denim material was soaked to a darker shade, but it was her hair that she hadn't shaken out properly. 'Sorry, Dad.'

Heading into the back office, she collected the "Caution — Wet Floor" sign and planted it strategically to avoid any injuries. Health and safety was always at the forefront of their minds at the resort; their liability insurance premiums were already sky high.

'What's the go?' she asked after locating a towel and drying her hair.

'What's the go?' Davey repeated.

'With the newcomers. Do they have a booking?' She moved closer to the desk and traced a finger down the large planner diary that sat on top, searching the entries for today, Sunday. 'Infinity Developments. Is that them, the three cars that just arrived. I don't remember taking that booking. Who are they?'

Her father leaned his back against the bench and shrugged. 'Yeah, I took that one only last week. Group of six. And,' he drew out his syllables, 'all separate accommodation. A scoop, so happy days for us. They're staying a week in the cabins.'

'What? They each have their own cabin that sleeps five? That's crazy.'

People did odd things. Nonetheless, Hannah understood her father's excitement. A week booking was good and five days in six cabins, more expensive than the powered and non-powered tent sights, was even better. 'Okay, but who are Infinity Developments?' she repeated.

'Unlike you, love, I don't cross-examine the guests when they make a booking. I just let them in. If they pay, it's no fuss to me where they come from.'

'Yeah, agreed. But most people don't book under a company name.'

The screen door banged shut with the arrival of a

customer. Her father turned away, seemingly bored with the conversation. Her brother, Davey, piped up and started singing.

If you wanna be my lover, you've gotta be my friend.

Spice Girls songs were his current favourite. As Hannah watched, he added in a few dance moves, swinging his arms left and right with his index finger pointed.

Hannah checked to see if the customer required assistance. She caught the look before it disappeared from the woman's face. Without fail, every time it happened, Hannah's heart hitched, and her mood slipped. Most people were pretty good, accepting and understanding. Others not so much.

Davey with his broad and open face with slightly closed eyes and puffy cheeks was oblivious. That was one saving grace, he usually was. The reactions of most people to his having Down Syndrome simply washed over him like water down one of the backs of the ducks in their creek. At least they could be grateful for that. Except she caught the look and reacted for him instead. That's okay, she was tough and could handle it.

'Can I help you with anything?'

'I need sunscreen please, preferably fifty plus.'

Davey, having paid attention to the conversation whilst still singing the lyrics had rushed away to extract the tube of sun protection. He handed it to the lady with a broad smile. Every task was a pleasure to him.

'Thank you,' the lady said softy, tentatively as she took it from his grip.

The phone started ringing.

'Davey, can you get that for me, please?'

With a curt nod, he raced away again. If her eighteen-year-old brother could run instead of walk, he would. Well, more like a shuffle, but faster than a dawdle.

As soon as the woman had gone, another customer came in. Sometimes it felt as if her full-time job was in retail. Selling ice and lollies over the counter was not the most scintillating part of her job. But it helped pay the bills.

This person didn't dawdle but appeared in front of the counter before she could ask if they required help.

'Hi there,' he said as he approached.

It was one of the young men who'd just arrived. This guy had dark skin and she picked up the slight twang of an accent. Unlike his companions, he looked more like he belonged in the outdoors. Fit and muscular and, well, adaptable.

'I've checked into cabin three. We booked an en suite and there isn't one.'

Hannah drew in a large breath and planted a smile to her face while counting to three in her head. Drawing out the moment she glanced at the diary entry.

'Mr Singh, we're very happy to have you here and welcome to *Boondaburra Bush Resort*. You've booked one of our quality cabins that does have an en suite. Some of the cabins in the park do not have a bathroom, but I assure you, yours does. If you exit the screen door and go to the left, there is an additional building attached to the cabin. It looks like a water tank, I guess, with the corrugated iron walls and steel door. If you enter, you'll find your en suite equipped with a toilet, basin and shower. I trust that will be suitable for you.'

The man grasped his hands together and placed them on the counter. 'So, to clarify, the en suite is actually located outside of the cabin?'

'Yes, that's correct,' Hannah said, and she maintained eye contact and didn't let the corners of her lips drop.

'Right,' he said and repeated it, 'right,' nodded and exited the shop.

From out the back, Davey started a rendition of *I'm in Chains*…and was wildly off-key.

Her father looked at her and raised his eyebrows. No point bitching about the exchange. It was her job to ensure guests enjoyed their stay and it was the best it could be. She did wonder though, why people didn't read the brochure or check out the internet accommodation options when they booked. It was pretty self-explanatory. She knew – she'd written the bloody thing.

'You go and have a cuppa, I'll cover out here,' she said to her father and moved away to sit at the computer and check out the weather forecast for the coming week.

CHAPTER 3

*J*ackson swatted at the fly that buzzed in his ears. He strode over and shut the flimsy screen door. Note to self: keep door shut if you do not want to be inundated with bugs.

His hand came away dirty from touching the doorknob. *Gross.* He ran his pointer finger along the make-shift timber shelf, and it was dusty. Splotches of grass and dirt were scattered across the lino floor. It was fair to say nothing was sparkling and clean about this place. But hey, they were in the country. Almost eight hours from Brisbane, in fact. And he wasn't outside in the bush yet. He was indoors in the best available cabin on offer *with the en suite.*

He could hear his team outside moving between their cabins, and their grumblings. Not really fair but he hadn't warned them. What was the point? They still had to come; they all did. And it would be worth it.

Jackson was sure the brochure advertising the resort had used the term 'glamping'. This wasn't his definition of glamping. The cabin was a canvas tent with a floor and enclosed sides. And it was true, the shower was private. You just had to battle the bugs and leave the safety of your cabin to use the toilet. He was pretty sure the pamphlet hadn't mentioned that. It seemed like camping, but what would he know? He'd never camped.

Jackson didn't care. It would do. They had a job to do and not for the first time since they'd arrived, a bolt of excitement raced through him. This place had loads of potential. And he couldn't wait to get started. He left his bag where he'd thrown it and went out to join the others.

'Jackson, have you seen the bathroom?' Monroe asked with her lips pouted.

'Yes, and it's functional. Would you prefer to be staying in the cabin without the en suite?' And he pointed in the near distance. 'See over there. That's the communal bathroom that the campers use. If you'd prefer you can shower there. Did you remember your rubber thongs?' He smiled, teasing.

'Urgh,' was her only response. He might have detected a slight shiver from Janessa who stood next to Monroe.

'Hey, what's that dude over there doing?' Hudson asked.

They turned their heads back in the direction of the toilet block. The building sat next to an open, covered concrete area housing picnic tables and what looked like barbecues and cooking equipment. In the middle of the space, a man danced. Fast, jerky moves to music they couldn't hear. A few of his vocals drifted up to them.

A small crowd of three or four young men had gathered around the dancer.

'Weird,' Hudson commented.

Jackson recognised the guy from reception. It was obvious he had Down Syndrome and enjoyed singing; he'd been singing in the shop too. Jackson was reminded of his younger brother, Samuel who had Asperger's. Sam mightn't look different even though often his intense glare and serious demeanour didn't always serve him well. But if anyone dare pick on his brother, well, it was one of the only times Jackson fired up. A similar feeling came over him now and his fists clenched. The dancing man's wavering voice and small shuffling steps backward made him suspect that his spectators weren't being kind.

'Hey. It's pretty obvious he's Down Syndrome, so give him a break, okay?'

Jackson marched down the small incline. Yeah, he was right. Snide comments were being flung around and the guy had stopped performing and stood still, his head slightly bent.

'I really love that song you were singing. Do you know any others?'

The young man smiled up at him with such gratitude, Jackson's heart juddered. After offering a reassuring smile in return, he turned to the spectators. 'And if it was the case, and I'm sure it's not, that any of you were teasing this young man about his singing, I might have to break some knuckles and have you thrown out of the park.'

The boys, no more than fifteen, scuttered in each direction.

'And don't do it again!' he shouted after them.

Jackson placed his hand on the young man's shoulder, 'I wouldn't have broken their knuckles, but it was fun saying it. I'm sorry they were mean to you. Are you okay?'

'Oh, yeah. Okay. Thank you for helping me. My name is Davey.'

'Hi Davey. I'm Jackson.'

'Hi Jackson. Thank you, Jackson.'

He gave a wave and walked back to his workmates who'd

moved under the shade of a tree. They exchanged glances but didn't comment. 'Only task for today is to set up our workspace. We'll convene in Roger's tent as he has most of the gear. Plus, there's happy hour back at the reception bar area later, that'll be a great chance to meet the owners and learn more about this place.'

His team nodded.

'What time does that kick off?' Roger asked. 'And I'm assuming there's no need for us to dress up?' He offered a twisted smile.

'Pretty sure it's four pm for drinks followed by an information session. And I'm guessing that we'll be the most overdressed there. Maybe we can wear our runners.' The group laughed, but Jackson meant it. They stood out like sore thumbs. Their objective wasn't a secret, but they could probably fit in better.

He pulled out one of the camping chairs he'd brought and set up under the shade of a nearby tree and nursed his laptop on his knees. Sweat dripped down his back and moisture gathered under his arms. And this was winter in the bush. Imagine summer! He didn't say any of this out loud, didn't want to be a whinger like the others in his team.

But he did understand from his research that the summer months were a time when few people visited this far inland because of the heat. He might have read the Gorge walk was closed then. Surely not? It was the only attraction for miles. He made a note to look that up later.

Jackson paused from scrolling through his emails and took in his surrounds. It wasn't hard to imagine himself sitting in a recliner beside a lagoon-style swimming pool right in the middle of that common area with palm trees and slides. That would attract visitors all year round. You can't have a successful resort running at low capacity at any time, it didn't make economic sense. It was implausible really, a business couldn't only run for a few months, could it? All answers he had to find out.

As he dreamed of the potential of the park, the woman he'd spotted at the creek earlier walked across the open green space, moving around a couple of kangaroos and into the covered common area. She placed her hand on the guy who was still wildly dancing, and he stopped.

Jackson muttered under his breath, stood too quickly and almost upended his computer. He recognised her. A fizzle of something zipped through him. What was she doing here? Was this fate? His mother would draw that conclusion, he was sure. After returning to the bar last night, the woman had vanished. His disappointment at the time was palpable and now she was here.

It appeared as if she knew the Downs guy. He offered her a puffy-cheeked and gummy grin, and she smiled warmly in return. He performed an exaggerated dance move for her, and she doubled over at the waist, laughing.

Last night, she'd had bare shoulders and wore a mid-drift that showed off her tummy, and her curly hair had flowed down her back. Now she was dressed for the middle of summer in shorts and a tee with her hair held in a high pony-tail. While not tall, she was slim and toned with tanned arms and legs but appeared strong and held herself with confidence, as if she could do anything, get herself out of any scrape. Was she a local? Was it possible she worked here? It sure appeared as if she fitted in.

She watched the young man as he walked away from her. From this distance Jackson could just make out the broad smile that spread across her face; a smile filled with affection and delight. They knew and loved each other.

'Jackson, can you come and check this out?' Roger sang out from indoors.

He glanced at the woman one last time before resuming work.

HANNAH HAULED THE BUCKET OF CLEANING PRODUCTS ONTO the picnic table and checked the contents. Occasionally, her father would sneak in some chemical-fuelled product that worked faster but killed the environment around them. He should know better, but he was lazy. Today all was well, only the usual, eco-friendly cleaning products were present.

The lunch rush was over, and Hannah wanted to give the outdoor kitchen and tables a wipe. The guests were fantastic at cleaning up after themselves, as was expected, there wasn't a trio of cleaners behind the scenes at the resort, but she always checked just in case. Today the kitchen looked tidy.

Two British backpackers were washing up their dishes in the sink. 'Oi, get a load of that lot. Pretty swish. New people in camp. Always makes it more exciting at happy hour, particularly when they look as hot as that.'

The girls laughed.

Hannah glanced up the small rise toward the cabins on the hill, where the backpackers were enjoying the view of the new group to camp, Infinity Developments. Two of the blokes gathered outside cabin three while the others lugged what looked like office equipment. That was weird. Why would anyone need a mobile office out here in the Gorge? Plus, the internet was shite. Getting a signal was almost impossible.

She squeezed the excess water out of her sponge, and stood watching at the basin sink. There was one camping-style table with a camp chair outside, barely catching the shade of the tree. Lucky it wasn't the rainy season, and even more lucky, in winter it was cool enough to be outdoors.

What on earth were they doing? Discomfort spiralled through her stomach but Hannah couldn't work out if that was from her confusion at what they were up to, or her brief encounter with the guy last night. She still wondered what his hot kisses trailing down her throat would have felt like. Hannah shook off the thought. Either way, something wasn't right. Her instincts went on high alert and usually they were spot on. Nothing about this fancy group gave her the impression they were planning a gorge hike. None of that bothered the British girls who were scheming a walk past the group on the way to the lookout. She could hardly criticise.

Hannah watched pub guy move into the cabin. Who was he? He was still dressed in his clean city-gear. She couldn't watch him without wishing he'd simply disappear so they could avoid any awkward moments that would surely follow. She sure as hell wasn't going to hook up with him out here, at her home. He might be on holiday, but she wasn't.

He left the cabin again. He needed a hat, that's for sure. His pasty white skin would burn quickly even in this mild winter sun. His skin matched his hair. Hannah could see his face without his aviator sunnies. He was youngish, her age possibly. Yeah, he was tall but slim, just like she'd thought earlier. His legs looked super lean in those dark blue jeans. She glanced at the group as a whole, they were all so darn good looking and polished and smooth and clean. Or had she simply lost perspective living out here in the wilderness?

Hannah glanced down at her outfit. It was all practical

workwear out here in the bush. Her shorts were stiff from the creek water and wore a couple of dark brown stains. Even her white *Boondaburra* shirt was turning an ugly shade of off-white. Maybe time to grab a few more clothes next time she was in town?

She'd give the visitors a day and then they'd resemble her too, so why worry?

'Excuse me. You work here, don't you?' asked a woman as she approached with a young boy in tow.

Hannah nodded.

'My son has a rash. I wonder if you have a first aid kit or any relief cream. I usually carry some with me but forgot this time and you know...' The mother shrugged.

The boy, around ten-years-old stood beside his mother with his head down. When he glanced up, Hannah saw the redness on his neck, spreading to his arms.

'We sure do. Follow me back to reception and we'll get you sorted with some light pain relief to take away the sting too.' Hannah chucked the cleaning gear back in the bucket, did one last look around including a quick glance up the hill, and walked with them across the green space.

'Hey. Matey.' She addressed another child. 'We love the kangaroos, but we can't feed them. They're wild animals and if they become dependent on humans for food, they'll not be able to look after themself. So, whilst they're friendly and will hang around here all day hoping for a scrap or two, can I ask you not to feed them?'

He muttered "sorry", and she caught his arm before he raced away. 'Want to know their scientific name?' The young kid looked blank. '*Macropodidae*,' she said triumphantly. He ran back to his cabin causing the birds in the tree to break into flight.

CHAPTER 4

The mystery woman he'd met at the pub ran the information session. She'd introduced herself and the moment she'd started talking, Jackson's attention was captured and time evaporated.

Hannah.

The sweet cadence of her composed and confident voice was seductive and commanded notice. His group muttered amongst themselves, and ordered fresh drinks, yet Hannah didn't break speed.

Jackson relished the icy cold beer he drank as he relaxed in the outdoor garden where happy hour was underway. Fifteen or so park visitors had gathered and he detected a range of dialects from German to Japanese to Canadian. That caused his gut to clench. Could the resort be an international destination?

Or was it Hannah who had his insides buzzing? Not only did she work here, in the last half-hour he'd learned about the Gorge and National Park and the local area. Hannah knew a lot; it was impressive and knowledge obviously derived from years on the land. Her passion came through in every word.

But Jackson had done his homework, too, and was familiar with the names and terms: Baloon Cave, Mickey Creek Gorge, the rock pond and the platypus pool for viewing the reclusive creatures at dusk or dawn. All nearby attractions. But there was one main drawcard, the Gorge. And he was getting the distinct impression the nice nature walk he'd envisaged might be a whole lot more than that.

His eyes roamed over Hannah's body; he couldn't help himself. She'd changed her clothes from this morning. She now wore a close-fitting, red top and jeans that clung to her body. His throat dried and he took a sip of his beer.

As guests shouted questions at her she brushed her hair from her face answering without hesitation. Those wild masses of curls spread down her back; in the dying dusk light of the day, the colour appeared more blonde than brown. As Ryder next to him asked a question, Jackson was thinking her eyes were dark like chocolate almonds.

At least his team were paying attention.

'I know it's hot during the day,' Ryder said 'but evenings get cold right? Can we light a campfire and toast marshmallows?'

The rest of his group chuckled, but Jackson remained quiet.

Hannah turned her attention to the group of six sitting in the front row, slightly to the right. Jackson glanced sideways at them, wondering what she saw. As he turned back Hannah scanned across each of them in turn. Did her gaze slow on him? Her chest rose and fell like she was controlling her emotion. Funny, she'd been animated as she'd answered the other questions. Were fires a sore point? Did he detect the slightest hint of disdain spread across her face when she looked at them?

'No, absolutely not. I know we're approaching the middle of winter, but we've had very little rain this year and we remain on high fire alert. No campfires, ever.' There was no smile.

'O...k...a...y,' Ryder dragged out the letters.

Davey, the dancing young kid, stood behind the bar and rang a bell. The man who'd checked them in appeared at his side announcing the special drink of the day.

Hannah shoved her hands in her pockets. It appeared as if she still had a lot to say and might be disappointed to be cut short. An elderly couple approached and had her captive for a few more minutes when they pulled out their map that they pored over.

Jackson stood as the older man approached him and held out his hand. 'I'm Robert. Welcome once again to *Boondaburra Bush Resort*. Nice to see you all again. More drinks anyone?'

The group put in their orders and Jackson followed Robert back to the bar.

'Robert, you're the owner, aren't you?' he asked as the older man bent down behind the counter to collect clean glasses.

He nodded. 'Yes, I run *Boondaburra* with my family. Son, here, Davey,' he smiled at his helper who was now expertly pouring drinks, 'and daughter, Hannah,' and he gestured behind him.

Davey is the son, and Hannah's brother.

'Hannah is your daughter?' He quickly made the connection.

'Yes.'

'She's very knowledgeable.'

'She sure is. If there's anything you want to know about the Gorge or the local environment or wildlife, she can tell ya.' Robert paused, held the post mix siphon over the half full glass of Coke. 'Have you met Hannah yet?'

Jackson shook his head.

'Hannah!' Robert yelled. 'When you're finished, come over here.'

BLOODY DAD. OF ALL THE PEOPLE SHE DIDN'T WANT TO TALK to, it was that group and *him*. It would be all shades of awkward, she knew it. Plus, his rejection still stung. She drew out the talk with the elderly couple who were planning their hike the next day.

'Best idea is to head along the Gorge track and stop at maybe the first two spots.' She pointed to the map. 'And then return. See how you feel. Many people walk out each day sometimes just to see one site. It's easier that way and if you have the time, it's a pleasurable way to see the Gorge.' They nodded their thanks and turned towards the bar.

Big breath, Hannah.

Plastering a smile to her face, she took one step towards the group who now stood drinking the cocktails her father had prepared for them, but a hand to her lower arm stopped her in her tracks.

'Do you know the scientific names of all the animals?' asked the little boy who'd fed the kangaroos earlier.

Hannah relaxed. 'Well, I know a lot, but perhaps not all of them.'

'What's another one?'

'Here's a good one – *Strigiformes*. Do you know that one?'

He shook his head and a long lock of dark hair covered his eyes.

'Owl,' she replied as his mother approached. 'You should think about doing our night safari. It's on each evening and we'll often see echidnas and marsupial gliders and Strigiformes. He might enjoy it,' she spoke to the mother but nodded in the kid's direction.

The man from the pub strode across and stood beside her so she smiled at the mother and son in good-bye and heard the boy begging his mother to do the tour.

'Your dad is waiting to introduce us. My name is Jackson.' Along with a loaded grin, he offered his hand to shake. His gaze bore down deep into her and her insides churned but she arranged her face into a smile.

Jackson didn't let on that they'd previously met, and neither would she. An implicit deal was made. But she couldn't ignore the sinking humiliation that this guy had rejected her for his mother. She didn't like the feeling one bit.

Hannah accepted the handshake and noticed his skin was cool and smooth. Geez, she hoped her hands weren't dirty. She pulled away first and then in an awkward gesture wiped her palm down her jeans before they moved to join the group.

'Here she is.' Dad patted her heavily on the back and spoke too loud. 'Our resident expert. If there is anything you want to know 'round here, Hannah's the girl.'

Six pairs of eyes watched her but didn't speak. Seconds passed until each offered their hand in greeting.

'Ryder.'

'Roger. We met earlier.'

'Janessa.'

'Hudson.'

'Monroe.'

'Lovely to meet you all. How're you settling in? Find the en suite, okay?' She looked at Roger.

He nodded. 'I did, thank you. Quite an ingenious idea. Provide an en suite that is an addition to the cabin. Tell me about the design of that.' He directed the question to her father who elaborated on the style of canvas tent and the requirement for a bathroom to be stand-alone but next to the sleeping arrangements.

'And you only have a handful of cabins with the en suite?' Jackson asked.

'That's right. There's a range of accommodation options available...' Hannah was about to launch into the variety provided when the woman interrupted.

'But don't most guests want a bathroom?'

'No. Actually, most travellers are here for the outback experience, not a hotel. So, they are happy to camp with their families. Others prefer not to lug around equipment and wish to avoid erecting a tent. They're also prepared to share facilities.' She dared them to contradict her.

'Have you had a chance to look around yet? There is so much on offer. Hannah can show you tomorrow, right, Hannah?' her father volunteered.

Her eyebrows rose in question. *Hell, no.* 'It isn't that hard,' she said instead. 'The roads are clearly marked and the map we provided upon check-in tells you everything you need to know.'

'No, that would be great.'

Bloody Jackson. His voice suited him perfectly. Light and breezy, pale maybe. Not weak but strength hiding in tenderness?

Really?

'Yes, let's do that first thing in the morning. We have a heli-

copter tour booked for mid-morning, so after breakfast say?'
He offered her a broad all-teeth smile. Those teeth were pearly
white.

'Settled then,' Dad said. 'If you'd like you can try your
luck at dawn with the platypus. Hannah knows just where to
look.'

'Yes, we might have time to spy an *ornithorhynchus anatinus*.'
And yes, she was a smart arse.

The group nodded, confused.

'Helicopter tour. What else have you got planned for your
stay?' Her tummy did somersaults, and she wished it would
stop. This group unsettled her, and she wanted to know why.
Well, perhaps it was just their fearless leader.

'What about the Gorge walk? Have you planned that yet?'
Dad asked. 'That is a must.'

'Sounds incredible,' Jackson agreed. 'We haven't thought
about that yet.'

'You've travelled all this way and haven't planned a gorge
walk? Most people only come here for the hike. It's its own
tourist attraction.' She couldn't keep the incredulity out of her
voice.

Jackson stared, and the group exchanged glances. Her
father looked like he wanted to jump in at any moment. And
damn it, he did.

'Hannah will take you. She takes private tours, on request
only, out to the Gorge and along the top, round trip. It's the
most amazing walk you'll ever experience, particularly with a
guide who knows her stuff.'

'You're just the go-to-girl out here, aren't you?' Jackson
smirked and this time his ocean-blue eyes lit up. He was teasing, but she didn't find it funny.

'Most people don't require a guide. It isn't a hard walk.

The tracks are marked and it's easy to find your way. I'm sure you don't need me.'

'Yeah, I think we're good,' one of the other men said. His chest might have puffed out a little.

'Do you carry gear?' one of the girls asked.

'Um, no. That's up to you. Pack light I say.'

'No, that would be fabulous,' Jackson again.

Really?

'We'd appreciate a local giving us the lowdown. It'll be much more efficient and less work for us. We're on a research trip.'

Research trip? They were conservationists? Scientists? These ones must have spent most of their time in the lab.

'Researching what?'

Someone tapped her father on the shoulder and called him away. Davey was flat out behind the bar and she needed to give him a hand.

'A potential new development.'

Hannah's stomach performed a funny flip. 'What sort of development? I haven't heard of anything?'

'Private development. A new and improved resort with accommodation and adventure options.'

'What? Where exactly? We're the closest accommodation to the Gorge.' The pitch of her voice rose.

'Yes, and that's brilliant. A real selling point. Here would be great. There is so much potential. This is our first choice but if not, perhaps next door or down the road.'

Hannah's hands went to her hips. Her voice lowered. 'What are you talking about? Does Dad know about this?'

'No. But he will.'

She leaned in close to him, paused and closed her eyes. Man, he smelled good. She was momentarily stalled by his city smell that hadn't yet evaporated. It was like soap on clean skin made moist by sorbolene cream with a hint of woody after-shave. Opening her eyes, she looked closely. His chin was free of even the slightest hint of facial hair. So clear she could see the follicles.

To their left, Davey collected empty glasses. They clinked as he stuffed them one into the other. His lips were moving with speed and when he had a tower reaching up to his chin, he paused and commenced to hum in a melodic and calming manner. Hannah always enjoyed the sound but the crowd around him stopped and stared. Some looked fearful, others amused.

'What is he doing?' Ryder asked.

Hannah bit her lip. She wanted to continue this conversation, needed to find out more. Get all the detail from these people and what they were doing and planning. But Davey was lost in his own imaginary and harmless world. With great reluctance, she walked away from Jackson and lightly placed her hand on Davey's back. It brought him out of his trance and back to reality. He offered his usual bright smile and immediately broke out into lyrics.

I wanna dance with somebody, somebody who loves me.

He did a little foot shuffle and got on with collecting the dirty glasses. When Hannah turned back, ready to pick up where she'd left off, the group had gone.

CHAPTER 5

*D*avey jumped out of the front seat of the ute and rushed over to the helicopter where it sat on the tarmac. Its blades were already twirling.

Jackson flung open his backseat door and chased after him. Davey had almost reached the chopper when Jackson slapped him on the back, placed one hand to his neck and forced him to bend at the waist. Davey was supple under his hands and complied. Jackson let out a breath of relief. He didn't want to see anyone decapitated today.

A third man, standing under the blades, laughed, and gestured for them to move to the left and away from the chopper and the dust swirls dancing in the air.

'I'm Simon. Thanks for taking care of Davey here, but he's been 'round these beasts since he was a little 'un. He knows how to look after himself. Plus, at his height there's no chance of chopping off that noggin.' Clearly Simon was the pilot and he ruffled Davey's hair which now stood at all angles.

Shit. 'Sorry, Davey, I panicked seeing you run toward the

helicopter. I didn't realise.'Hannah arrived with the rest of the group and stood next to Davey.

'It's okay, Jackson. Thank you,' Davey said and smiled in his direction, not the least bit disturbed that a stranger had tried to rush him away from non-existent danger.

Sweet kid. Again, like his brother, Sam. A sudden rush of homesickness came over Jackson, but he quickly squashed it.

Hannah smiled too, in an amused, what are you doing, sort of way. He shrugged. 'I didn't realise you knew each other.'

'Of course, we do.' Simon leaned over and kissed Hannah's cheek.

Simon was an older indigenous man with a greying beard. He wore his Akubra well, and was covered from top to toe with long-sleeved shirt and pants. *That's what I should be wearing*, Jackson thought, as he swatted away the millionth fly already that morning. They were dressed for the cool, not the heat. He'd learn.

'This is a great day's business. I can't thank you folks enough. You've ordered the deluxe flight and that's made this old fella's day.'

'Do you get a lot of business? Tourists wanting flights over the Gorge?' Janessa asked.

He nodded. 'Yeah, guess so. Varies a lot. Lot more during winter and,' he paused to laugh, 'if there are busloads of the Asian tourists out. They ain't doing no walking on the tracks. They want to fly above. And hey, why not? They're fabulous travellers.' Simon rubbed the tips of his fingers together and smiled.

'We're doing both,' Monroe pointed out.

'That's awesome. The real experience. Both are fantastic and from my point of view, necessary because both provide different vantages. From up here,' he pointed toward the sky, 'the vastness of the Gorge and surrounds will take your breath away. On the track, you'll notice the minor details that are just as awe inspiring.'

'Have you always lived out here?' Hudson asked.

Davey jumped in to answer. 'Nah, he was a cattle rancher on the chopper!'

'Yeah, that's right isn't it, Davey? Learned to fly on the cattle stations in outback Northern Territory. Now that was a blast. Chasing after herds of cows from the sky is lots of fun. Technically trickly too sometimes. Need to get real low to encourage 'em to move but not so low I'm touching the ground.'

'How'd you end up here?' Jackson asked.

'Born and bred from around here. So I saved and saved and came back. Wanted to keep flying so bought me own chopper and set up this business. The red tape, man,' he shook his head, 'but it's worth it.'

Jackson couldn't help himself. 'Well, we might be able to help your business in the future. We're looking at improving local accommodation into more attractive options for tourists.' He looked at Hannah who'd folded her arms across her chest. 'I mean the Asian market is a good example. I guarantee they do not stay at the bush resort. Do they Hannah?'

She remained tight-lipped.

'Davey?' It was unfair but he knew he'd get a straight answer from the kid.

'Nah, never. They want fancy!'

He was sure he saw Hannah control a jiggling foot. She obviously wanted to give her brother a fair kick in the shins.

'Exactly. Imagine those busloads of tourists who come out here. The money they could generate if they stayed. If they had a nice cabin…'

'With a bathroom,' Janessa interjected.

'Yes. With facilities, and a gift shop because they love buying souvenirs. Plus a restaurant because they don't cook on holidays. They want to buy their meals,' Monroe added.

'They can get all that at our resort.'

'Really?' Jackson challenged. 'Because they aren't staying. So, if they're satisfied with the available facilities, why aren't they?"

She stared him down but didn't respond.

A discussion for later.

'Simon, your business could expand with more visitors to this area.' The fixed smile had dropped from the man's face. He was backed into a corner. But he could see sense, couldn't he? Jackson wanted the support of locals, and Simon was perfect.

'I'm not just a tour guide,' he said. 'My choppers help out in emergencies. Significant weather events and injured hikers and stuff.'

Jackson sagged. Simon felt the need to defend himself and his business. That wasn't his intention.

'So, you have more than one chopper?' Ryder asked.

Simon turned behind him and pointed. 'Yeah, another one, there in the shed. I have a team of pilots but it's not their full-time job...' His words petered off realising he was veering back into dangerous territory. Simon stared at Hannah, but Jackson didn't understand the exchange.

'Let's get moving. You guys are in for a treat,' Simon clapped his hands together.

'You guys are in for a treat,' Davey repeated.

'Do you like to fly Davey?' Roger asked.

'Oh, yeah. Love to fly.'

'Why don't you join us?' Hudson suggested looping an arm around his shoulders.

'That's impossible,' Hannah intervened. 'The chopper can only take six and there's six of you. Davey, you'll have to sit this one out.'

'Bummer. Davey sit out.'

Simon commenced his instruction talk and safety guide. Jackson listened intently while his team checked their phones. He elbowed Ryder in the arm to gain his attention.

Ready, they moved forward.

'Have a great trip,' Hannah said. 'We'll be here to pick you up when you return.'

Jackson glared at her and lifted his sunnies.

'Yes,' she said. 'Dad's orders,' and she gave them a formal salute.

Davey's wave was more friendly.

HANNAH WATCHED THE GROUP EMERGE FROM THE HELICOPTER after the flight.

It was always the same. The rosy cheeks as if they'd been exerting themselves, and the flushed expressions and broad smiles. She'd seen the transformation a million times. People underestimated the Gorge. And it always delivered.

She waited in the car as each member of the group shook hands with Simon and when he moved back to the chopper, he gave her a wave.

Would Simon's business improve with a luxury resort? She hadn't stopped thinking about that since she'd dropped the group off this morning. She knew times were tough for everyone in outback Queensland, but he did all right, didn't he? Maybe she and Dad could have a chinwag with him about other ways to help out?

Jackson jumped straight into the front seat. 'That. Was. Incredible.'

'You sound surprised. What did you expect?'

He shrugged. 'Big rock formations. But that was something else. The colours, the range, the depth, the vastness.'

Hannah nodded, amused, but also impressed. There was a tiny part of her that had wondered if the Gorge might not work its magic on Jackson. The man was focused; focused on his fancy resort so much, that she wasn't convinced he actually saw what was already here.

The others climbed in the van making similar exclamations.

'If I was an artist, I'd paint a picture of the Gorge. Imagine the colours you could achieve,' Roger exclaimed.

The group cracked into laughter.

Roger was affronted. 'What? You belligerents. You take one hundred photos and post them to social media instead. That's a crap form of expression, especially when you're in it!' He sat back silent.

'When you do the walk, you'll see the aboriginal paintings and artwork. It isn't artwork of the Gorge itself, of course. But of their way of life. How they lived. It's incredible.' Hannah caught Roger's eye and he nodded in acknowledgement.

The passengers fell silent. 'You understand that's the point, don't you?' She half-turned to Jackson. 'The Gorge is a natural wonder. It's special and historic and to be treasured. It isn't a manmade construct where people pay an entrance fee and traipse up and down and ruin it with their human traffic, litter and graffiti.'

'Don't you want the world to see it?' Jackson asked.

'The world?' Her voice mocked.

'Yes, the world. It's not something that should be kept a secret or hidden.'

An adrenalin surge pulsed through her. 'It isn't a secret. But people who visit now, want to be here. It's an effort. A destination. It isn't necessarily a journey. Perhaps if we had a nearby domestic airstrip more people would come?' Sarcasm dripped off her words.

'Good idea,' Hudson shouted from the back.

Hannah groaned and turned up the radio.

'Thanks for showing us around this morning. Shame we didn't see any platypus.'

Was Jackson trying to mollify her? She simply nodded and kept driving.

~

'WHAT THE HELL IS GOING ON HERE?' HANNAH STORMED INTO the back room of the office and slammed the door after her.

'Hannah Elizabeth. That's enough. We don't speak like that. I'm terribly sorry everyone,' Dad said, always the pacifier.

Well, Hannah knew that attitude never got you anywhere.

Local state member, James Howard, grinned conspiratorially up at her. 'Didn't take you long, did it, Hannah? Did you smell the meeting in progress? Hear us whispering? Did the local spirits tell you?'

Jackson's head jerked up at the member's tone. His expression was one of confusion.

'Now, James. Come on, let's play nice,' her father again.

Hannah clenched her teeth as anger surged through her, but she could look after herself. Sometimes, though, it was like she was the only one looking after the Gorge and the natural environment while conservative liberal pigs like Howard did everything they could to get their own way and *improve the economy*.

'Looks like I'm just in time.' She pulled out a chair and sat with a thump.

'Sorry, Hannah, I invited your father as he's the owner, I didn't realise you might want to be present.'

'Yes, you did, and you didn't invite me on purpose. Dad is a pushover and that's why I'm here. To keep everyone honest.'

Hannah balled her fists in her lap. Otherwise, she might just punch each of the men in the face, her father included. The world of misogyny lived on. At least the rest of Jackson's team weren't here to add to the testosterone-fuelled energy. Three men, two in power-suits, was enough. At least her father hadn't dressed up for the occasion. Glancing at him she grimaced. She loved him and all that, but he looked like he'd just dragged himself out of the creek like she had yesterday. Perhaps he could have put on a clean shirt?

Howard was clean though; sitting across from him, his strong cologne tickled her nose. If she had to guess she'd say he wore Old Spice. An old cologne for an old man who no longer fitted in and had prehistoric ideas. At least Jackson smelled less city-clean and soapy now. She sneezed.

'God bless you,' Jackson said.

Refusing to be distracted by him, she ignored the comment and picked up a piece of paper lying on the table. 'What's this?'

Her eyes bulged so wide from the words she read that she thought they might pop. Hannah looked at her father. 'Did you know about this?'

'No. Not until just now,' he shook his head.

'Well, let me explain,' Howard said. Even his voice grated

on her. Making an exaggerated effort to remove his jacket, he slung it over the back of the chair.

'Jackson works for Infinity Developments. The company believes *Boondaburra* is perfect for development into a world-class resort and to maximise not only on the potential of the holiday destination but the local area, that is, to date, untouched in their view. I agree.' He paused.

Her fury threatened to choke her, her breath burning in her throat. Once she would have jumped up and down, screamed and shouted. She'd matured slightly over the years and had learned that acting that way wasn't always the best idea. Unfortunately, she still often felt like it. Instead, she gripped the cheap tabletop and collected her thoughts. They might just explode out of her yet.

'We've met a few times...'

Hannah's back went ramrod straight and she sucked in her breath. Infinity had met with Howard a few times?

'... and I fully support the idea. As you well know, Robert, I'm a big fan of development of my electorate. Moving toward the future, more money, more jobs, more opportunity. And I see this as a wonderful prospect for the entire community.'

Hannah picked up the glossy brochure. It was a small booklet, but the images were professionally altered to demonstrate what any potential development might look like. To Hannah, it depicted an impossible Utopia in the middle of nowhere. Happy, smiling families around an outdoor pool, surrounded by low rise accommodation. We aren't the Whitsundays she wanted to sneer. It did resemble *Boondaburra* but that was only the embellished blues and greens and the brown of the canyon. Otherwise, it was transformed into something beyond her comprehension. The images and the words accompanying them blurred.

'And you are here, why?' she asked, directing her question towards Jackson.

Howard answered. 'To show you the potential.'

She glared at both of them.

Howard changed tack. 'To help you see reason. To advise that if you agree to the development, the state government, me as the local member will support it. Pass the necessary approvals and applications etcetera.' He tapped his nose as if it was top secret business. Which it probably was as the shonky shark would pass it through parliament as quietly as possible, not putting it out for expressions of interest to the local conservationists and greenie groups, of which there were many. Hannah was a member of most.

Hannah looked to Jackson for his reply.

'As I said, I'm here to do my research. To confirm that this is a project that we'd like to be involved in. To satisfy the company that it is worthwhile and that there is potential. To secure a mutually satisfying deal.' He stared at her with those bloody ocean eyes. They were miles from the coast and that's where he should be, sunning himself at a proper tourist destination, not here at her resort. Now instead of drowning in those eyes, she wanted to poke them with a pencil.

'A mutually satisfying deal,' she said repeating the words and sounding like Davey. 'To make money you mean? Are you here to make us an offer so you can develop…your development?'

Nice Hannah, very articulate. They knew what she meant.

'Yes.'

'Should we talk about offers now?' Howard jumped in.

'No! The resort isn't for sale.'

Her father had remained silent and now raised his head.

Oh no, his eyes were hooded, and his look did not encourage her in her vehement stance. *Please, Dad.*

'I think I need to talk to Hannah. It's true the park has been struggling...'

'Dad!'

'Hannah, they've read the financial returns and business reports. We can't hide it,' he spread his hands wide showing the first hint of desperation.

'Dad, no.'

He refused to meet her glare.

'We understand things have been tough for a long time. It would be a very generous offer.' Jackson's tone had mellowed, offered hints of sympathy. As if they were here to help them.

'And if we refuse?'

'We have various options. We'd hate to locate another suitable nearby sight and enter into competition with you because that would destroy your resort. With the alternatives available at our luxury resort, I can't see that anyone would choose to stay here.'

'Gee, thanks. So, kind of you.' Hannah spoke through gritted teeth. 'There is a whole range of people who will not be able to afford your accommodation with its en suites and Egyptian linen and tiled bathrooms. Perhaps the chocolates on the pillow.' Her voice cracked and she hated herself.

'It is not our intention to cut those people out. There'll be affordable facilities of the highest order. Lots of sophisticated options in one place. You can cater for everyone.'

The room fell silent for a breath.

'Of course, another option is that you fund my company to design and draw up the plans and project management any development and pay us for the pleasure.'

'Sure, I'll just arrange that finance now, shall I?'

Jackson sat back and Hannah kept going. 'You are forgetting one of the most important factors. The environmental impact.'

Howard emitted an audible sigh.

'Yes, I'm well aware that is of little concern to you and your party, Howard. You're forgetting that this resort was built to fit in with the environment and make as little impact as possible. What you're proposing could potentially cause major environmental damage and risk wildlife habitat. And not let's forget the Aboriginal cultural history and sacred grounds.'

Howard let out a bigger sigh.

'Okay, that is something to be considered.' Jackson surprised her.

'Yes,' added her father. 'You haven't been out into the Gorge yet. Flying over the top is wonderful but entirely different to walking on the trek. You'll see the bush and the wildlife and the aboriginal artefacts. Makes a difference.'

'Okay,' Jackson said again. 'We leave for the big walk tomorrow. We can reconvene after that.'

'You can forget about that. I'm not taking you on the big walk just so you can size it up for redevelopment.'

'Hannah,' her father warned.

'We'll go on the walk with or without you. Either way. Do you want us to understand the significance of this environmental site or not?'

Cheeky bastard.

'You've agreed, Han. Let's do the right thing.' Her father's words almost made her lose it once more. Almost, but she held it together, glanced down at the Formica table and drew in large gulps of air.

Hannah had known from the moment they drove those three big guzzlers into the park, there'd be trouble. She'd been right. Her gut rarely let her down. But it wasn't just trouble, it was way more than that. They were fighting for their livelihood, their home. What would Infinity Developments do when it was defeated, and Dad refused to sell? Develop another site, she guessed, just as Jackson had threatened. And he was right. That would be catastrophic. Often, she refused to accept it, kept a blind eye, she knew, but the park had been on hard times. It was seasonal though. Damn, if she had to pull out a pile of excuses.

'I'm a busy man. Come back to me when the deal is done.' Howard stood.

CHAPTER 6

a gaping wound, exposed and raw could have explained the pain in her chest. But no, it was angst and frustration with the situation holding Hannah in a relentless grip.

Standing outside the reception area, in front of their home, the whole park lay before her. Man, she loved this place, could not imagine living anywhere else. She and Davey had been born and raised here, belonged here, they knew no other life. Understanding people yearned for more, but Hannah didn't, she not only enjoyed living here, she loved the Gorge and the surrounding environment with a deep passion. It had always been more than enough. *Boondaburra* was home, and it was all she needed. At the thought of losing it, the pain in her chest worsened.

Sweat balls dripped down her back as the heat of the day continued to bake the ground. She hardly noticed the high temperatures anymore. It was always stinking hot, but she never cared. And today, there wasn't so much as a puff of air to cool them down. Instead, hundreds of coloured butterflies fluttered around her. Followed closely by bright blue and orange dragonflies. Where else could you see these creatures? Not in the city. Probably not in the smaller regional towns, either. At her feet a frog hopped past and on the lush green grass nearby, kangaroos gathered for dusk.

Other people could deny it, but this place was special.

Well, perhaps that was the problem. They didn't deny it. Others were finally seeing what she saw. It was unique and this wasn't even inside the Gorge where the beauty increased tenfold.

The arrival of the local inhabitants, right now, at this moment, was pivotal. It was a sign. Why else had they arrived and surrounded her? It was a reminder of what she had to lose. At the beauty and wonder of where she stood, a calmness overcame her, and she was certain, certain of what she had to do. It was up to her to save the resort.

Yep, they needed to get smarter. Work smarter. Her guts churned with a mixture of emotion. A fierce protectiveness overwhelmed by a sinking feeling of dread; could she do it?

As it did every afternoon, the sun slowly sank over the ledge of the uppermost tip of the Gorge and the light dimmed in the park; it would be dark within minutes. The temperature was already dipping.

Her father came and stood beside her and draped his arm across her shoulders. Davey joined them on her other side.

'Is it really that bad, Dad?' she asked, her stomach roiling as she knew the answer.

'Love, it hasn't been great for a long time. Enough to keep us afloat only. You know that. You aren't silly. You try to ignore the figures, but they're real. Perhaps the time has come to work out whether we battle on or not. Is that what we want to do?'

'The problem is, Dad, that isn't the question for me. The question is, what do we do if we don't?'

Davey broke into the lyrics of *Lean on Me*. That kid didn't speak much but the emotion he could convey with song almost killed her. She reached out and dragged him closer to her side. He continued to sing. Deep down inside her Hannah felt something shift. With undeniable certainty she knew life from now on was going to be different.

IT WAS EARLY, SO EARLY, THE SUN WAS BARELY UP AND THE THIN layer of frost covering the grass crunched under foot as Hannah walked the short distance to the reception area and met the group from Infinity Developments.

'Did no one pay attention at the briefing the other night?' The words were out of her mouth before she could stop them.

'Huh?' Ryder grunted.

Charming.

'We ask guests not to feed the animals. They're wild and need to fend for themselves and not rely upon humans for food. Plus eating our food changes their tastebuds and digestion and everything.' She sighed. Sometimes Hannah hated hearing her own voice.

'Sorry.' Jackson stepped forward and grasped the last remnants of food out of Ryder's hand. He gestured to Janessa, but she held her palms up, empty.

'We'll just wait for the others and get going. Always a good idea to get some solid walking in before the sun heats up.' Hannah tried to lighten the mood after her harsh introduction.

The trio exchanged glances.

'What?' Hannah questioned.

'We decided to split up. The other three left yesterday for the big walk. Thought we'd try and get a couple of different perspectives on the Gorge, not just yours.'

Ouch. He was right though, but still. 'Experienced hikers, are they?'

Jackson stared at her but didn't respond.

Hannah had no right to comment. Most people did the simple return walk unguided. Sure, the groups were bigger if you were taking the long way round, but three was enough to ensure everyone kept safe. There wasn't much out there to hurt you, anyways.

'They did let someone know they were heading out, didn't they?' she asked.

'We know,' Janessa replied and turned her back away.

Hannah stood still and paused, head down. *Sanctimonious little upstarts...* She had a choice: lecture them, again, about their lack of responsibility, or let it go. Why was she always the cranky old school matron? Urgh! This time, she'd let it go. What did it matter if there was three or six people to guide? Less for her to worry about.

'Is that your gear?' She nodded toward the three small backpacks.

'You said pack light,' Janessa again.

'Yes, but you do have tents, right? Equipment?'

More exchanged glances. 'Well, to be fair Hannah. We didn't realise we'd be camping out. We thought we'd be staying in the luxury cabin option, not out in the wild.' Ryder had a fair point.

'Did your research well?'

Jackson smiled at her. 'Well enough.'

'We've got spare tents and sleeping bags.' She smiled her most saccharine smile back. She could play this game too.

'I'll grab them.' Hannah walked away and the kangaroos followed. *See,* she wanted to scream, *that is what happens when you feed the animals,* but for the second time this morning, she controlled the barbs wanting to shoot from her tongue.

And she'd leave a note in the book that a group of three had left for the big walk yesterday. 'The shop isn't open yet but if you need anything last minute before we go, help yourself and we'll fix it up later.'

Hannah retrieved two small tent bags from the storeroom. She gave one to Jackson who proceeded to attach it to his bag and one to Ryder. Sexist? Maybe. She wasn't sure but it didn't look like Janessa was built for carrying twenty kilograms. Janessa picked out red jelly babies from the packet she held in her hand and Ryder chewed on gum.

Good choices. Would she ever stop being critical of others? Hell no, not when they acted irresponsibly, she justified.

She lugged on her own pack. It was twice the size of theirs. Usually, they'd drive to the start of the walk but that would mean keeping a car there for the next few days and hey, if they were walking this far, why not a bit longer? Inside she giggled. It did add an extra kilometre or so.

They walked in silence until they reached the Information Centre at the entrance to the Gorge walk, then crossed the narrow timber bridge spanning the creek. Hannah advised, 'This is the last toilet stop, best to make use of it,' and the group paused for a break.

'There's Boolimba Bluff off to our right. It's a nice three-hour trek to the top of the bluff and back. An easy day walk. Of course, uphill one way, downhill coming back. An idea for another day as we have a full day walk ahead of us to reach Big Bend by this afternoon.'

The start of the trek was sedate. Hannah had walked it a

million times and she realised people must take comfort in the wide, flat, gravel path with bush surrounding them on all sides. In this section, you could still see the vast sky above and bright daylight. The environment and the track changed dramatically over the course of the day.

Hell, she might as well play tour guide. The trio might actually come to respect where they were walking.

'The Gorge is located in our central highlands and is about thirty kilometres long. Water flows in from numerous side gorges, and it was originally created by water erosion. The cliffs are sandstone, and we lie directly between Roma and Emerald. Some would say we are now in an oasis in the middle of the semi-arid heart of Queensland.'

Someone stumbled behind her.

'Watch your step. There're heaps of boulders lining the track and the Gorge. And keep your eye out because the Gorge is home to a significant range of plants and animal species. There's something like one hundred and seventy-three bird species. You'll see many ferns, including a special ancient range I'll point out, palms, flowering shrubs and gum trees. On this walk you'll see a range of landscapes and they will change constantly as we progress. Let's see if we can find any *tachyglossidae* today. That would be quite a find.'

'It's obvious you want us to ask. Which animal is that?' Janessa spoke.

She smiled without turning around from her position in front and called back, 'an echidna!'

Laughing, she continued walking. Despite the circumstances, this indeed, was her happy place. 'This is our first deviation off the track, The Moss Garden. So, we've walked about seven kilometres so far.' She walked them off to the left of the track until they reached a timber walkway that had been specifically designed to show off a stunning water pool surrounded by boulders and rocks and cliffs covered with moss. Wet, moist and cool, a haven of green. Such a striking difference to the open track. The group took a breather on the provided seats. Nearby, water trickled down the rocks into the pool.

'See here.' Hannah pointed to large plants lining the edge inside the timber railing filled with foliage. "These are *cycad macrozamia moorei*, otherwise known as cycads and they are an ancient palm, millions of years old. There is an abundance of them here which is incredible because they are at risk of extinction. They only live in certain habitats and grow slowly and don't reproduce often.'

'Incredible,' Jackson said, still catching his breath.

The others remained silent and gazed up at the moss-covered rock walls.

Ryder guzzled water, looking particularly flushed.

'Are you okay?' she asked.

'My heels are rubbing and feel a bit sore.'

'Do you have Band Aids or plaster? I have a first aid kit.' Hannah rummaged around in her pack. 'We can fix you up before moving on.'

She found the kit and sat next to him as he pulled off his boots. She picked one up in her hand.

'Are these new?'

He nodded.

Her adrenalin spiked. 'Have you worn them in?'

'What do you mean?'

'Have you taken a few shorter walks in them, made sure they're comfortable and fit well?'

'Nup. Didn't realise I had to. Plus, we weren't supposed to

be taking long walks, right?' He shrugged, like a belligerent child. And yet he had expensive hiking boots.

'Okay, take off your socks and let's take a look.' She crouched down in front of him.

Removal of his rather thin cotton socks revealed bloodied heals with the skin punctured and puckered.

'Man, that must hurt. I don't know how you've walked this far.'

Hannah looked at Jackson. He raised his eyebrows.

'I can patch these up but you're going to be in pain, and this is a long walk. I can't recommend you proceed. Continuous rubbing on these spots is going to cause more bleeding and bruising so that you won't be able to walk for a week.'

Hannah sat back on her haunches. People were silly and lacking in common sense. That's why the rescue teams were kept busy each year.

No one spoke as she patted on disinfectant and soothing cream. She admired Ryder for only flinching slightly.

'Okay. Let that air. Never ideal but I think you'll have to pull out your thongs and walk back in them to let this breathe and keep the pressure off. You'll be sore for a while.'

'Sorry, Jackson,' he said to his boss.

'Best not to walk alone so, Janessa, I'm sorry you'll have to walk back with him, particularly because he's injured. Seven ks back.'

1 AUGUST 2001

Oh, it's been the most exhausting but happiest of days. Little David is here. I woke early this morning needing to go to the toilet but that's been like any other day of this pregnancy. On my return to bed, a sharp pain crossed my middle. And then again. They came fast and caught me by surprise. One is never really ready, I don't think, even though we long for our swollen feet to reduce, for the indigestion to ease and the ache in our back to lessen, for the act of delivering your baby. I woke Robbie who jumped from the bed but then tiptoed too, we didn't wish to wake dear Hannah asleep across the hall.

Robbie rushed to the telephone the midwife. Sally only lives a few towns over and wouldn't be long she said. The sun wasn't up and there'd be no traffic.

Robbie rubbed my back and held my hands, but the pain was gripping. It hurt. I don't recall this much pain with Hannah. The tightening of my middle, clean stole my words away and there was no time to catch my breath in between the rapid contractions.

I'll admit a trickle of fear crept up my spine and I prayed Sally arrived quickly. But David wouldn't wait, and I couldn't stop the urge to push. Robbie told me to stop, to wait, but only a man would say that to a woman who cannot ignore the urge to release her baby.

We talked about getting in the car and heading to the hospital, but it was more than an hour away. Likely I'd be in the car and we'd have to stop anyways. Safer to be here, I said, no matter what. Robbie was panicked and I tried to stay calm.

In the end the little bugger slithered out like an eel. Without any graces, Robbie scooped him up and for what felt like agonising minutes he was still. I was still reeling, the cord attached and tugging and feeling rather uncomfortable. Robbie held him and I think he said later he slapped him on the back. A few moments more and he cried, and we did too. He was okay. Excepting, Robbie didn't look okay. He looked at the baby and then at me and I couldn't read his expression. He mouthed words but I couldn't hear them and after a short while the door clicked open, and Sally arrived. Sally walked in and took over and then he stared at her, looking, waiting for her reaction. My blood was curdling by this time and my body shook.

Sally ordered Robbie to hold the scissors she extracted from her bag and cut the cord. For me the relief was instant and the tension between my legs gone.

Sally wrapped baby David and handed him back to Robbie who now stood in the corner. He watched me.

Sally was speaking kindly and urging me to deliver the afterbirth. She knelt beside me on the tiled bathroom floor. Her knees must be hurting I thought for some reason. I leaned against the wall and did as I was told and felt the final release after a wee while.

Robbie stood near the open door and the baby cried. His body rocked from side to side like I'd seen him do a million times before with Hannah.

Sally attended to me and cleaned me up, gave me a sip of water. Eventually I found my words and asked for the baby.

'It's a boy,' Sally whispered, and my heart expanded with love. Robbie still looked startled. I held my arms out and craved to hold him,

meet him for the first time. I lifted the blanket and counted his ten perfect toes and checked his tiny fingers that scrambled to clutch onto something. His head drifted across my chest, his mouth opening and closing. There was a little tuft of soft velvety hair. I looked at his precious face and then the fatigue hit, and I was lost to my exhaustion.

CHAPTER 7

'We've lost time and it's almost lunch. Are you okay to keep walking for a while longer? We need to make up ground to avoid setting up camp in the dark,' Hannah addressed Jackson but walked away before he replied.

They were alone.

Walking in single file, the silence between them was deafening. Jackson heard each step she took, the rustle of leaves in the trees, birds chirping high up in the canopy. Would they walk in solitude or fight the entire way? Either was possible.

With his next step he walked through a fresh gust of cold air. His skin crawled and he twirled on the spot to check for hikers behind them, but nothing. He peered around Hannah, no one in front, either. They hadn't passed people since they'd veered off track to view the Moss Garden. Another cool breeze chilled his skin. He was usually a pretty level-headed guy, but he'd felt *something*. He shook his arms and legs frantically as if the invisible force covered him like a shroud. At least his wild movements scared away the flies.

Hannah walked on unperturbed.

The wind picked up and barrelled through the valley. A branch cracked and he checked to his left and right. Nothing. Hannah still didn't slow. He strode a quick two steps to bridge the distance between them. It would be disastrous if they were separated. But Hannah wouldn't leave him; she was responsible. Particularly out here in her precious nature. She'd worry he'd desecrate something significant.

The wind whipped past his ears once more and then all was still.

Too still. Like there'd been no breeze at all. Then he heard indistinct sounds and his body tensed. He twisted his head around, but again, nothing but bushes and trees and boulders. Birdsong?

He held his breath the next few steps.

What if something happened out here? He'd had a recent health check and received the all-clear, but you never knew, right? What if he overexerted himself and his heart raced uncontrollably and wouldn't settle? It had gotten out of control before, often did unusual things. His blasted heart had its own rhythm. His mother's words echoed in his head; declarations of caution from his childhood. Some habits were hard to break.

Oh, man, he was being ridiculous. First of all, he was fit and healthy. He had regular check-ups; everything was fine. He was unlikely to need medical intervention for years yet. It would come though, but not soon. Just the prospect of more open-heart surgery and his mood dipped. The recovery was not fun. But he wasn't here to think about that and there was no point worrying about something into the future.

Perhaps the solitude of the bush was getting to him? Did the noise and hustle and bustle of the city with its skyscrapers and bright lights drown out his fears? It helped to be busy. Right, he needed to get his mind back on track and think about the development and his reason for being here.

Hannah paused up ahead and he rushed to catch up to her. His heart didn't race but his legs were heavy. Or was that from the ridiculous pack he carried? Was this why he'd never camped? Well, no, it wasn't. He hadn't been allowed as a child, and who starts going bush as an adult? As a person who could choose where they went and stayed. And could afford it. Not him anyway. It was those childhood fears still hanging on too tight. Not that he didn't like camping. Well, to be fair he wouldn't know. But as his crazy thoughts settled, along with the environment around him, he detected the calm out here. A serenity that couldn't be captured in many places; a quiet seclusion. Clearly, it made you confront things.

Hannah paused at another side-track. 'This is the next attraction, the amphitheatre. Because we're heading up to the top of the Gorge, you'll need to see all these spots on the way, otherwise you'll miss out. Guess you could come back, but given we're here.' She shrugged but the movement was hardly discernible. Again, she didn't wait for his response. He wondered why she bothered telling him. He'd follow regardless, particularly at the moment when he detected a strangeness around them.

Up ahead was a steep set of stairs. Bugger carrying his pack up that. He went to remove it to give his back a rest but before the pack had hit the ground, Hannah sang out, 'Don't leave your gear. We'll grab a bite to eat up here and you'll need your food.'

Jackson held in his sigh. *Bloody woman,* but regardless he heaved his pack back on.

'Lucky, I didn't have too much breakfast,' he joked as he

sidestepped through a narrow crevice of solid rock. No response. Maybe she didn't hear him?

'Wow!' Solid, vertical cliff faces extended on each side reaching metres above his head revealing an open-topped cavern with a ceiling of blue, cloudless sky.

Hannah heard him then. 'This is what you call natural architecture. It's a sixty-metre-deep chasm. Quite hidden, isn't it? You'd never know it was here unless directed. They say it's been created over tens of thousands of years.'

Jackson craned his neck to take in the cavernous space. They were mini figurines in amongst the vastness, and for the first time today, he didn't feel like a blanket of heat engulfed him.

Hannah offered him a cup of coffee.

'How'd you make that so quick?'

She smiled and her face lit up. It reminded him of a cute pixie, maybe a pixie who could bite.

'Don't get too excited. It's instant but it'll revitalise you. Even though I'd recommend more water because the coffee will dehydrate you.'

Yes, Mum, he wanted to say sarcastically but didn't want to spoil the kind gesture. Instead, he said, 'Are we going to ignore the fact that we met the other night?'

That stopped her dead in her tracks. The cup was halfway to her mouth when she lowered it without taking a sip.

It was a low shot. He'd detected her softening, mellowing out here, in the place she loved and he'd taken advantage of it.

'Um, no.' Hannah Wallace was lost for words. It made him ridiculously happy to have caught her off guard. So far, he'd only ever seen her in control, and he'd frazzled her.

He placed his cup of coffee on the nearest timber seat, moved over to where she stood and pulled her in close with one hand to her back gently propelling her forward. She gasped, emitting a cute 'O' sound.

'I thought perhaps we could continue what we started?'

Eyes on her mouth, he leaned forward, zeroing in. She smelled earthy and raw, and of caffeine. Up close, this woman was intoxicating. Alluring. Her lips parted like they had the other night, and he recalled the tiniest of tastes he'd experienced then. He wanted more.

And yet, she twisted away. Her eyes flickered, darting left and right. He saw the moment she made her decision, and then it was swift. One flat palm to his chest and he was pushed backwards, removing his hand from her back instantly.

Steadying himself on two feet, he recovered quickly. 'If you hadn't done that, I'd have been disappointed.'

The look she gave him was quizzical. 'Let's forget about the other night. You were obviously busy and had better things to do.' Her lips drew into one thin line.

'What? You think I gave you the brushoff? Honestly, my mother was on the phone, and I had to take the call.'

'Yep, whatever.'

She didn't believe him. That's why she was pissed. Well, one of the reasons anyway. She was a pretty pissed-off sort of girl in general, he was guessing. But she thought he'd dumped her and used the phone call as an excuse. She was wrong. He'd wanted her.

'In fact,' he challenged her, hands on his hips. 'It was you who didn't wait. I came back and you were gone. So, it was *you* who ruined our night.'

'What! You disappeared outside the pub to speak to your *mother*,' she said it like a dirty word, 'and I was supposed to stand around waiting. Last time I checked it was uncool to leave a girl hanging.'

'Well, we're all alone now and probably for the next few nights. We can reconvene.'

'In your dreams, lover boy.'

'You can deny it but there's fireworks going off between us each time we're close.'

Hannah scoffed, drank the remainder of her coffee in silence, packed up her stuff and walked away without a further word. A pattern was developing that he'd have to get used to. A thrill raced up his spine at the thought.

The day proceeded with a plethora of sights. His inner well was fit to burst. Ward's Canyon—moist and green and such a relief from the heat that kept climbing. And different again to the Cathedral Cave where they walked a long valley of rocks. It smelled musty and as if the air was struggling to be fresh, caught in amongst the low-lying ground of the Gorge. High rock walls formed on each side and at times, the walk was wide, other times narrow. The air was cool despite the smell.

But it was the art gallery that most impressed him. Not because he was a lover of art, although he didn't mind it, but the sense of place and history was overwhelming. Jackson knew nothing of Aboriginal history that hadn't been taught in school. And that had been slanted toward the white invasion as opposed to the history of the natives of Australia. Left to his uncultivated mind, the painted wall in front of him looked like a sea of ochre. But Hannah pointed out objects and suddenly they were obvious: leaf-shapes, boomerangs, stone axes, hands, arms, stencilled feet. It was an entire mural on the rock face and at angles he could only contemplate how they reached.

'See over there,' she pointed. 'That's a coolamon and there in white is an echidna and goanna.'

'Coolamon?' he questioned. 'Okay, is that another scientific name for an animal. A kookaburra or snake?'

She laughed and Jackson liked the sound. He suspected Hannah didn't laugh often. Or have much fun. But where was the fun to be had out in the middle of nowhere? Surely, she could see the sense in having a bar where young people could meet and drink and listen to music? Could they get live bands out here for an annual music festival? Honestly the options were endless if you were open to them. Hence the problem.

'No, it's not an animal. That's the word for an aboriginal carrying vessel. A dish, I guess you'd call it. See the shape. Does that look like a kookaburra to you?' Her eyes sparkled with mischief. It was a relief to sense a young woman did live inside that body. An impressive body he had to admit.

But too soon the moment was over, and she lugged on her pack and strode away without waiting for him to follow.

CHAPTER 8

*J*ackson stood in awe. Hannah had to admit she adored it when people fell in love with her gorge. How could they not? And Jackson kept surprising her. Bloody man. So, he was human after all.

Big Bend was special, though. While there was water throughout the Gorge, hell, it had been shaped by water over the years, and there were many creek crossings, Big Bend was literally a bend in the river where the campsite hugged the water. The water met the sandstone walls, and it was like being in a safe cocoon. When you were at the bend, the Gorge surrounded you. And you became one tiny speck within something greater.

'Nice, huh?' she said.

'Incredible. The clear water and the sound of it trickling through the rocks is mesmerising.'

Hannah nodded. He'd captured it perfectly. 'I agree. It's unique.'

She'd erected her small light-weight tent while they

talked, and it was done quickly. Jackson was two steps behind her and hustled to do the same. Did he think they'd be sleeping in the same tent? Was that why he delayed? Wishful thinking! Hannah smirked. Not only was he a city slicker trying to take her home, but he'd also already rejected her once. It wouldn't happen again. As she hammered in her last corner peg, she watched him. Her thoughts strayed to what it would be like lying next to him in the close confines of the seriously tiny two-man tent. The flush crept up Hannah's neck so fast she couldn't stop it. She pulled her eyes away.

'It's only going to be daylight for a little longer. Best we get organised before everything turns dark. When we lose the light, it's pitch black out here.'

Jackson held up one tent pole and tried to fit it together. When the two pieces didn't fit, he tried another, and another. 'No one else camping here tonight?'

'Doesn't look like it. And they should be here by now if they were.'

He nodded.

He finally had his tent poles ready but the base layer wasn't yet in place. It was excruciating to watch. 'I'll just have a quick wash before dinner.'

'There's a shower?'

'You wish. No, a bucket.'

'Oh, right.'

The light was fading fast as she made her way across to a small clearing, not wandering far, only enough so that Jackson couldn't see.

Hannah filled the bucket with creek water and stripped down to her underwear and tipped the cool liquid over her clammy skin. It was sweet relief. She washed under her arms, down her legs and closed her eyes as she rubbed the washer around the curves in her neck.

Opening her eyes, a figure stood in shadow, close by. 'What the hell!' she exclaimed as she scrabbled for her micro-fibre towel and held it to her chest.

'Shit, sorry. It's only me. I didn't see you there.'

'What are you doing?'

'I needed to pee and didn't realise you came this way. Sorry.' He sounded genuine.

'You realise there's a toilet block right there, near the camp site?' and she pointed behind them.

'Yeah, but a bloke doesn't need to go into those stinky places. I can go anywhere.'

Whilst she couldn't see his grin, she knew that smile would be wide.

'Nice towel,' he said. 'So tiny. Must save a lot of room in your bag.' She looked down and the miniscule cloth was barely covering the lace of her bra cups. Her undies and bare legs were on display. Jackson's eyes grew phosphorescent in the dusk, and they raked boldly over the length of her and smouldered and darkened when they paused at the creamy expanse of her neck and shoulders. She shivered.

'That's the second time I've seen you in your underwear and I've only known you for a few days.' A slight pause. 'I think you're making a habit of this.' He chuckled but made no effort to move away.

'Ha. Ha. Funny. And both times I was enjoying a private moment.'

He stepped forward, his eyes captured hers and her breath hitched. She hoped that he couldn't see her inhaling deeply as her chest rose and fell. Those blue pools lowered to her chest and flickers of longing erupted deep down inside her. But

Hannah couldn't discern if it was lust, or a longing to be held and loved.

Did it matter?

The towel slipped revealing one breast as a branch cracked and fell to the earth. Quickly, she covered herself once more.

'Understood,' he said. 'Leave you to it.' His boots crunched on the gravel as he walked away. Oh, thank goodness, Hannah wasn't sure she could have controlled herself if he'd pounced on her again, like he had earlier in the day. Strangely, disappointment spiralled through her.

Back at camp the light was lost, and the sun had sunk behind the higher edges of the Gorge. The sky was midnight black with a sparkling of diamond stars. Jackson was still mucking around with his tent. The frames weren't even up. 'Do you need help?'

'Nah, I'm good.' He kept working.

'Well, let me get the light and I'll hold it up so you can see at least.'

'Okay, thanks.'

Hannah directed the beam of light onto Jackson's tent that still sat in an uneven puddle on the ground. She watched, amused at first, as he couldn't get the pegs into the hard ground and fit the elasticised frame together. She tapped her foot silently and held in a sigh. She admired that he was trying, but really? After fifteen minutes she intervened.

'Jackson. Hold the light.'

His pause was only momentary. Silently, he took the lamp and held it aloft. In swift movements, Hannah connected the inner frames and placed the tent into position before stomping in the pegs with the sole of her boots and the tent was up. With one hand he helped her trawl the cover across the top and fix it into place.

'Thanks,' he said. 'I never camped as a kid.'

'Sometimes these tents can be tricky,' she replied. Why was she being kind to him? The man couldn't put up a tent. Camping 101. 'Have you camped as an adult?'

'No.' He didn't elaborate.

A man who couldn't erect a tent. Said a lot.

'Okay. Let's eat.' She moved towards the picnic table next to their site. Various items were lined up ready. Jackson rummaged around in his bag before she heard, 'Shit,' and the bag drop to the dusty ground.

'Ryder had the food in his bag, and we didn't transfer it over when he turned back.'

'Ryder has your food for the entire walk?' Her intonation rose too high.

'Yep. Sorry.'

Breathe, Hannah, breathe.

'It's okay. I packed way extra. There's plenty.'

'I'm sorry.'

She waved her hand in the air indicating it was nothing. Two strikes for the city boy. 'Maybe you can pour the wine? I have a cask here.' She handed over the bladder without its box and two plastic cups.

'Clever,' he commented. He poured and held up his glass. 'Cheers!'

She paused her lighting of the camping gas burner and joined him but added, 'Cheers to Carnarvon Gorge.'

'Geez, I haven't drunk cask wine since I was a teenager.'

'Tastes good in the bush.'

'Sure does,' he agreed.

Jackson pulled out his mobile phone. He swiped at it and held it up in the air.

Strike three. Couldn't live without his phone. City folk had a lot to answer for.

'There is no reception in the Gorge. There's hardly any at the resort. No chance out here.' Her voice was stern.

'Damn it,' he said and kept touching the screen.

'Jackson. It will not work. Put it away.'

A look of anguish crossed his features.

'What's so important anyway? Can't it wait? You're out here to enjoy a natural and environmentally significant experience and you're working anyway. Surely you can take a break?'

He looked contrite at least, and hung his head. 'I need to call my mother. Despite what you might think I do actually speak to her every day. I didn't ring her before we left camp. I hope she's okay and not worried that I haven't contacted.'

Hannah's first reaction was to laugh. A grown man calling his mother every day? But then she saw his expression and her heart jumped into her throat and lodged there. 'Oh, shit. Sorry. And here I was lecturing you. Is she sick?'

'No,' he shook his head. 'But she's alone. I always check on her and I forgot to let her know I'd be out of touch for a few days. Bugger.'

Hannah glanced at her tent where a satellite phone was safely tucked away. But it was for emergencies, no exceptions. Not for checking on mothers.

'Surely you don't need to speak to her every day?'

'Well, I guess not. But I do, without fail.'

'Don't you exhaust topics of conversation?'

He smiled, amused, but she was genuinely interested. She could detect the white of his teeth in the dying light. 'You haven't met my mother. But no. I'm checking in mostly. She might need a lightbulb changed or the lawn mowed or some groceries.'

A familiar ache pierced her chest; all that was lost to her. The pain behind her sternum thrummed.

'Do you have siblings?'

'Yes, they live with her, but they're younger and aren't much help. They rely on her. And me. I've become the father figure none of them have.'

'You don't have a dad?'

He shook his head. 'My mum hasn't had an easy life. She fell pregnant with me and my father didn't hang around. Then fell into a succession of relationships and had three more children. He hung his head. Embarrassed? But he loved her so much.

'I'm the first to admit that my mum, her name's Jaclyn, has made mistakes. But despite that, she's raised her children and loved us ferociously. I owe her everything and now it's my turn to give back.'

Hannah's chest swelled, dismantling her own heartache. 'That's how I feel about my dad. He's always been there for me and devoted his life to me and Davey and the resort.' She looked pointedly at him then. 'We are real people, with dreams trying to keep our family business alive. No different to your family.'

The dinner bubbled, signifying it was ready.

'Thank you,' he said inspecting the bowl he was handed.

'It's nothing fancy. A rehydrated meal and the other is a microwave dinner except heated on the gas top.'

Jackson took a mouthful. 'It's delicious.'

'I'm sure it isn't, but after our long walk, it will fill the spot.' Hannah focused on eating.

'And in reply,' he said after a few moments, 'my company is *not* trying to destroy your family business. We are legitimately trying to enhance it if you'll let us.'

'But only on terms that you think are enhanceable? Is that a word?'

'There's no getting around the fact we're a business and we are in the business of improvement and usually, we make a lot of money from our developments, but only because we choose the best ones. That's why I'm here. To confirm this is a worthwhile venture.'

'Okay. That's easy then. You go back to your HQ and advise them there's nothing in this option. It's just a simple bush resort doing well.' Her voice had almost become a whisper.

'I can't do that.'

'Can't or won't?'

'Can't. It's not the truth.'

'And…'

'They know enough already. I'm expected to return with a sealed deal.'

She digested that for a moment.

'So, I'm clear. What you've said so far isn't exactly true. You said you're scoping us, but you're not, your boss expects a positive result?'

'Yes.'

'And if you don't?'

'Failure is not an option.'

Hannah looked at the kaleidoscope of stars. Gazing at them she felt small, insignificant. 'There's something in it for you, isn't there?'

Jackson pushed his bowl aside but didn't answer.

'And what does your mother say about you ruining a family business and developing a fancy resort in the middle of the natural environment?'

'Ouch. You sure have a way with words.'

A loud grunt and snort came from the nearby bush.

'What was that?'

'Wild pig. They live out here and come out at night to forage and hunt. They make quite a mess actually. Tomorrow you'll see the massive holes they dig. But I haven't seen one up close for years.'

'Oh, so we're quite safe from the feral pigs, then?'

'I'd say so. But don't avoid the question.' The grunts continued and Jackson kept his head to the side for a few more moments. He sipped more wine and refilled their glasses. Then the trees closest to them rustled, and he jumped up and moved around to sit next to Hannah. Their legs touched and they looked at each other. The skin where they connected burned.

His hot breath brushed her cheek. The closest she'd been to a man for a while. But this guy was infuriating. Infuriating for who he was but also, because even out here he smelled good. Was useless at anything practical but was damn good-looking, and she sensed a soft spot. Could she be wrong? What if he was playing her to get what he wanted?

He reached for his glass of wine and accidentally brushed her hand. His lips parted into a perfect O.

She didn't know quite what was going on, but Jackson made her heart skip too many beats. It felt like her heart was a beating living thing that was about to jump out of her chest. It rang in her ears so loudly, surely, he must hear it. His touch on her leg and hand sent tingles racing to her core.

'Why are you so opposed to making things better? Have you looked at the preliminary plans? Tell me what kid wouldn't love a zipline from the top of the Gorge down into the valley? Tell me the tourists wouldn't love ready access to their own helicopter rides from a pad located centrally in the park? A fine meal at the end of a long day walking? A spa to ease out the kinks and relax worn-out feet?'

Her body fizzed all right. With pure rage. She stood and bumped into him roughly as she lifted her legs over the seat. She gave him an extra shove with her hand for good measure but he didn't flinch. But she needed space, and suddenly didn't want him anywhere near her. He had a different idea and inched closer on the seat and his too-long hair on top fell forward. She would not fall for cuteness right now, damn him.

'What people want and what they should have, are different issues. Right now, we are in the heart of the Gorge. Not only a culturally significant site to our ancestors but a natural wonder created over thousands of years, that is home to wildlife and plant species. All of those things you speak of are manmade constructs for human pleasure. When what most people need is to restore their wellness naturally by healing in places like this.' She took a further step back. 'I hope you're prepared for a fight. I will *not* let you ruin this special place with your fancy spas and food. Let alone destroy livelihoods like those of Simon.'

'Huh. No, that's not our intention. He can work for us…'

'Urgh!' Hannah stormed off with the light and left him sitting alone in the dark.

CHAPTER 9

*J*ackson pushed the sleeping bag aside for what must have been the hundredth time. Sleeping in that thing was like being slowly suffocated. And since dawn, the heat had been unpleasant to put it mildly. He'd been hot and cold all night. It was a damn horrible sleep, and he couldn't stand another moment in the claustrophobic enclosure.

He unzipped the opening and emerged. It was still early, but the air was cool unlike inside the oven the tent had become. Stretching, his body temperature lowered, and he breathed in deeply, the fresh air going straight to his lungs and his grouchiness seeping away. Except for the pesky flies that buzzed around him immediately.

The tantalising creek flowed in front of him, and he dipped in his toe. The quiet lapping of the water at the edge teased him until he couldn't resist and he stripped off his gear and waded in. A quick glance at Hannah's tent and all was still quiet.

He let his body sink below the surface and the water splash over him. Within an instant he felt more like himself.

But it was short-lived. Emerging from the water, Hannah met him on the shore with her hands on her hips and wearing an expression not unlike the one from last night before she'd stormed off. The ferocious look distracted him from her mussed bed hair that was wild and unruly.

'It's forbidden to swim in the creek.'

Shit.

'I'm sorry I didn't realise.'

Her pointer finger directed him to a nearby sign that clearly indicated swimming was not permitted.

Double shit.

'I'm really sorry. I wouldn't have jumped in if I'd seen the sign.' But still, the water was so inviting, torture not to enjoy it. Bugger. He wandered out; rivulets of water running down his legs. Damnit, he didn't have a towel. In her mood, he sure wasn't going to ask Hannah to borrow her tiny one.

He glanced up but Hannah hadn't moved. With each step he took, her eyes became wider.

Oh, triple shit. He wished he could run and hide. Not normally shy but under her intense scrutiny he wondered whether his man-bits in his boy-cut undies had shrivelled and she'd be able to tell. Nothing to do but own it, he guessed. Bare-chested he stood before her and matched her stance, his own hands on his hips. But then he lowered them. This wasn't a stand-off. He shouldn't have worried; she was just working out her next caustic barb.

'You're just like every other tourist, aren't you? Beg off with apology after doing the wrong thing. The damage is done, Jackson. You didn't wash yesterday and the chemicals from your sunscreen and deodorant are now in the natural creek. Rules aren't made up for the fun of it, you know?'

'Of course, I understand. Do I look like a rule-breaker?'

She scoffed. 'I reckon you break the rules of ordinary folk all the time. Simple folk trying to make a living. You demolish their dreams and develop your own despite the damage you might cause along the way.'

He held up one flat palm. 'You might want to investigate our previous projects before you keep spruiking off. They are well-built and designed hotels and apartment blocks and large-scale houses. They are built to specification and within regulations. Our clients love them.'

'How many environments have you ruined before? How many innocent jobs have you stolen? Not everything needs to be modernised.' And with that she turned and walked away.

His skin had dried during the short exchange and he went back to the tent and dressed in the clothes he'd worn yesterday. Only one set of hiking pants and a couple of shirts to see him through the walk. Would Hannah criticise that too?

'Can you smell that?' she asked as he arrived at the table. At the same time, she handed him a cup of coffee. At least she didn't hold a grudge.

'Thank you. What can you smell?'

'Smoke?'

'Nope, can't smell it.' Pause. 'The coffee is great, thank you.' Would the entire walk be filled with this endless tension? He knew they had different objectives but surely, they could be friends. The possibility of being more than friends popped uninvited into his head and he squashed that thought down quickly.

He sipped his coffee as she returned to her tent and

retrieved something. When she came out, Hannah was punching some buttons on a hand-held gizmo and talking to her brother. She was asking about the weather and seeking information about any incidents on the trek. She listened and nodded, and the conversation ended quickly.

'Is that a satellite phone?'

Nodding, she sipped her own drink and started making them simple bread rolls of cheese and ham.

'So, I could have used that last night to call my Mum?'

'Technically yes. But it's only used in emergencies. It isn't a mobile phone and isn't used for that purpose.'

She was a real piece of work. A wave of disappointment washed over him. He could have called his mum and simply let her know he was okay. Then neither of them would be worried. Hannah Wallace was stubborn and always trying to make a point.

He made no further comment. 'I had to ring the resort and get a status check. I think I can smell smoke and I shouldn't be able to. There's a fire ban as you know. I guess it could be cigarette smoke but surely it would have to be nearby to smell so strong.'

Did she feel bad that she'd acted like a petulant child and forbade him to use her toy? He wasn't going to make her feel better with baseless platitudes, so he remained silent.

From their left came the splinter of twigs and snap of dried leaves, and a couple approached through the thick scrub. They walked spritely despite being their senior by at least twenty years.

'Well, hello,' they shouted in greeting.

'Good morning,' Hannah returned. Jackson held up his hand in a wave. 'Gosh you must have got an early start to be out this far at this hour,' she said.

'Sure did. Was barely daylight but ever so cool. We didn't stop at any of the sights—seen them all before—and made straight for here. We're doing the Big Walk and want to tackle most of the hiking each day before the heat hits.'

'Very clever,' he commented. The couple sat and joined them for a drink and snack.

'I'm Earl and this is Hazel,' the man said and held out his hand.

'Nice to meet you both.'

'So, you've been out to the Gorge before?' Jackson asked.

They both nodded enthusiastically. 'Yes, Earl, what do ya say? Three or four times, I'd guess.'

'Yeah, I'd say so, love.'

Hannah smiled. 'And what keeps you coming back?' she asked and threw Jackson a pointed look.

'It's a good, solid and hard walk. Tough terrain and a fantastic work out,' Earl said.

'Yes, all of those things, but also the serenity,' Hazel added. 'The environment and the isolation. It's returning to the land. A chance to enjoy what this fabulous country has to offer. It's real. It's authentic. We love outback Australia. The beaches are nice, but those fancy resorts aren't for us. A cocktail by the pool, nah.'

Jackson could almost feel Hannah's excitement bubbling over. Her chest puffed out and she stopped eating and listened to them intently wearing the broadest grin he'd seen yet. To emphasise her point, she delivered a swift kick to his shin to make sure he was listening.

'And you're staying at *Boondaburra*?'

'Oh, yeah for sure. Nowhere else for miles,' Hazel said.

'In our van. We're travelling around,' added Earl.

'And what are you two lovebirds doing? The Big Walk? Camped overnight, have you?' Earl asked.

'Yes, the Big Walk. We're heading the same direction as you. Probably see you again, I'm sure. We've got another smaller group up ahead we're trying to catch.' Jackson jumped in so fast there was no chance for Hannah to clarify.

'It's my first time. But Hannah here is an expert.'

Hannah looked at him amused. It made him strangely chuffed to have her attention.

Earl ate two Scotch Finger biscuits and drank tea. Hazel packed away their gear as quickly as she'd arranged it. As soon as Earl took his last sip, that cup was rinsed and dried and placed strategically away. These two were experienced hikers.

They rose.

'Before you duck away, tell me your favourite thing about hiking?' he asked, genuinely interested.

The couple smiled at each other conspiratorially, as if they kept the world's greatest secret. Jackson felt their electric connection and he envied them. To reach this age and still be so in love. Hannah was paying particular attention too.

'The tranquillity, it allows you to reconnect; reconnect with yourself and nature and that rejuvenates the soul. Plus, it keeps you fit and healthy. There's nothing like it,' said Earl.

Hazel placed her hand over his and gazed adoringly at her husband before saying, 'See you up ahead, no doubt. Have a great day!' And they were alone again.

Silence hung over them like a cloak, the absence of the vivacious couple obvious. And yet it wasn't quiet. Jackson heard birdsong, animals rustling in the trees and the water trickling over rocks. The heat also blazed with the sun having fully risen now and burning everything in its path. He pondered what the older couple had said and thought perhaps they were right.

'We'd best get moving too,' Hannah got up and moving, always on the job.

CHAPTER 10

They had to circle a few hundred metres back through Boowinda Gorge to follow the path to the Big Walk. In usual circumstances Hannah would have joked with her companions about walking in a gorge within a gorge, but not today. Yeah, she was being spiteful, but it was way more than that.

Jackson confused and unsettled her. One moment her body lit up simply being near him with his magnetic pull that she was unable to control; the next, she wanted to hurtle something at his head.

Yes, she was being mean. She knew he'd be interested in the narrow walkway where they had to step over literally thousands of boulders towards the ascent to the bluff. He always soaked up the information on offer; she'd give him that.

Surreptitiously, and every now and then, she checked behind her to ensure he followed. He was never far behind. Usually his head was bent, his longish fringe covering his eyes.

Regardless, she enjoyed the silence. Like the older couple

said, hiking was transformative, rejuvenating and calming. That was part of the tonic and why people loved it. It was eerie sometimes too, she agreed. Particularly in this section of the walk, a narrow, enclosed area where the sun light barely reached. The air was dank and unused with no plant life covering the ground or walls. Worn-away rock face protected them on each side.

It didn't last long though, and quickly they were ascending six hundred metres within four kilometres on the steep climb to the Gorge edge.

Hannah loved the confines of the lower gorge like secrets hidden inside a box. But on top, well, that was an entirely different experience. Vastness, open spaces, bright light, and a never-ending sky.

She turned behind her to watch Jackson admire the changing landscape. Except, he wasn't. His body was bent over, forearms resting on his knees while his chest rose and fell with force.

She closed the distance between them in an instant. 'Hey. Is something wrong? Are you hurt?'

He lifted his head. His face was blanched of colour, his skin glistening with moisture. He opened his mouth to speak but struggled to form the words.

'Jackson. What's wrong?'

'It's nothing. It'll pass.'

'What's nothing?' She placed the back of her hand to his forehead. It was clammy. He continued to heave air into his lungs and make exaggerated noises on each intake.

'I have this heart thing and sometimes it causes me a bit of strife.'

A heart thing that causes him strife? What the …

'What does that mean exactly?'

Jackson stood to full height. 'It's receding now. Sometimes my heart races too fast. Officially, I think it's called a heart palpitation. Skipping beats and all that but mine are so strong it causes an ache to shoot across my chest and makes me catch my breath.'

'You're having chest pains?' Her voice took on a frantic wobble.

'No. I mean yes, but I'm not having a heart attack.'

'How do you know?'

Colour returned to his face turning his cheeks a faint rosy pink. He breathed with less effort and took a couple of steps forward.

'Um, let's stop for a breather then.' And she led them to a couple of large boulders and helped him remove his pack before releasing hers. And then retrieved his water bottle.'It's empty. You didn't fill it up this morning?'

'I've run out of sparkling water. I don't like tap water.'

Hannah gritted her teeth so hard her jaw clenched. 'You're kidding right? We're in the middle of the freaking bush and you don't have any water because you only drink sparkling? Please tell me that isn't true?'

'I'm allowed to have a preference.'

'Not in the bush, you aren't!' she yelled, but she wanted to scream. 'Bloody hell. You're telling me you're having chest pains and now you have no water. What were you planning to drink for the remainder of the walk? Your own urine like Bear Grylls?'

'Now you're being ridiculous…'

'I'm being ridiculous? Can you please lower your standards for a moment and drink this?' she resisted throwing the water bottle at him. While he drank, she extracted another full bottle she'd prepared earlier this morning. He could keep one.

'We just don't agree on anything, do we?' he commented as drips of water dribbled down his chin.

'It doesn't appear so.'

'I'm fine. Let's keep going.' He rose and picked up his pack. She watched him to ensure he didn't keel over. He walked on and she pulled in step beside him.

'If I'm not going to worry and watch over you like a hawk the remainder of this trip, you'll have to give me more info.'

He nodded but she had the sense it was reluctant. They walked in step along the narrow ridges.

'I was born with aortic valve disease. It's a congenital heart condition. So, essentially, I have a faulty aortic valve. The valves around the heart are kind of important as they allow blood to flow in one direction and not backward. Anyway, I had it replaced a few years back with a pig's valve. It'll eventually wear out, too, and it'll be exchanged for a new and better version. Should have a good ten years in me though.'

'I'm fine as long as the replacement valve continues to work. The open-heart surgery is a bugger, unpleasant as you can imagine, but a necessary evil. I have a large scar. Want to see it?'

He pulled up his shirt and sure enough from just under his collar bone to his navel was a long, narrow scar. It was ridged and she had the urge to run her finger along it and feel the smoothness of the repaired skin. Strange how she hadn't noticed it this morning when he'd been standing like a bronzed beauty in the water. His skin wasn't as pale as she'd imagined.

'So, you live pretty much a normal life? But how can that be when you were struggling to breathe only moments ago?'

'I'm not even sure it's related. Shortness of breath is a symptom of a deteriorating valve, but I've had my check-ups and been given the all-clear for the moment. Lots of people have palpitations. Has your heart ever raced so fast it makes you stop what you're doing?'

Yeah. When you're around, but she didn't say that. 'No.'

'Okay. You're one of the few. I get it regularly and more often if I'm stressed or exerting myself. It always settles back down.'

'So, are you stressed or overdoing it?'

He stared at her, holding her gaze a moment too long. She squirmed.

He shrugged.

'Well, that sucks for you. How has that worked out for you over the years?'

'Honestly. It's not a big deal. I can do anything.'

He paused for too long.

'When I was a kid, I wasn't allowed to do much. I guess less was known about the condition then. So, often I wasn't allowed to go outside and play with my friends.'

'You weren't allowed to play?'

'Oh, well. Of course. Sorry I meant sport more specifically. No team sports or where there was a chance I'd get hurt or yeah, over do it.'

'Bummer.'

'Yeah. Because kids want to kick the ball around at lunch or play tiggy or be a member of the rugby team. So, when you can't do any of those things, you don't make friends and people ignore you, well, because what's the point of asking the kid who always says no and isn't any fun? My mother overprotected me too, being her eldest and first child. She was daunted by my health. It held me back a lot.'

'Plus, she was a single mum with no support and I'm guessing not a lot of money.'

'Spot on.'

'I guess that explains your rubbish camping skills,' Hannah tried to lighten the mood.

Jackson pulled up sharp and Hannah almost ran into his back. 'Holy shit. Will you look at that?' he pointed across the flat plain; they'd reached the top of the Gorge. Talking had made those four ks go so much faster.

'Yeah, wild brumbies.' Her face lit up with a grin. 'They're everywhere up here. You won't see them in the lower gorge, they're a treat for the top only and to reward walkers who hike this far.'

'That horse is magnificent,' he said and lowered to his knees, captivated by the creature. The snowflake-coloured wild horse stood on its hindlegs and neighed. The horses bunched close-by twitched their ears and pounded the earth with their hooves in response. It was like they enjoyed an animated conversation.

Within seconds the mare was back on four legs and racing away.

Jackson watched it gallop into the distance across the flat plains. He shook his head, 'I don't have enough adjectives for this place. It's incredible.'

'Welcome to *Battleship Spur*.'

Hannah was shocked again at his appreciation of the power and splendour of the Gorge. It was a wonderful reminder that Jackson wasn't immune to beauty and was human after all.

Standing at the upper rim of the Gorge was like being on top of the world. If they raised their fingers, they could touch the blue, cloudless sky and yet reach for the horizon as well that spanned hundreds of kilometres in front of them.

Hannah released the clips around her waist and dropped

her pack. She unzipped the top pocket, extracted the satellite phone and handed it to Jackson. He took it and she nodded.

'Thank you.'

∾

HANNAH BUSIED HERSELF MAKING WRAPS FOR LUNCH BUT eavesdropped on Jackson's conversation with his mother. How could she not?

Her limbs went gooey and the cheese she held almost landed in the dirt. Right at this moment, Hannah wanted to devour him and not the food she prepared; she wanted to eat him all up in one gulp.

Oh, the way he spoke to his mother. There was no faking that affection. He genuinely cared for her and had been worried about her since they last spoke. He told her he loved her and Hannah nearly wept.

Jackson Kelly was a living breathing cliché; that one about how a boy treats his mother. Well, Jackson had passed with flying colours. OMG.

Jackson rang off after only a few more moments.

'You could have spoken for longer. It's okay.'

'No way. Thank you. That was enough. She's fine.'

'I'm glad.' And she handed him a wrap. 'Gourmet today. My specialty kebab with cheese and salami sticks.' She smiled warmly at him and meant it. For the moment anyway.

He peered inside. 'That's clever. The pre-prepared sticks don't require refrigeration and encased in the trusty old white tortilla makes it delicious.' He took a big bite to prove it.

'What's your mum do?'

'For work, you mean?'

She nodded.

'She didn't work for a long time. Raised us kids only. But she's super-smart so later in life I encouraged her to study, and she went to uni and trained to be a social worker.'

'Are you serious? That's incredible.'

'Yeah, she's pretty amazing. And she absolutely loves it. One of her fortes is caring for others and she excels at it.'

'Gosh, that must have been hard, studying and being a single mother. Plus, the cost.'

Jackson dipped his head, went silent.

'What?'

'I owed my mum. So, once I was working and earning money, I paid for her studies.'

She wanted to eat him with custard and cherries.

'Do you love what you do?' It was a loaded question and Hannah knew, somewhere, deep, down inside, she wanted to emphasise his flaws after all the nicety. He wasn't perfect, right?

Jackson paused and she jumped on it.

'That says a lot.'

'No. It doesn't. It indicates that I'm thinking about my answer. I do enjoy my work and I need to put it in context for it to make sense. You know my background and understand that we weren't a prosperous family and life was tough some-times. I left school too early and became a labourer. I mean, look at me, Hannah, do I look like a builder? This frame isn't designed for lugging around bags of concrete or timber slabs. It was brutal and I didn't fit into the male landscape. I didn't bond with my fellow workers, you might say. Those blokes are tough and hold a certain view of the world. It wasn't for me. But working on building sites you meet all sorts, and I watched the developers arrive in their new shiny cars, wearing their suits...'

He looked at her.

'Yes, I'm thinking exactly what you think I am,' she said and controlled her eye-roll.

'But you have to understand. To me it looked like they had their whole world at their feet and well, at the time I had nothing. It took time but eventually I secured a position at one of those companies and things improved dramatically.'

'What? You had money?'

'Yes. We needed it. And I had great motivation. I wanted extra for my Mum and my siblings. Plus, for my health.' He held up his hand pre-empting her. 'It's fine and there shouldn't be any complications, but I need to make sure I have the funds for a rainy day. After surgery, I need time-off as you can imagine. So, give me some credit, it hasn't been entirely selfish.'

'I understand we need money. I need money. The resort needs customers so we make a profit and can stay afloat and pay our bills. But there is more to life than making a million dollars. Particularly when there are other stakes. Like the environment. You can never justify ruining something irreplaceable on the basis of greed.'

'At the risk of getting back onto dangerous territory, you still haven't told me how I'm ruining the environment.'

'C'mon. You're playing games with me. I can tell you with absolute certainty that the plans you have do not co-exist with the natural environment. The bush resort is minimalist to cater for and work within those surrounds. And you know it. That's what makes this worse. You keep saying the environment will not suffer with authority, but you know that's simply not true. You can't construct new and modern buildings and accommodate fancy spa baths and pools without it affecting the water supply and the very basic foundations of the natural world upon which it is built.'

'Don't you ever desire more?'

'What?' the words spluttered. 'What are you talking about?'

'You've always lived at the resort. Born and raised here, and as an adult you now help your dad.'

'Your point?' She controlled the snarl curling at the corners of her lips.

'Well, what does Hannah Wallace want? Surely as a kid growing up you wanted to be something, go somewhere, do other things?

'Life isn't always that simple,' she said.

'No, I know life isn't simple. But you can still dream.'

'Why? Why dream about something you can't have and that will never be?' Her voice rose and her body trembled. 'Yes, I had dreams. And you know what? They were torn away when my mother decided that having a disabled son wasn't to her liking. It was too hard for her, and she couldn't cope and left. Left behind a baby. And me, to find a better life. A life without children. So, yes, I dreamed I might be a vet or environmentalist or a scientist. Anything to do with the environment. Anything to save the world we live in. It's what I care about. But to do that I had to move away. Away from Davey and my dad. They needed me. Need me. And I will never shirk from my responsibilities like my mother did.'

The words sat heavy in the air.

'Whoa. I'm sorry. It wasn't my intention to attack you or open old wounds. I know what it's like to have responsibility. I'm driven too. To provide for my family so they are not hungry and can have the things they need. I was that kid who didn't have school shoes and a homemade lunch. Because of me, my family is independent...'

'And I really admire that,' she interrupted. 'You obviously

work hard but surely there are other jobs that pay decent money and allow you to care for your family?'

He wasn't finished. 'And I admire your passion for the environment. Man, the natural world doesn't realise how lucky it is to have you on its side.' He smiled, but he was he making fun of her? 'I do enjoy my job…'

'You keep saying that like you're trying to convince yourself.'

'I'm not,' Jackson shook his head. 'But I'm not going to say it's my passion. I like nice buildings and designs that I've created. I do. It is a satisfying sense of achievement. But I imagine it's not the same as saving a one-hundred-year-old tree.'

Hannah laughed and packed up their lunch. The brumby appeared at the edge of the grassy plateau where they rested. Tufts of grass sprang up across the space mixed in now with smaller boulders and rocks. The horse shifted and rested quietly under a tree.

Jackson moved close and placed his fingers over hers, stilling them. She gazed at their cupped hands. His, smooth and pale covering her weathered and tanned hand. The contrast obvious, and making it apparent they weren't a match. She snuck a look at him under her lashes. His eyes had that sparkle of excitement, of wonder, again. She followed his gaze.

The horse was near. It stood still, ears pricked, listening. Like before, the pack remained at a distance, as if waiting for her call. Then it reared on its hind legs and repeated the action again.

'What's up with her?'

Hannah shrugged. 'They're very intuitive. Maybe there's a predator or it's been spooked by something. Occasionally a storm will work them up, but the sky is cloudless and blue, and I can't smell any rain.'

'I'm going to name her Tiffany.'

She laughed. 'Tiffany? Why?'

'Because she reminds me of a white diamond.'

Tiffany paced back and forth in front of them as the pack tittered and neighed nearby.

'And that's exactly why we're opposites. You see a white horse and picture diamonds from an expensive brand. I see that wild horse and imagine it roaming free and living in its natural environment away from the harm of man. And with a name that suits her habitat and spirit, something tough yet liberating.' She turned away to collect her gear, reluctantly pulling her hand free. Once the pack was on her back, she said, 'Let's keep moving. We have a few hours ahead of us before we hit camp.'

Before she hurried away, Jackson grasped her forearm. 'I'm really sorry about your mum.'

Hannah nodded but didn't reply. Without waiting for him she strode ahead.

CHAPTER 11

The whinnying of horses close-by woke Hannah. Brays high-pitched like a child's squeal, quick and in succession.

Fully awake now, she smelled smoke. Climbing out of her sleeping bag she ripped the tent open and observed a grey-filled patch of sky.

'Jackson. Wake up!' she yelled at his tent as she fumbled through her gear to find the satellite phone.

He emerged from his tent, sleepy and rubbing his eyes. She saw the moment he realised. His eyes went from half-closed to wide-awake and alert when he registered the threatening sky and the smoke-filled horizon. 'What's going on?'

'There's a fire.' Hannah worked the phone and held it to her ear praying her father or Davey were already awake. It answered. 'Davey! Thank goodness. Has anyone reported a fire on the top of the Gorge, somewhere near Gadds?' She used the abbreviated name for *Gadds Walkers Camp*, the spot they'd camped last night. Hannah listened and waited while Davey checked with her father and emergency services.

'Okay. Well, I'm telling you there's a fire. I have no idea about details or the exact location but contact the authorities and I'll find out more.' She threw the phone down and told Jackson to pack up his gear. 'We need to move.'

He did as he was told. 'Are we heading for that? Shouldn't we be going in the other direction? Toward safety?'

'Yes, of course, but I need to get more info to advise. The Gorge is huge, Jackson. To isolate a fire, they'll need to know specifics. Damn!' she said and slapped her thigh. 'I forgot to ask about the number of hikers on the walk. Bugger. I'll have to check again. But Jackson, I won't put you in any danger, I promise,' she said registering his concern.

He nodded.

The half dozen-or so herd of horses circled the camp site. Tiffany led the pack, her brilliant white coat looking more faded in the eerie light.

'What about the horses?'

'They're wild, remember? They wouldn't be led to safety even if I insisted but they'll run if it's necessary. They're smart and won't deliberately put themselves in danger and, trust me, they gallop fast.'

'Okay. Let's go then. Got everything?'

'Do you have a scarf or jacket or something to place around your mouth and nose? It will help you breathe. I reckon the smoke's getting thicker by the minute.'

'Um, no I don't think so. My jumper?'

'Here, use this.' Hannah threw him the small micro towel. He followed her lead and placed it mask-like around the bottom of his face.

'Hudson, Roger and Monroe are out there.'

'Yes. That's why we need to push on. See if we can find them. I'm sure they're fine.'

Was she?

It was against her natural instincts to walk towards the black plume of smoke.

'How do you think it started? There's a fire ban.'

'I don't know. But it's a disaster. At least the horses can run, but there's hundreds of animals that may not be able to outrace flames or smoke. Or maybe they will, but their habitat will be destroyed. Do you know how many years it takes to rejuvenate?' Hannah didn't wait for an answer. 'Decades. Not to mention all the plants and tree species. And the Gorge. If there's no walking in the Gorge, there's no *Boondaburra* resort, luxury or otherwise.'

She walked briskly, breathing in and out through her mouth, the bitter taste of smoke on her tongue. Visibility was declining and she kept her eyes downcast on the pebbled path. Hearing a sound, she jerked her head upwards.

'Earl! Hazel?' she said and rushed forwards.

The two of them sat huddled together at the edge of the path. She noticed Earl's hand on Hazel's knee.

'Earl, Hazel,' she yelled louder and caught Earl's attention.

'Hey, lassie. You aren't proceeding up ahead, are you?' He coughed and couldn't catch his breath. Hannah handed over her water bottle and he skulled greedily.

'Did you see the fire? How far ahead is it?'

They both nodded and Hazel pointed. 'The smoke is too thick. You can't see your hand in front of you. We could feel the heat but didn't see any flames. It's hot as blazes.' Hazel rapidly blinked her eyes.

'Hazel, are your eyes stinging? Here, pour water over them.'

Shit.

The smoke stung Hannah's eyes and lined her throat too. A cacophony of noise exploded in her head, but it was only her own heartbeat thrashing in her ears. The situation was serious, and she was here and responsible for people that needed her. How many others were on the Big Walk? She couldn't remember; couldn't remember if she knew in the first place. They had to get out. She had to get them all out. Panic rose up from her toes like a real live living beast and arrived in her chest. It burned like the worst heartburn she'd ever experienced.

Scenarios raced through her mind. As she considered what to do next noise came from their left, up the path. More hikers! They limped forward one step at a time and collapsed to the ground in front of them.

'Roger!' Jackson said. 'Oh my God, are you okay?' His friend was on his knees, palms flat on the gravel, his head bowed. 'Hudson?' Jackson said as a second person stumbled and fell. Hudson collapsed onto his bottom; his head craned toward the sky as if collecting fresh air. His mouth was open, and his eyes scrunched closed.

'Hudson. Roger!' Jackson sounded frantic.

Hannah knelt beside them. She felt their foreheads, one of her only tricks, and ran her hands down their cheeks searching for signs of injury. She grabbed her quickly emptying water bottle and splashed both of their faces in turn. Their mouths opened like baby birds, sucking up the water droplets.

'Monroe,' Roger whispered, his voice croaky and rough. 'She's still back there. Her ankle is sprained, I think. She can't walk. So much smoke. We've raced ahead to try and get help.'

'Monroe is still back there? How far?' Jackson ripped off

his makeshift mask and ran his hands through his hair. He threw his pack on the ground.

'I don't know. Five hundred metres, maybe more. Not far. But in this, feels like a long way.' Hudson rubbed his eyes. Roger's nose was running, and the mucus left a wet trail through the grime on his face.

'I'll call for help. We can air-vac you out. I need to get notice to helicopter rescue.'

Sweat rolled down Hannah's back and her shirt clung to her. She reached once again for the phone. With a quick check to ensure the four of them were okay, and breathing normally, she turned away to speak to her father. She worked hard to keep the panic out of her voice and simply tell him the facts: they needed help and quickly; four victims suffering smoke inhalation. Dad gave her basic advice; get them away from the area as quickly as possible, monitor them for headaches, nausea, chest pain and loss of breath.

Yes, yes, she knew all of that. Whether she could actually do it was another thing. It was all well and good to learn first aid, but no one taught you how to react in stressful situations. But how could that ever be taught? Her father confirmed he would get the chopper as quickly as possible and that she should get everyone to the nearest flat plain. 'Thanks, Dad. I love you.'

As she turned back toward the quartet, a figure ran away from them and down the track. Was she hallucinating? Who was it? Was it Jackson? It looked like him. She checked the group. They were all accounted for, but Jackson's pack abandoned on the ground, toppled to its side.

Her words stuck in her dry throat. Her insides screamed and her fists balled and hung at the end of her stiff arms. Jackson's tall and lean frame disappeared behind shrubs at the turn of a slight bend.

'No!' she screamed when she found her voice. 'Jackson!' But her words only reverberated back in an echo. *No, no, no.*

Fire. Burns. Smoke. Danger. Images ricocheted off the walls of her mind. Hannah had only just met Jackson and she liked him. Not all of his ideas or his plans for her resort, sure. Did she more than like him? He was a decent bloke. More than decent as she recalled his behaviour on this trip. So much more so than any man she'd met recently. An authentic guy from a hard upbringing that had given him thoughts and opinions and dreams. He wanted more than a simple roll in the hay and a cigarette after with a can of beer. That seemed to be all the boys wanted out here in the bush. Either that or they talked endlessly about their cows, their crops and return on investment and not much else.

Hannah didn't know what Jackson meant to her. But he couldn't die. Not on her watch. And oh, what about his heart. What if the smoke affected his breathing and made his heart race and he suffered chest pains again? He might collapse…or worse.

'Hannah?' It was Earl. His voice soft, kind, concerned.

Pull yourself the hell together, Hannah. There are four people here in front of you that need assistance.

It was like someone slapped her. 'Okay, let's move. All of you. We need to shift away from the smoke. It's blowing in this direction, straight onto us. Let's find a place behind a group of rocks or under a ledge.' She looked frantically around, scanning their environs. 'Yes, over there. C'mon. I'll help you.'

'I'll support Hazel and we'll walk together. You assist these gentlemen.' Hannah nodded at Earl, grateful and watched him guide his wife, together they took small steps. She lifted

Roger to one side and Hudson to the other. Her body lagged with the weight and her shoulders cried in pain. The men weren't hurt but weak and dragged their feet unable to balance properly. If their throats were anything like hers, they would be severely parched, too.

It took a few agonising minutes, but they made it. Hannah positioned each man under the secure ledge and out of the direction of the wind. The moment their weight released, her body spasmed and sagged. The smoke lingered in the air of course, but their exposure was less. Catching her breath, she sank to her knees, keeping an ear out for the chopper. Now where the hell was Jackson?

JACKSON RAN BLINDLY. UNABLE TO SEE, HIS EYES STREAMED with unbidden tears. He'd been a fool to toss away the towel in his rush and panic. Because now, he desperately wanted to stop the flow of smoke into his mouth and eyes. After only a few hundred metres, visibility was so poor, he dropped to his hands and knees and crawled like a baby. The pebbled path grazed his flesh and bruised the skin through his long pants. It hurt but stopping was not an option.

By fluke he ran into Monroe, their bodies colliding on the ground. If he'd had to guess he would have assumed she was further along the path. Surely, he hadn't come five hundred metres. Who knew? If he had to advise where he was, he'd have no idea.

Monroe was on her back, lying flat on the track alone and his heart lurched at the sight of her, and he blinked through his watering eyes. He couldn't tell if she was alive or dead.

'Monroe,' he roared, but his voice disappeared into the wind. He crouched down lower and lifted her head.

Her eyes opened. She was conscious, thank God and suddenly Jackson could breathe again. 'Monroe, are you hurt?'

She opened her mouth and tried to speak. Her lips were so dry they cracked, and a drop of blood formed on her top lip. He hadn't brought any water. He was an idiot who didn't think before he acted. Stupid. Instead, he wiped the red spot with the corner of his shirt sleeve. Monroe's words didn't form, and she nodded to answer his question.

Of course, her ankle. He wasn't thinking clearly, and his brain was turning to mush. He rested her head back gently on a shrub and moved his hands down one leg. With her boots still on, it was impossible to tell which ankle was sprained. However, when he touched her left foot, she jumped.

'I'm going to gently lift you and carry you out of here, okay? There's a fire and we need to move pronto.' She acknowledged him with a slight incline of her head.

Jackson had never thought of himself as the strongest bloke, but now, from somewhere he called on his reserves. His body had to perform and get them to safety. Monroe wasn't dainty and small, but he couldn't dwell on that. Adrenalin kicked in and he rolled her to her side and squatted to his knees. He placed her lifeless body onto his shoulders and reared upwards with all his might.

As he stood to full height, a thunderous roar echoed around the valley followed by whooshing sounds as if cyclonic winds were swarming. He paused. Seconds before it had been silent, none of the usual birdsong or echoes or those strange eerie noises he'd once heard. But now the roar bellowed in his ears and stopped as quick as it started.

Then the heat hit. He fought to keep his eyes open. His

skin sizzled and he thought his clothes might catch alight. Jackson swung in each direction thinking that a blaze of flames was about to engulf them. A strange clearing occurred in front of him, and the blue sky emerged but quickly, became a haze and everything around him distorted. He blinked several times in quick succession, but nothing changed the environment.

Another roar boomed and he frantically searched the horizon again. A narrow but bright orange fireball advanced at speed, racing across the landscape, and charring everything in its path. It came straight for them and not a metre either side.

No more time for gentle, they needed to get the hell out of here. Too quickly he placed one foot in front of the other, stepping onto tree roots and other debris almost causing him to overbalance. His instinct was to hide, seek safety but there was nothing surrounding them but bush. His foot slipped and they went down in a heap, one of the ditches dug by the wild pigs. Perfect! Dumping Monroe under him, he covered her body with his own. Then he burrowed them down into the hole and covered them with fistfuls of dirt. Almost impossibly, the heat built and was so intense he couldn't see, and he scrunched up his eyes and pushed his face into the ground. Within seconds, a raging swirl of fire and wind and anger was on top of them and so loud in his ears he thought he'd gone deaf. He pushed so hard down upon Monroe he worried she was squashed and suffering further injury. A twinge spiralled across his back, like a sting, and suddenly all was quiet. Silent. Still. Cautious, Jackson waited not wanting to emerge from their safe cocoon. Curiosity won and he lifted his head. The world around him was a charred and blackened mess, everything cooked beyond recognition. He gulped in air that was still tinged with smoke but not the blackness of before. It was possible to breathe easier.

A wave of light headedness hit him, and his head lolled. Jackson gave in to the pressure, closed his eyes, and willed the experience to be a nightmare that would be replaced by the beautiful gorge in its green glory. Opening his eyes one at a time, of course, that didn't happen, but the blackness did pass.

He rolled to his side to take the pressure off Monroe. She groaned and he placed a hand to her back.

'It's okay. We're okay.' Were they? How long until more fire advanced? His urge was to move again, and fast. He felt a funny stretch to his back, like a tear and slight discomfort. Jackson ignored it and prepared to put Monroe in a position to lift her once more.

Reaching for her hand it was slippery and came away from his grip. He tugged again and paper-thin strips stuck to his fingers. Skin. He retched. Monroe's flesh had slipped away from her hands and was dangling in his fingertips. He had the strangest compulsion to save it, but there was nowhere to preserve the skin, so the strips slithered away and into the blackened earth. He glanced back at her hand and the taste of bile burned his throat.

Her hand was nothing like he would have expected. It was red, but not blistered or weeping. The top cover had been removed to reveal the inner pink, fragile, layer. It was the dangling loose skin that undid him. Grotesque and wrong. He diverted his gaze to her other hand, but it was hidden, tucked above her head. Somehow when she'd landed on the ground, her hands had flayed forwards rather than being safely cocooned by her side. With nausea swirling in his stomach, he lifted the arm from the elbow and grimaced as he saw the same burned mess. Both of her hands were singed, and he didn't have any first aid or water. He had to get her out and fast.

Putting aside her injuries, near impossible to do, but he tried, he manoeuvred her into position. Ignoring her whimpering cries, Jackson listened to her chest to check her breathing. The dirt in the ditch was soft and gave way under his feet as he shifted.

Satisfied she was stable and on firmer ground, he crouched and placed her back into the fireman's lift. She lay half across his shoulders with her body dangling down his back, lifeless and heavy. Another sting zipped across his back, and he shifted uncomfortably.

Gaze focused, he searched for the track. The ground looked unfamiliar, but he recognised the charred remains of the larger shrubs and bushes that lined the boundary. Jackson followed them praying it was the right direction. Occasionally the soles of his feet came alight with the heat of the ground permeating his thick rubber boots. He danced down the track as it got hotter and hotter. Plumes of smoke rose from smouldering plants, and he walked around them.

Thinking he'd walked a thousand metres, he paused. He must be close? Where were the others? Where was Hannah? And for the first time he feared they might be heading directly in the path of the fireball. He hoped he wouldn't come across any charred bodies like the plant life around him.

In the end she found them. Hannah appeared like an apparition in the dull and grey world, and for a moment the air around her cleared.

'Jackson! Are you okay?'

'Yes. Yes, okay. Thank goodness. Is everyone else all right?' But he didn't let her answer. 'Monroe has a sore ankle and her hands,' he paused, the words choking him, 'are burned. The skin…' He stopped and watched Hannah's eyes glance downwards. She nodded, her face grim.

'We're safe over here waiting for the chopper. Can you make it to the ledge?'

Automated, he moved one step in front of the other, adrenalin and panic propelling him forwards. His grip on Monroe remained tight, he was not going to drop her. Reaching the group, Hannah helped him place her against a boulder. In position, Monroe stirred, alert.

'Hannah, she needs water.'

Hannah obeyed.

Freed from the weight, he collapsed onto his knees and rolled onto his side and laboured in heavy, deep breaths. He righted himself sitting on his bottom, knees towards his chest and hands hugging his legs. Commotion, confusion and fear threatened.

CHAPTER 12

*W*ith everyone stable, Hannah focused on Monroe. The young girl had her eyes closed but her chest rose and fell in an exaggerated fashion. Hannah didn't know if that was from the smoke, her burns, or something else. She was conscious, that was the most important thing. Perhaps her foot might be broken? Hannah dithered about what to do and uncertainty clouded her thoughts.

Jackson sat close, but with his back to her and leaned his head on his knees. Exhausted. What had happened out there? Geez, it was a miracle he'd found Monroe, but it had clearly taken its toll. He needed her attention, too, but Monroe first.

The foot, she'd start there. Monroe was unresponsive so she lay her down on her back and elevated her left foot on a pack. Undoing one loop to her lace, then the other, Monroe didn't flinch. Encouraged, Hannah loosened the shoelace further until it hung limp from the boot. Next, the hard part. These bloody hiking boots were sturdy and difficult to remove even without a hurt ankle. True, the boot should have nicely supported her ankle, so perhaps the sprain wouldn't be too bad. She took a big breath and yanked the boot down. Monroe sat bolt upright and moaned. Hannah stalled.

Jackson winced.

'I need to get her boot off to wrap a compression bandage around her foot for support. It's gonna hurt.'

He shifted, sat at Monroe's head and applied pressure to both shoulders to force her to remain supine. Leaning in close, he whispered assurances into her ear while caressing her forehead with his fingers. Jackson avoided her hands.

With Monroe distracted, Hannah wrenched the foot free. Monroe buried her head into Jackson's chest and muffled her scream. Hannah finished by unrolling her sock. The ankle was swollen and tainted blue and black but not so bad it might be broken. A relief. It needed ice but that was a luxury she didn't have. The bandage would have to do. She wrapped it as tight as she thought Monroe could tolerate and left her foot elevated on the bag.

Next, she used the dwindling supply of water to trickle over Monroe's hands. Hannah's breath caught. No skin remained over any of her fingers and up to her wrists. *Shit.*

Was that the distinctive swirl of chopper blades? Straining, she listened. Nope, nothing. Wishful thinking.

Jackson moved back down the ledge and sat, hunched over. His T-shirt was ripped, hanging in remnants, and clung to his back in a strange, bunched up fashion. It was hard to distinguish between the shirt and his skin. Icy tendrils twisted around her heart and squeezed too tight. Without alerting him she crawled nearer for a better inspection. At the top where his collar ended, his neck was bright red with patchy skin. At first glance it looked sunburned, but she peered closer and the top layer of his tanned skin was missing. Examining the remainder of his back, the shirt was burned, crisp and stuck to his dorsal area. The entire fabric or what remained of it, moulded to the contours of his spine.

Hannah lifted a tiny corner of cotton just below his waist, and he jumped.

'Ow,' he said. 'What is that?' He glanced over his shoulder.

It must have been the terror in her eyes.

'What is it?' he asked but his voice was soft, too low, as if he didn't want the answer.

She hesitated. Should she alert him to the fact that his entire back was burned? The shirt was so embedded to his charred skin it had become one. The thought of removing that shirt made her break out into a sweat.

No, instead, she pulled herself together. 101 of first aid— don't panic. And she wouldn't. It took a great amount of effort to make her cheeks and mouth agree, but she managed to pull those lips into a semi-smile. 'It looks as if your back has sustained a little bit of fire damage.'

Fire damage? Jesus Christ, Hannah.

'Um, I mean it looks like you've been burned a little. Can you show me your hands and um, not your feet, I guess? You've still got your boots on?'

He nodded. She wasn't making any sense. Instead, she reached for his hands and sucked in a breath. No, they were intact. She rubbed her hands up and down his legs in their pants and they seemed okay too. The material wasn't singed.

'Were you directly in the path of the fire?' she asked, her voice sounding sickly sweet.

'Um, yeah. It was after I found Monroe, and it headed straight for us. Like a singular wall of fire only a metre wide. It was the strangest thing. If we'd been slightly to the left or right, it would have missed us entirely. So unlucky. Anyway, I'm thankful for those nasty wild pigs. I literally fell into one of their ditches. I didn't know what to do...' His voice waivered but he kept speaking. 'So, I lay on top of Monroe and piled us with as much dirt as I could before it hit. I didn't realise that Monroe must have laid down with her hands out and exposed.' Jackson shook his head.

Hannah's heart squeezed tight again. Was that sensation anything like Jackson experienced with his heart? And that reminded her.

'What about your heart? Is it racing? Are you okay?'

'Strangely, I can't feel a thing. You say my back is burned, but it's numb. It was only when you touched it before and it felt, I don't know, like it was stretched, the skin too tight. But my heart rate is fine, and I don't have any chest pain. I'm bloody thirsty though.'

'Jackson, dude, you should have said.' Hannah retrieved her last water bottle. 'Sparkling, sir?' and she handed it over.

Jackson got the joke and managed a weak smile.

'It probably tastes like carbonated water because this one is from the creek and purified with a tablet. You like?' she smiled for his sake, but it was fake.

'No,' he said, and she followed through with the obligatory chuckle.

The chopper would have water.

'I'm going to dribble this over your back.' With the greatest of delicate care, Hannah slowly released a trickle of water at the top of Jackson's spine. He sat upright, as straight as a rod at the light touch of water striking his back. She placed one hand to his upper arm, communicating that he shouldn't squirm and continued to pour until the bottle was empty. If it hurt anymore, he didn't let on. Man, he had stamina, and, in these circumstances, she admired him enormously for that. Lesser men would have been rolling in agony.

What she wanted to do was hug him tight. Lay her head against his scorched back and circle her arms around his middle and not let go. Feel his body warmth, hear his heart beating and close her eyes. Even for a moment.

Voices drifted in to burst her bubble. Hannah glanced around and the group was quiet, lost in their own thoughts. But the sounds continued, and she realised it was from above them, outside their protective shelter. Her legs were like lead and didn't want to co-operate and she wobbled to her feet. The voices were closer now and she made out warbled cries. Her stomach swooped but she was on her feet and moving. Lucky, she'd had no breakfast this morning. She'd have lost it ten times over by now.

Crawling, one step at a time to the edge of the ledge, she came out onto the flatter plain. More people, a large group. Or where her eyes playing tricks on her? She rubbed them roughly and felt the grit behind her lids. Hannah didn't know what hysteria felt like, but the stone sitting on her chest, pressing in so hard that her breaths came short and sharp, felt like rising panic. More people. All relying on her. And worse, kids. Two adults and a group of kids.

You can do this, Hannah.

'Hello, I'm Hannah. Is anyone hurt?'

A man stood at the head of the group. 'Oh, I'm so glad we've found you.' He was breathless.

'It's okay. I can help and there's a chopper coming. You'll be okay.'

Relief spread across his darkened and wearied face. 'Thank you. I'm Mark and this is a group of students from Kilmore High. I'm their teacher. We were hiking the Big Walk trail. No one is hurt but the smoke is affecting a few of the kids, one has bad asthma.'

'You haven't encountered the fire? No one has any burns?'

He shook his head. 'No, thank goodness.'

Hannah didn't swear, but she wanted to now, loudly. Smoke inhalation by an asthmatic wasn't great, but she was immeasurably relieved that there was no more ravaged skin. And because she had no more water to relieve any such pain.

The indistinguishable sound of blades moving at full speed filled the air and travelled to them on the wind. She had to yell at the teacher, 'I need you to move them downwind, see over there. We're sitting under that ledge, out of the direction of the sun and wind and smoke. Those people are hurt and will need to be air-vacced out first but when they've evacuated, your group can sit there.'

She didn't wait for a reply and raced over to where the chopper had landed. Simon jumped down from the console and she leapt into his arms. His slow reaction told her he was surprised by the welcome but after a minute, he held her tight. His strength helped, but when she looked up at him, tears pooled in her eyes. She knew this would be a sign to Simon that things were serious.

'You're a sight for sore eyes.'

'Seems like you've got everything under control,' he said, his smile broad and wide, reassuring.

'No, Simon, I've got a couple with burns. Hands and back. And an older couple with more serious smoke inhalation and the rest of the group have been exposed as well.'

Simon turned serious in a millisecond. He gripped her by the forearms and held her in place. 'Okay. You've done a great job so far. Now let me take over. I can take six. Lead me to the most serious.'

'You didn't bring medical help?'

'No. Evacuation is more important. You cannot stay here. The other choppers are gathering water for dropping but the risk is too great because the fire isn't contained yet. We can't treat here. We must get out.'

Okay, yes, she understood. She raced away and Simon followed. She pointed to Monroe first and Hannah directed the others to get to the chopper as quickly as possible. Earl helped Hazel, and Jackson assisted both Hudson and Roger. It made Hannah grimace. Both men leaned on his shoulders. If Jackson couldn't feel that pain, he was more badly burned than she thought. Anyway, he'd receive treatment soon.

Monroe was in first. After Jackson supported everyone else on board, he stood back, the force of the wind from the spinning blades wildly tossing his hair around. 'You next, Jackson,' Hannah said.

'Me, no I'm staying. The kids need to get out.'

'What? No. I mean, yes, they do, but they aren't hurt. You need to get medical treatment for your back. You're with this group.'

He turned those facts over in his mind and tentatively touched his neck. The sensation of his fingers on that raw skin registered and it was like the first time he realised he might be injured.

'Thank you for helping me. But you need to leave now, and Simon will take you to the nearest hospital and he'll come back. He'll do as many trips as he must to get everyone to safety.'

Jackson stared at her before he leaned in and kissed her lips. Those lips that she wanted only those few short days ago to be caressing the hidden parts of her body. Their mouths met, hot and burning, like the heat radiating off the ground.

And the sensation sent pleasure like a jolt to her core. But just as quickly as her body reacted, it was over, and he'd moved away. It was too quick, and she desperately wanted more of his touch. Hannah wondered when they'd have the opportunity again. Her throat closed, and a sob rose up travelling through her chest before getting stuck there. She watched him grip onto the rail of the helicopter and hop in and she slid the door shut.

CHAPTER 13

*H*annah shaded her eyes with her hand and watched until the helicopter flew out of sight. A mixture of relief and sorrow zipped through her. It was a relief all on board would receive the medical treatment they required. But sadness, because regardless she wanted Jackson by her side. Of course, that wasn't possible. Her gaze slid from the hazy grey sky to the ground, and she hoped, not for the first time, that Jackson's back wasn't too badly burned, and he would heal quickly.

Her fingers lightly touched her lips, lingering there, recalling the sensation of his touch. Would they kiss again? And did she want to? She and Jackson were on different pages with different goals and dreams and desires. And she knew where that got you. Alone like her father.

Didn't stop her thinking about him though. This man that had only entered her life a few short days ago, rejected her and infuriated her and all the emotions in between.

Would he recuperate and head home? That would make

sense. His mother would be frantic. If Hannah had the details, she'd call herself, but Jackson was lucid and capable, she knew he'd call when he was stable.

Maybe now Jackson would give up his hare-brained scheme of developing the bush resort into a fancy version of itself? Like her, she recognised the determination within him. He'd even said a promotion weighed upon his success. He'd give that up now, after this, wouldn't he? A seed of doubt remained. She hardly knew him. How would she know what he'd do?

A crack of a twig brought her landing heavily back to earth. This group was not out of danger yet. They were quiet, but the silence was eerie. This gorge was a different place to the one she knew. It carried a sinister feel, as if evil chased them but momentarily it was lulling them into a sense of hope, as if the immediate danger had passed. The intensity of the heat had lessened, and a slight breeze had returned. But all around her was black, charred, cooked, and crunchy under foot.

Hannah checked on the young asthmatic girl and she breathed easier but still laboured. The others seemed okay. The teacher was doing a brilliant job of keeping them calm and hydrated, sharing around their own reserves of water. She was parched but wasn't going to ask for a sip. She could wait.

The satellite phone crackled to life, and she fumbled to answer it. Hearing her father's voice, she had to fight down another sob. He was so close, yet so far away.

'Hi, Dad. Yes, all fine. Oh, thank goodness. So, they're at the hospital. That's great news. Yep.' He talked on and she listened. 'Um, okay. Gosh. Right, yep. What do you reckon?'

Fighting down further tears, she rang off. This wasn't a time to lose it but really, how much longer could she hold it together and remain stoic and in charge? She longed to be back at the resort with her father and brother, hearing Davey sing and watching him dance. But not yet, soon. She called the teacher over.

'Mark, the conditions have changed, and the chopper can't make it safely back into the Gorge. The fire has shifted and is still causing significant smoke and the visibility is poor. The pilot can't take the risk and if he does, he may not be able to return and then we're all stranded here.' Hannah didn't react to the teacher's anguish. 'No one is significantly injured, if there was, he'd take the risk, but in the current conditions, I have to agree it isn't worth it.'

The teacher regained his composure, nodded. 'Of course, I understand. These kids are tired but not hurt. So, we walk out?'

'Yes, but you won't be alone. I'll guide you and after speaking to my father, it's agreed we head back the way we came. Not forward. There is damage to the upper edge and rim of the Gorge in front. We need to get back down into the safety of the lower gorge. As an added bonus there's plenty of water down there. We all need to refill.' And drink gallons of the stuff, her mouth salivated.

Hannah had a mammoth task ahead of her and she'd be lying if she didn't feel it upon her shoulders weighing her down. But Hannah Wallace had walked this gorge a million times. If she had to, she could walk it blindfolded. They'd get out safely. Admittedly she'd not completed it with the threat of fire and smoke, before, but hey. She mightn't breathe a proper breath until she got this group of ten and herself over that last bridge and stretch of water and into the visitor centre car park, but she'd do it. She had to.

'We need to get moving as quickly as possible. Can you tell

the students to have a drink and a snack, and we'll head off in five minutes?' Mark agreed and walked away to prepare the group. As expected, there were a few cries of despair. These kids were frightened and desperate to get back to loved ones.

~

A WELCOME PARTY OF MEDICS AND STAFF MET THEM AT THE visitor centre two days later. There was no question of walking another step today. The students were ushered through triage and examined. As far as Hannah could tell they were all doing okay. Exhausted, but shit, everyone was.

They'd walked for forty-eight hours on a stretch that required an overnight stop. Instead of resting, they'd curled up in the dirt and slept for snatches of time and moved on as soon as they had the strength back in their legs. Hannah had not shut her eyes. Each kid had been her responsibility and she didn't let them out of her sight.

'Hannah! You've done amazing, girl.' Her father's arms wrapped around her in the hug she'd dreamed of, and her legs finally collapsed. Davey supported her and gave her a sloppy kiss. She would never mind those loose lips again.

Against her reluctance, the ambo gave her a cursory once over. He wanted her to be transported to hospital and admitted for observation. She wasn't having any of that. She wasn't hurt. Exhausted and dirty and wanting to sleep for a week but not hurt. She told him to focus on the others who needed him instead. Her father drove her home.

'What the heck is going on?' she exclaimed as they drove along the gravel path entrance to *Boondaburra*. She'd have described the upper gorge as a war zone, but this was chaos.

Cars lined up outside reception, doors open and people

milling about. Others raced in and out of the shop taking all the supplies they stocked. Children ran around being chased by parents. Guests were pulling down their tents with haste.

'People are scared, Hannah. They're leaving as quickly as they can,' Davey advised.

'But why?' It was a silly question. Their guests were hundreds of metres from a wild bush fire. The attraction they'd come to walk and enjoy was no longer an option nor was swimming in the creek pools. These people didn't live here and if you didn't need to be here, why would you risk the life of your loved one? The prospect of heading into the Gorge in the next few days, gee, the next few weeks, was low. Of course, they'd leave. She couldn't blame them.

Janessa and Ryder were outside one of their cabins, packing up their gear. Hannah leapt from the ute and went to rush over but her legs seized up and turned stiff. She gave them a brief rub and took slow steps up the incline towards them, each step causing a shooting pain up her calves. They spotted her and raced to close the distance. Janessa pulled her into an embrace that made her body erupt with aches and pains. Hudson did likewise and once again, sobs bubbled up in her chest. The girl who never cried wanted to blub at every opportunity.

'I'm assuming you've heard?'

They both nodded. 'Hannah, you're a hero. You've single-handedly saved all of those people. You're incredible. Without you, I'm not sure what our group would have done, let alone the others.'

She inclined her head. 'That's not the case. And anyway, I was the most experienced out there and with a phone. That's all. If I hadn't been there, help would still have arrived. We keep a track of people hiking the Big Walk. We would have found them.'

'Well, Jackson and Monroe are both getting the treatment they need. They aren't too bad from the reports. A bit sore and sorry but it could have been so much worse. Thank you,' and Janessa clasped her hands in hers.

Dropping those hands, she moved a step back, the usual Hannah resolve returning. 'Ryder, how are your blisters and heels?'

'Good.' He still wore thongs and lifted his feet and showed her. The bruises remained deep purple but not red and the spots were healing.

'That's great,' she said. 'You heading back to Brisbane now?'

'Yes,' Ryder said. 'Monroe and Jackson are being treated at the burns unit in Brissie. We'll get our stuff and skedaddle. Bit hectic around here, so no rush. The road is going to be chockers.'

That caused Hannah to look around at her beloved park again. The place would be a ghost town within thirty minutes. How quickly life could change.

A large roar traversed above their heads and they craned to look upwards. Water-bombing helicopters were loaded and heading to the Gorge. 'It should be over soon.'

They kissed her on the cheek once more and re-commenced their pack up. Hannah had started walking away when she paused and turned back. 'Hey, have you spoken to Roger or Hudson? Do they have any intel into how the fire started?'

They both jiggled on their feet and cast furtive glances at the other. 'We're sorry, Hannah. Hudson didn't listen. He started a campfire, a small one he says, and he swears he put it out, never left it unattended, but, you know,' Janessa shrugged, 'maybe he didn't and it smouldered and got out of control.'

Hannah's fists balled and she locked her jaw tightly shut to prevent speaking. Without a word, she turned and walked away. By the time she'd reached her home, her body trembled, and thoughts of a long hot bath and a deep sleep were forgotten.

CHAPTER 14

*S*he had to be mad. Hannah didn't do spontaneous but here she was driving the more than seven hundred kilometres to Brisbane to visit Jackson in hospital.

The idea had come to her last night in between dreams of her mother. She had those dreams, or rather nightmares, frequently. The same one replayed over and over where her mother left and never came back. Waking from the terror, she was shaking and dripping in sweat, but Hannah knew with absolute certainty that she needed to see Jackson.

There were various reasons it was a hare-brained idea. She hated cities; didn't matter which one, the bigger the more she disliked them, and she didn't do crowds or hustle and bustle. Plus, it was an eight-hour drive. And she hated leaving the resort. Her dad was a wonderful host; fantastic at recommending walks and attractions, and spinning a good yarn, but he forgot, or deliberately chose, not to actually run the place and open reception and show people to their cabins or replenish the stock in the fridge or empty the bins. Ironically it was Davey who would remember those tasks over Dad. It wasn't that her father was lazy exactly, sometimes he simply didn't feel like *working*. And she used that term lightly. And occasionally, he'd get in a *mood* and life seemed to topple him sideways and render him incapable of doing much at all. And at those times Hannah was always around to pick up the slack. And if she was engaged in other work, Davey did whatever was necessary; it was never work to him. Her brother was like her apprentice, but more so a very capable righthand man.

Hannah didn't think she was indispensable; she was. Not because she was amazing and proficient at managing the affairs of *Boondaburra*, but rather because she got on and did it. She loved Dad without limit, but she ran the place.

She was only thinking about the bush resort to avoid the real issue at hand. What the heck was she doing? What would she do when she saw Jackson? What would she say? What would he do? More than once during the trip she placed her hand on the blinker ready to indicate and turn the hell around. But she didn't.

There was no getting around it—she was confused. A state she didn't like. Turning on the local radio station and playing the music too loud, didn't distract the voices in her head, only gave her a headache. She switched it off in frustration.

Hannah wavered between loathing Jackson and what he represented, and longing to hear his soft chuckle again and see his cheeky grin. But most of all she hated that she was experiencing any feelings for him at all; she'd become quite adept at ignoring her emotions. Since the fire, Jackson had consumed her thoughts too often; in all his infuriating glory, the good and the bad bits. It helped that she'd convinced herself he'd have given up his ridiculous scheme for the resort and that idea would be well behind him and his team from Infinity. They'd move onto another project. She was sure because they'd be embarrassed wouldn't they, to show their face again anywhere near the Gorge after what they'd done? After what his team member had been responsible for. Surely? Hannah reminded herself it wasn't Jackson who'd acted so stupidly by starting a fire in a banned zone. It was a member of his team. The team he was responsible for. The team that should have stuck together.

Her father had said, *what's done is done* but that was simplifying matters. What Hudson had done had huge ramifications for their livelihood and the environment. It was unforgivable. Her father refused to act. Hannah wanted to report Hudson to the police so he could be punished because his act was more than reckless, it was criminal. Thinking about it now, a ball of fury formed in her stomach and her hands gripped the steering wheel tighter.

Jackson should be responsible, but she didn't blame him.

Hannah stopped well outside the skirts of Brisbane for a drink and toilet break. There wasn't a chance she'd be stopping on the busy roads or in the congestion of the city. The GPS was set for the hospital and that's where her journey would end.

Hannah drove slowly through the hospital car park trying to find a spot. It was crazy they tried to cram this many cars into one place. The space she found was tight, but she made it and got out of the old beaten-up ute. It was out of place next to the shiny new cars that wouldn't last a moment out in the bush.

Her legs were cramped from the long trip, and she stretched them out before heading for the entrance. The slip of paper in her hand cut into her palm and she checked the details. Janessa had kindly provided her with the room, floor, and directions.

As the doors of the hospital slid open, the ridiculous notion of what she was doing, hit her with the blast of cool air. It could be one of her stupidest ideas. She hardly knew the guy. Getting stuck in a raging firestorm, she'd admit, created a certain level of familiarity. But they weren't the only two people involved. For Hannah, though, the intimacy had been building since the night in the pub. Not unlike the fire that had surrounded them, a simmering hot blaze full of longing festered within her, unsated.

Walking the narrow corridors, she rubbed her bare arms revealed by the tank top she wore. With each step, her nerves grew, not helped by the flock of swooping birds in her stomach. Hannah tasted the cheap and weak coffee she'd drunk at the servo stop as it threatened to rise up her throat. Strangely, her feet kept taking steps and her body propelled her forward. Despite her fear, she simply wanted to see Jackson and make sure he was okay.

Flicking her eyes to the numbers displayed on the walls, Hannah found his room. Laughter drifted out through the rim of the closed door and her step faltered. Letting a patient in a wheelchair pass, she moved to the side and peered through the glass panel.

Jackson. Wearing a green gown, he sat up in a hospital bed that was circled by people.

He had visitors! Three sat on the bed, their feet dangling. Another had pulled over a chair at the base. They laughed, talked, and a couple moved their hands animatedly like they were telling a good story.

Of course, he had visitors. She was an idiot. The prospect had not crossed her mind. Did she think he'd be sitting and pining for her and passing the hours until she arrived? Hardly.

Jackson smiled at someone, and her insides melted a little. If nothing else the trip was worth it for that alone. He looked well. Her mind had gone crazy about the extent of his injuries ranging from hideous disfigurement to barely a scratch.

Given he remained an inpatient though, she imagined the truth lay somewhere in between. His feet were bare and peeked out the bottom of the sheets. The skin of his soles looked soft. It reminded her of his hairless chest with its long and ribbed scar from his morning swim in their sacred creek.

Dragging her gaze away from his feet, she noticed there was something bulky about his back. Three or four pillows and cushions were behind him, but he didn't lean against them.

She heard the word *Mum*, and the older woman with long blonde hair sitting in the chair turned her head. Of course, his mum would be visiting. Given how close they were, she'd probably spent days at his bedside. The woman smiled and spoke, responding to whatever he'd said. She reached across and touched the head of a child in front of her and pulled them in for a cuddle.

His siblings.

His mother.

Despite the hospital setting and his injury, it was a scene of joy. Love oozed from the room; it was in their looks, their touch, and the way they held themselves close. They loved Jackson and each other. A tiny crack in her heart fissured open. She might be a bit lacking in that department, but it brought her immeasurable joy that so many people cared about his recovery. Imagine being so adored. Hannah Wallace could not complain. The love of her father and brother was boundless and she revelled in it most days. She was loved too, but this was something else. She was lost for a moment wondering what it felt like to have one's heart bursting.

But it meant only one thing – he was okay.

Someone brushed past her, and she fell against the door. She motioned to duck but wasn't quick enough before his mother turned. The woman spotted Hannah and her brow furrowed and her eyes squinted in question. Everyone else in the room was oblivious as their eyes connected through the panel. Hannah scrunched down, her back swivelled against the door and she crab-walked sideways along the wall until she reached a corner. She swore she heard the door creak open and then she turned and ran.

HANNAH DROVE STRAIGHT HOME WITHOUT STOPPING, CRYING most of the way. Arriving in Roma, she was exhausted, her eyes red and raw and puffy. God, what was wrong with her?

She pulled over to the side of the road in the main street. The resort was still three hours drive away and no one was expecting her return this quick, plus it was late.

It was not a coincidence that she'd parked across the road from the pub. She wound down her window and the cool night air wafted in. Hannah lay her head back on the seat rest and closed her eyes. The music from the band playing at the pub drifted across to her. It was crass and loud and for the moment, she wanted nothing more than to lose herself in a large crowd. Then she wouldn't feel as lonely. How could you when surrounded by hundreds of people? And she knew that if she entered the bar, she'd find a friend. A tingle of excitement raced up her spine. The anticipation and thrill of the chase didn't get old, but it wasn't the game she liked, it was that someone wanted her, chose her, desired her over all others. At that exact point in time, she was loved and wanted. Right now, she wanted to be adored, have someone honour her and help her forget the reality. Yep, old habits die hard and hell, she was desperate to feel something.

Hannah ripped down the sunshade and checked herself in the reverse side mirror. Not one for make-up or glamorous dress-ups, she looked pretty much like she would any Saturday night in town. Fluffing up her wild hair was easy and then patting it back down into a semblance of control. A pinch to her cheeks made them rosy and she was set. Phone and keys in her back pocket and that was all she needed.

The pub was at maximum capacity and as she entered, she scanned the crowd checking out the scene.

At the bar she ordered a tequila shot and skulled it, asking for another immediately. The drink warmed her from the inside out. The barman knew her and offered a sly smile. Yes, he'd helped her forget before but he was on duty tonight and she couldn't wait until closing time. She found a tall bar stool and perched at its edge.

Within minutes a nice young guy working out on one of the remote cattle properties was by her side. He was joined by his two friends and a small group gathered. On the way to the bathroom another fellow stopped and said hello and brushed his fingers against hers and asked her to come and find him later. Another bought her a drink, a scotch neat, and a clear invitation issued by his eyes.

Instead of revelling in their attention, the room zeroed in, and all of a sudden the oxygen was sucked from the cramped space. Hannah smelled stale beer and body odour. Noise became garbled like she was underwater, and a buzz commenced at her temples. Her chest became tight. But worst of all, was the realisation she didn't want any of these men. Her body quivered as repulsion swept through her. Being wanted briefly by a stranger didn't make her loved or loveable. Why had she ever thought so? It didn't take away the fact that her mother had abandoned her. It didn't take away the fact that her mother didn't love her enough to stay. It didn't change anything, except providing a few blissful moments of forgetting.

Hannah had forgotten about her childhood trauma when Jackson had spoken to her, shown interest in her and her opinions. When he'd expressed his pride about her passion for the environment. Hell, Hannah realised with a sudden clarity, she'd experienced similar warm sensations at those times, plus she had forgotten, had felt worthy and when they'd disagreed, which was often, he'd kept coming back for more. Jackson had liked her and he hadn't even slept with her.

Was she rejecting these guys for...for Jackson? He had made her feel different, special maybe, but still...she refused to accept the proposition.

Just because her mother hadn't loved her, did that make her not capable of being loved? Surely, she was worth so much more than being adored briefly and then nothing but a fleeting memory?

These men circled her like prey and her desperation to feel loved, even for a moment, had allowed it to happen.

A man whispered in her ear and placed his hand on her arm. The touch burned her skin, and she shook it off and scowled at him before he scurried away.

Hannah signalled for the barman. He assumed she wanted another glass of something, instead she bought a bottle. Avoiding eye contact with the men around her, she walked through the crowd, bumping into people as she went and left the building. Outside she gulped in heaving breaths as if she were drowning. The air didn't help the cavern in her chest that felt open and exposed and made her physically ache.

She brushed away the tears that rolled down her cheeks and wiped her hands down her shorts. Jumping back into the ute she revved the engine too hard with her foot on the accelerator and drove away, far away from the pub. In a quiet country road on the route home, she parked. The world around her was dark, no streetlights only the sparkle of the stars in the sky. Hannah took one sip of the whiskey and then another. She'd drink the whole bottle straight and then she'd well and truly forget.

CHAPTER 15

*H*annah returned to the resort late morning, her eyes still crusty with sleep. As she drove, she hoped for a miracle and that the world would have miraculously returned to rights during her absence. Wishful thinking once again.

No guests wandered the grounds; no children squealed or splashed in the creek in the warm midday temperatures, nor did backpackers fight for space to prepare their lunch in the communal kitchen. Already feeling wretched, her stomach swirled further like a washing machine on spin cycle. It was the bottle of whiskey and lack of food, she knew, but still, the sight of *Boondaburra* was enough to sink her into despair.

Not even in the height of summer was it this quiet.

Thankfully a handful of grey nomads, with no time requirements or specific itineraries, remained and their caravans dotted the grounds. That would barely keep the business afloat. Yes, they paid for the powered parking spot, but the retirees were self-sufficient, rarely enjoying the weekly cook-up. Would she bother baking the roast this week?

The fire had been contained before she left on her road trip to Brisbane so now it was a matter of ensuring no more spot fires ignited or embers burned. She'd leave that to the experts, but at the resort, they'd be waiting with anxiety for the call that the national park would re-open. And by the time it opened its gates again, it would take days for the tourists to return. Some wouldn't. Many bookings had been cancelled; others delayed.

Hannah sighed as she jumped down from her ute. They'd be okay; they always were but her heart sat heavy in her chest.

She slammed the car door shut and Davey appeared on the timber decking to the reception entrance. That old saying was true, he truly was a sight for sore eyes. Hannah immediately felt lighter, and her heart skipped a beat at his beaming full smile and the twinkle in his eye. He stood on the top step and belted out song lyrics.

...you'll always be my baby...

Hannah laughed and cried at the same time. God, she'd missed him. This kid with his own struggles always had a smile on his face and her, well, she was usually a grumpy old bear. This kid, who loved her regardless of how prickly she behaved.

This was unconditional love and she had it in spades with her brother, Davey. His love made her light-headed and caused a gentle thrum to buzz inside her body and the blood to flow through her veins. Regardless of her pathetic life, Davey loved her. And she loved him back. No one could take that away.

The adoration she so desperately needed; she'd get from Davey.

He continued to sing and climbed down each stair, and she met him half-way and pulled him in close. The lyrics ceased while they embraced. She revelled in the sweet smell of sweat in his hair and of his body warmth. Home, this is where she belonged. Her headache receded and her brain cleared.

'You okay?' he asked and held her at a distance.

Davey was intuitive. Plus, she must look like hell.

'Okay, Davey. Could drink a whole horse trough though.'

'I'll fetch you some water. You have a visitor.'

Her stomach somersaulted.

'One of the ladies from Infinity, the one you saved.'

Her tummy settled and she shook her head. 'I didn't save anyone…'

Davey didn't let her finish and held up his flat palm to quieten her. 'Yes, you did. And she's here to thank you.'

Following Davey into the office she saw Monroe sitting at one of the indoor tables. A man sat with her who had his hand to her knee. Both of her hands were bandaged and laid on the top of the Formica table. When the door clicked shut behind her, Monroe turned.

'Hannah!' she exclaimed and rushed over. 'I can't thank you enough.' She engulfed her and held tight. Hannah acquiesced even though the embrace went on too long for her liking. A quick squeeze was enough.

'How are you? How are your hands? I'm so sorry about everything,' she said to Monroe as they pulled apart.

'You're sorry? Don't be ridiculous. None of this is your fault. If we'd done the right thing in the first place, it wouldn't have happened. We should have stuck together as a group and with you as our guide. So, I'm sorry we made your life difficult. And about Hudson. We told him not to light the fire, but he didn't listen. I'm so sorry, the devastation must be huge. We never meant for it to happen.' Tears glistened and sat at the tip of Monroe's long, dark lashes.

Usually, Hannah would give her a mouthful of how stupid they'd acted. But she had no fight left in her today. Hudson wasn't here apologising when he should be. Monroe who'd suffered the most severe injury was here to express her regret. That was bolshie.

And plus, her apologies wouldn't miraculously bring customers back or rejuvenate the bush but that would occur, over time. Too much time but she couldn't keep dwelling on that.

Davey came out with three bottles of water, a toasted ham and cheese croissant for her and a plate of mint-slice biscuits to share with their guests.

Hannah smiled. She had everything she needed right here.

'When were you released? Hannah asked realising Jackson was still an inpatient. Were his injuries worse? She wanted to ask but she wouldn't.

'Only yesterday. And I've come straight here. My hands will be fine. They're sore, of course, and need to be bandaged for a while but they will heal. And while I was in hospital, Evan proposed.' She beamed at the handsome dark-haired man behind her, dressed impeccably in dark denim jeans and collared white polo. Quite a catch.

'He said he was so frightened he'd lose me that he didn't want to delay a moment longer.'

'Oh, that's wonderful! Congratulations.' Kissing them on their cheeks, she bathed in the happiness that sparkled between, blinding her with its force. Hannah focused on pushing down the deep wave of envy bubbling up inside of her.

Monroe gestured to the necklace dangling at her throat and Hannah moved in closer to examine it. A sparkling

square-set diamond in a gold band sat on a loop-gold chain.
'Just until my fingers are better,' she explained.

'It's beautiful.'

Hannah's stomach rumbled and she directed them back to
the table to eat and drink the food Davey had delivered. Poor
Monroe, she couldn't grip the bottle to sip the water, but Evan
assisted. In quite an unladylike fashion, Hannah demolished
her sandwich and drank the whole bottle of water. Monroe
laughed.

They talked for a while longer but not of the issues
Hannah was desperate to hear of–Jackson and the further
plans of Infinity, if there were any. Monroe was on sick leave
until further notice, so she wasn't aware, anyway.

Hannah waved as they drove away. The visit had touched
her unexpectedly and she stepped lighter on her feet. It was
kind of them to travel all this way to simply apologise and offer
their gratitude. It made her realise she needed to stop
wallowing and get on with things. There had to be heaps of
jobs neglected by her father. She'd gather Davey and together
they'd tackle whatever was required. When the tourists did
return, Hannah would be ready–the cabins would be clean,
the rubbish bins empty, the kitchen gleaming, the green spaces
raked of leaves and the grass mowed. Everything would be in
tiptop shape. She might use the downtime to write a wish list.
Some odd painting she knew of, minor repairs they could do
themselves and what they always ignored, marketing. Yes,
there was heaps to do and no time to waste.

HANNAH STARED AT HER LIST, SO LONG, IT OVERWHELMED HER.
Once she'd started looking for jobs, she remembered so many

it would be impossible to achieve them over an entire summer, let alone a week. Well, she hoped it was no longer than a week, two at the most. If tourists didn't return with haste … it didn't bear thinking about.

No, she wouldn't be beaten; she was tired, that was all. Her legs ached in their stretched-out position on her bed and moisture clung to her skin. She and Davey had worked hard today but with urgent tasks always popping up, they'd achieved little.

It was unusually warm for a winter's evening, and she had the portable fan at top speed. The cool air caught the corner of her sheet, and it blew out of her hands and down beside the bed. She rolled over to retrieve it, but her fingers were too thick to fit into the narrow space. She rose and pulled the bed out an inch to help. Sliding her hand down the wall, she came to something else. Something hard and square. Pinching with her pointer finger and thumb she slowly dragged it upwards.

It was a jewellery box. It looked familiar but she couldn't place it. Hannah never wore jewellery. It usually got caught when working outside, and plus, it was hardly necessary. No need to dress up out here. She had a few pairs of plain earrings that she rarely wore and were safely tucked away in one of her chest drawers.

This was a green velvet box. Hannah rubbed her fingers over the soft material. Dust had formed a fine layer on top and the dirt formed into small piles. She wiped her fingers on the bedspread. It was larger than a ring box but still tiny enough to hold in the palm of her hand. Hannah lifted off the lid.

A necklace sat cocooned inside a light sheaf of tissue paper. Her mind came immediately alive with a memory. Of anger. Disappointment. Of flinging the box away, out of her sight. She couldn't recall why she'd been so upset.

Gently she lifted the necklace out letting the paper float to the ground. The necklace had a fine delicate gold chain, so slight, it slipped through her fingers. At the end was a charm in the shape of a book. It was dirty gold, tarnished, with a miniature key and lock as if it was needed to open the sacred text. It was all so tiny, like it belonged to an elf.

Hannah took a deep breath; this was her mother's. Out of nowhere she remembered her mother had loved to read. Hannah recalled something else; her father clearing the house of books after she'd left, pile after pile. His rage palpable so that his lips were set and his neck rigid, but he didn't say a word. Still today, most of their bookshelves were empty.

Hannah held the chain up to the fluorescent light of her bedroom. Even in the artificial beam it sparkled. Was it special to her mother? If it was, why didn't she take it with her?

It was left for her. The thought came to her unbidden, but she knew with certainty she was right. Also, that when she'd discovered it, she'd been so angry that she'd thrown it, never wanting to see it again.

She held it up to her throat and let it dangle there, feeling its coolness against her skin. Unlike last time, now she never wanted to let it go; to let it out of her sight again. This was her only link to her mother. She undid the clasp and fastened it around her neck. It sat perfectly, the book sitting just at her sternum. Hannah glanced at the mirror and down at it again before letting it drop and her fingers returning to the box.

Her mind raced; where would she keep the container? She lifted the lid from the bed to replace it and saw inside was that old fashioned cushy sponge where the necklace had lain in its delicate paper. The edges were tattered with age and she touched one corner with her finger. Little pieces formed balls and gave way. Perhaps she should discard it and she commenced lifting out the soft bed. Underneath was a piece of card or paper. It took a few tries, but she managed to lift out the sheet folded into quarters.

Inside was handwriting, of the old cursive style in flowing letters. Age had deteriorated it and some of the words had faded. She couldn't make out the salutation but, could this be what she thought? A letter from her mother? To her? Her fingers fumbled then, and a tear appeared at the bottom.

Damn it! She needed to be careful. Up to now she'd been rushing, but she slowed her movements wanting to saviour what it might say. Once it was read, she could never take it back. What if it was filled with vitriol and hate? Telling her all of the things her mother hated about her and Davey. She'd engineered her own list over the years, wondering of the reasons to abandon them. Her father had always cited Davey. Her mother couldn't tolerate having a Down Syndrome child. Sounded plausible. In other conversations Robert had revealed she hated living in the country, isolated and away from her family and friends. Again, seemed fair. It wasn't the life for everyone. But wouldn't they move away as a family?

Hannah rose off the bed and paced the small space of her room, back and forth. All this time with nothing and now something in her hot little hands and she couldn't bear to look at it! Nausea swirled in her stomach and thinking about what those words might say made the vomit climb her throat until she tasted the bile. Would her questions finally be answered?

But she'd never get any sleep if she didn't read it. It would only consume her thoughts anyway…This time she unfolded the four corners like the material was delicate spun gold.

…*filled with despair at leaving you*…

Hannah sprung her head up jerking it too hard. Her mother didn't want to go? Her eyes trawled across the page taking in the letters too fast.

I cannot bear it here any longer. You are the most … child and so is your brother, Davey despite his difficulties. It is me. I have … fearful of myself. I am … sleeping. I am …. eating properly. I listen to your brother cry in his cot and …. You are more patient than me. You, Hannah sing to him and calm him. You will be good for him and your father. You will do a better job than me. I cannot …. for you both, particularly with your broth-er's additional issues and caring for your father and the resort and doing everything. I need to rest. I feel like I could ….

Your father … is busy … resort, there is much to do and time to devote to the business that hasn't been going well. This adds pressure and stress and while I've tried to speak to him, tell him how I'm feeling, he … is … working all day.

I'm not leaving to … I am … mother…

The paper had watermarks and Hannah imagined her mother's tears falling wet and large and heavy onto the paper as she wrote. Her hand clutched her chest at her mother's despair. Was she unwell and didn't realise?

…this necklace…memory…love you

'Urgh!' Hannah said. The bottom of the letter was impossible to read and she fluttered it in her hands in frustration. She wanted to read the parting words, the last words her mother had written, so desperately a pain shot through her chest and caused her to hunch over. Her head rested against a pillow and silent tears rolled down her cheeks at the injustice of it.

She'd acted tough through her teenage years, told anyone who'd listen that she didn't need a mother or sometimes even want one. She'd banished thoughts of the woman who she had conjured as a monster. Who could possibly leave their own children and particularly their disabled baby? Only someone so incredibly nasty and mean, and that is who her mother became. In fairness, it was the only way to cope.

Now, now, there may have been a different reason. Hannah didn't know a lot, but it sure sounded like her mother wasn't well. Whether that was bone-crushing fatigue or depression, she didn't know. Anyway, it was enough to make her run away from their family.

She'd have to talk to Dad. The man who always refused to speak of their mother. Hannah had understood over the years that it caused him great distress and she'd shied away from causing him any more pain. Didn't stop her as a teenager though wanting to pummel his chest with her fists until he talked, and once she'd tried and failed. He was much stronger than her. It was different for Davey; he had no recollection of their mother. She wasn't slighting his loss; he was still motherless and that was unfair. But Hannah had memories of happy moments.

Thoughts of her mother usually made her stomp around in a fit of anger. Now, she didn't feel rage, instead, a wretchedness of mind came over her, an anguish so deep and unresolved, that it turned her weak. Her body wouldn't co-operate even if she compelled it to do so and her mind was a chaotic mess of incoherent reasoning.

She flopped back onto the bed clutching the letter and the box and wearing the necklace. Her knees came up to meet her chest and she stayed there curled in that position. Eventually, tears exhausted, sleep claimed her and for the first time, she dreamed of her mother as the loving and kind person Hannah so desperately wanted her to be.

CHAPTER 16

hree months later…

A bunch of firecrackers detonated in Jackson's stomach. He rarely got nervous. But today was different. Now that he had turned down the driveway entrance to *Boondaburra*, it felt like a New Year's Eve celebration in his body.

Jackson was the first to admit he hadn't been badly hurt in the fire, but trauma was a funny thing, and this was the first time he'd returned to the scene of the crime, such as it was. He wasn't frightened of the Gorge, but if a campfire raged out of control, he wasn't sure how he'd react.

Anyway, none of that mattered now, he was safe at the bush resort. And he was here for a reason.

It was the prospect at seeing Hannah that had him sweating buckets. Three long months and he'd thought about her every day. Did she remember him? It was easy to scoff at the notion, but they hadn't kept in contact. He'd thought about it; commenced writing a few texts, punched her number into his phone but always disconnected or deleted the text at the last minute. They hadn't exactly seen eye-to-eye when he'd last visited, even if they'd shared a goodbye kiss. Hannah might have been very happy to utter good riddance.

Remembering Hannah and that incident was easy because he had daily reminders. Simply sitting in the driver's seat properly agitated him. His back had healed well, and he'd survived a situation that could have been much worse, and for that he was grateful. One thing his heart condition had taught him was not to dwell on possibilities or *what ifs*. He was lucky and the scarring was only slight. Really, he bore more pain thinking about Monroe's hands and their disfigurement that was his fault. If he'd only thought clearer and taken a second to check where she'd fallen... It was hard not to replay those few seconds over and over and yes, he had to confess, he wasn't sure how he could have handled it better. It happened so fast. But still…

Arriving at the reception area, he cut the engine and sat for a moment. Yes, he was delaying, gathering his thoughts before he saw her. But as if he'd conjured her up with his presence, Hannah strode across the common area carrying two black garbage bags of rubbish. She wore a broad-brim hat that sheltered her delicate face from the brazen sun, but her long hair hung loose. She paused, the bags seemingly too heavy and she placed them down to rest and blew out her cheeks with the exertion before lifting her hair off her neck to let it cool.

Jackson gripped the steering wheel. She was more beautiful than he remembered. Her pale skin dazzled in the sunlight. There was nothing glamorous about what she wore, but she was all woman, her well-defined calf muscles on display and the sinew on her arms evident. After a short break, she lugged the bags back up and continued on.

He should help her, but he was stuck in place. Like a voyeur he wanted to keep watching her undetected a few moments longer. With the engine off, the car was sweltering and sweat gathered on his chest and forehead. Either that or, the sight of her had him hot and bothered.

A tap to the window and he swivelled in his seat to the bright and beaming face of Davey. Jackson smiled back and slipped out of the car. The kid engulfed him in a hug fit for a long-lost friend but that made him grimace with the pressure to his back.

Davey noticed, pulled back and his lips dropped their smile. 'You okay, Jackson? How is your back?' Davey walked around and lifted up Jackson's T-shirt. His hands were rough and thick-fingered, but his touch was gentle. With a solitary finger he traced over the scar tissue on his lower back. It wasn't sore to the touch though he imagined it looked ghastly. He hadn't yet had the courage to look.

'It's okay, Davey. I'm well. My back is fine.' He offered him a reassuring grin.

Davey relaxed.

'How are you? Is business better?'

He lifted his hand and shook it side to side and shrugged. 'Okay, Jackson. Okay. You want to see Hannah?'

'Yes, I do want to see Hannah.' Now Davey grinned, the smile taking up all of his broad face.

'Come.' He pulled him by the arm. Davey seemed as excited as he was.

He dragged him into their personal offices behind reception and called out to Hannah. Davey repeated her name a few times with no response. 'You sit and I'll find her.' He raced away.

Minutes later the back door slammed open and she

entered. She clearly wasn't expecting him as she rushed inside and went straight to the bar fridge in the corner and extracted a cold bottle of water that she proceeded to roll over her face and arms with her eyes closed. Her cheeks were flushed.

His groin might have fluttered.

'Hello, Hannah.'

Her hand stalled mid-flight and her eyes opened wide before she turned her head and took him in for the first time. 'Jackson?'

He nodded.

'Oh my God, Jackson.' She gulped down a sob and rushed towards his arms that he held wide open, welcoming her. His body sagged against hers in relief, until he flinched. Damn back, and she pulled away too quickly.

'Oh my God,' she repeated, circling around him like her brother had. 'How is your back?' she asked 'Is it still sore?'

Before he could respond she asked if she could check.

With greater care than Davey, she lifted the cloth like it was still stuck to his back.

'Hannah, it's healed. You don't have to be so delicate. Pressure on it does hurt a little.' And he lifted his T-shirt over his head. She gasped and he more desperately wanted to kiss those lips.

'I am so sorry,' she said. 'At the time it took me awhile to realise you were hurt. You seemed okay, acting normally. It wasn't until I noticed that your shirt sat funny that I thought something might be wrong and then when I got closer, the fabric of your shirt was stuck to your skin like glue. Geez, it must have hurt when they removed it.' Hannah used both hands to glide down the backs of his arms but not touch his back.

He turned around to face her. 'It didn't hurt, well, if it did,

I can't remember. I can't remember too much; my memory is patchy. Some recollection of before the helicopter and not a lot after. I think I hung on until then, until I left, before I gave in to the pain. I remember a lot more since then, but not the initial pain.'

She gazed up at him, her eyes watching his lips move.

'I'm relieved you're okay.' She stepped one foot forward, closing the gap between them. 'I didn't know, wasn't sure…' she rambled and dropped her eyes and stared at his bare chest. Unlike his marred back, she traced her fingers down his chest scar at the centre of his stomach, following the narrow trail of dark hair, to the elastic band of his shorts. His stomach convulsed at her caress and she snuck a look upwards at him under her lashes.

Jackson swallowed, his mouth suddenly dry and he stepped closer still until their bodies touched. Hannah's hands dropped as her nipples grazed his chest.

Jackson held back because if he stepped too close, she would feel exactly how happy he was to see her.

He held her gaze and watched her already dark eyes, blacken with desire. His breathing shallowed and he grasped her around her middle and pulled her in fiercely, not caring about his evident desire now. With bent knees, he lowered his body until their hips and groins aligned in perfect symmetry and Hannah groaned, deep in her throat catapulting Jackson into ecstasy. He cradled her head and pulled her in closer still forcing their lips to meet and it was like they'd been starved, their lips moulded to each other, their tongues clashed, and teeth connected in a wild frenzy.

Hannah wrapped her leg around him until they were a tangled mess of limbs. He ran his hand through her hair and took in quick, sharp breaths between kissing her. Hannah's caress was no longer gentle as she rubbed her flat palms down his chest with unsated need until they reached the crotch of his pants. She rubbed him there, feeling all of him through his jeans. He paused at her stroke, the momentum building. He hung his head back and it connected with the wall, where he let it rest. The temperature in the back room soared and his skin became slick with moisture.

Jackson wanted more. Bringing his head back down, he drank her in, wanting to feel each part of her, he cupped one breast, then the other. Her lashes flittered closed, her mouth a perfect 'O' and her head swayed to the side. He felt the soft flesh and rubbed his thumb over her nipple. He was rock-hard.

Hannah reached for the nape of his neck and yanked his head towards her and pushed with her body. The force propelled him into the wall, and he exclaimed in pain.

'Oh, shit! I'm sorry,' she said and reefed him away from the wall and peered around to examine his back.

'It's fine, worth every bit of agony.' He flashed what he knew was an irresistible and devasting grin.

They stood now gazing at each other, his heart rate slowing, and he watched emotions flick across her face. Her pink tongue licked her lips and her teeth nipped at one corner. 'Is there somewhere we can go?' he asked his voice so husky he hardly recognised it.

He watched Hannah's expression change, his words breaking the tenuous connection of desire between them.

'What are you doing here?' There was a steely edge to her voice now, gone the tenderness of moments ago.

Not now, Hannah. He wanted her so bad. *Please don't ruin it.*

But, yep, she pulled away, the room cooled, and her demeanour altered. Prickly Hannah was back, the version that guarded her emotions fiercely.

He had to be honest. 'There's a meeting tomorrow, don't you know?'

Now she increased the distance between them ten-fold. 'Before I lose my shit, what do you mean by meeting?'

His mind cleared and everything came back into focus. The lust haze evaporated.

'With your dad and the local member.'

Now her eyes squinted into skinny slits. 'Are you kidding me?'

He didn't reply but stared back at her, softening his stance. This wasn't a battle.

'You've returned to finish what you started, is that it?'

Jackson looked to the ground and around the room and sighed. 'This is my job, Han.'

'Don't call me that! Only people I love call me that.'

'Look, I have one last chance to do this otherwise I'm out of a job. This is serious. Business.'

'Don't patronise me. I know how serious this is. Do you? In all those days you lay in that hospital bed did you not think about how you were destroying my family business? I think I was pretty clear about it last time…'

It was her turn to carefully regard the lino floor. She shuffled her feet back and forth, heaving in large breaths.

'If it isn't me, it will be another developer, maybe not tomorrow, or next week. But it will happen. Let it be me. Infinity can make this place great.'

'Fuck you.' She shoved him hard and this time when his back connected with the wall, and a deep shuddering pain ricocheted through his entire body, he closed his eyes and collected the breath he'd lost. When he opened them, Hannah was gone.

CHAPTER 17

'What on earth are you doing?' her father exclaimed as a heavy old atlas flew across the living area narrowly missing his head.

'There has to be more of Mum's things. Where are they?'

'What do you mean? She took her possessions with her when she left.'

'She left nothing behind?' Hannah slumped onto the ground into a heap and leaned against the lounge chair exhausted. She didn't want to believe it but hadn't uncovered anything in her search.

The room had been ransacked; the cushions and pillows from the couch were on the ground, ornaments were out of place on the shelves leaving behind marks in the gathered dust, the oriental rug curled up and each cupboard door open.

'What's gotten into you?'

Hannah sat up taller then, this was her chance because she thought he was lying. Her voice was shrill as she said, 'I don't believe you. You never told me she'd left me this necklace.' She held it up from where it hung at her neck. 'So what else aren't you telling me?'

Only those few short months ago, she'd confronted her father with the necklace. It had been an explosive scene where he'd denied any knowledge, well, of anything. Afterwards he'd clamped up and refused to talk. For her entire life her father had drip-fed her information about her mother, at his convenience, and dependent upon his mood, and now, he was simply tired of talking about her.

She left because she couldn't cope with looking after a Down Syndrome baby and another child, was his catchcry. She'd give him full credit; he never altered his story. Robert Wallace said the same words verbatim each time Hannah asked. If you said something often enough, did it become truth?

'I didn't know about the necklace. As far as I'm aware there isn't anything else that belongs to her unless she perhaps left an item for Davey too.' Her father's eyes were hooded. Well, good. He should be shrinking.

Yes, something for Davey. She would have, must have. That's what she would find next.

'You never said she was sick.'

'Hannah, your mother wasn't sick. Yes, tired like any other mother carrying the load of caring for two children and helping me run this place. It wasn't easy, I'll admit...' There was a heavy dose of frustration in his tone.

'Did you help her?'

Robert placed his hands to his hips. 'I was working. You know how much there is to do around here and I worked alone back then. I didn't have any help'.

'Sort of like me right now. I do everything.' She was being a bitch; she knew it and was quite enjoying it.

But Hannah remembered her mother's words in the letter. She'd loved her. Didn't want to leave her.

'What if she's better? I could see her.'

Her father glared at her; his expression clouded in anger. 'She knows where we are. Where we've always been.' He held his hands up in a measure of defeat not needing to say more.

That was true. If her mother had been unwell, surely, she'd recovered and why hadn't she come back, even to visit? That familiar ache returned, like someone pushing too hard on her chest.

'I'll tidy the room later. I'm searching outside. Perhaps what she left Davey is out there somewhere.' She slammed the door shut.

It was the middle of the day and too hot to be outside. But she couldn't bear the prospect of being indoors with her father and in the house that she had totalled from top to bottom in her crazy quest to locate something else of their mother's.

Dad was right though, there would be a memento for Davey, she was certain. And she'd damn well keep looking until she found it. Unfortunately, that would have to be later as Jackson strode along the pebble path, rocks flicking up with each step. Hannah noticed the grass was too long and needed trimming. In the middle of October, the heat had serious bite to it now and the longish blades of grass were browning at their tips.

It wasn't a coincidence that her frenetic search coincided with her emotions going wild at the return of Jackson. Like every time they met, he both infuriated her and left her longing.

That kiss! It made her blush which was all kinds of ridiculous. It's not like she hasn't been kissed before. But this one, it made her skin burn hot. It was deep, intimate, and tantalising.

Was it passion? Lust? What was it? Hannah wasn't sure. Just thinking about it made her want to run a thousand miles in the opposite direction from Jackson while simultaneously staying close.

She wasn't stupid, though. That's one thing she wasn't—she wouldn't fall for Jackson Kelly while he ruined their resort with his fancy development and then returned to Brisbane, leaving her behind. There was no way she'd be the one rejected. And as for having her heart broken, she'd never allow that to occur.

First things first, she had a meeting to attend.

'Hello, Susan. So lovely to see you again,' Hannah said as she entered the meeting room with Jackson on her tail. She strode faster to reach the room before him and was conscious of him right behind her, so close she felt his presence, smelt his expensive city aftershave. Her stomach swirled. She kissed the woman on the cheek and sat next to her at the table.

Robert was already present. Jackson stalled when he tumbled into the room, glanced at the occupants before remembering his manners and extending his hand. 'Jackson Kelly from Infinity Developments. Are you from James' office?'

Susan jutted out her chin ever so slightly and smirked. She tidied the pile of papers in front of her.

Before giving her an opportunity to respond, Jackson continued, 'While we wait for him to arrive, do you think you could make five copies of this report and these plans?' And he pushed a bundle of material across the table with a saccharine smile and took his seat.

Hannah bowed her head and swallowed her laugh. Admittedly, Susan Mitchell with her meticulously groomed blonde bob and made-up face with pale pink lipstick and tailored slacks and white cotton blouse could easily be mistaken for an office worker and she guessed the secretary of *an important man.* That was the way Jackson viewed his pal, James Howard.

While Hannah found it highly amusing, she couldn't let the farce continue and allow Jackson to be embarrassed any further. Even though he deserved it.

'Jackson Kelly meet Susan Mitchell, the new local member voted into the electorate of Gregory and representing the Greens Party. Susan came into office last month when she defeated James Howard,' Hannah said and simultaneously collected the bundle of papers Jackson had provided and pushed them back in his direction. 'So perhaps you'd like to do your own photocopying.' Her face split into a wide grin.

Realisation dawned and for the briefest moment Jackson's lips parted and he sucked in a breath before he pulled himself together. Those lips, she could still taste them, him.

But Jackson had committed a massive faux pas thinking that the local political member for the area was only someone to perform his basic administrative work. Innocent mistake yes, but costly, Hannah imagined when your objective was to impress and garner the support of the government, the support you required to perform a major development. Maybe this meeting wouldn't be so bad after all?

Jackson jumped in. 'I do apologise. I wasn't aware there'd been an election and a change of the seat. Please understand, no offence was intended.'

'None taken,' Susan said. 'There was a state election last month where I defeated James Howard. I'm the first Greens member to hold this seat in over twenty years. As you can imagine, James was most disappointed to not only lose to a greenie but to a woman. I understand he didn't take the defeat well and has decamped, perhaps to Western Australia, is that right, Hannah?'

Hannah was downright enjoying herself. It wasn't often the cards were stacked in her favour and she planned to make the most of it.

'I understand he has moved some distance away, yes.' She looked directly at Jackson. 'And that governmental enquiries into corruption might be following him.' She turned back towards Susan. 'This area is immensely lucky to have someone with your environmental knowledge and passion to save the natural world. It's what we've been lacking and I'm super excited to be working with you on the *Greenies Unite for the Environment Committee*. I think our first meeting is next week. Hopefully we won't have to put on the agenda saving the Gorge from major development.' Another pointed stare in Jackson's direction had him shuffling his feet back and forth under the table and sitting up ramrod straight. A steely determination entered his eyes. It was timely, it acted as a reminder to her that he and the company should not be underestimated.

'You are bipartisan of course though, Ms Mitchell. As I understand it, you are to represent the interests of your entire electorate. Business owners, farmers, tourist operators, families, etcetera. And what I understood to be part of the previous member's agenda was the economy and keeping the local area great and strong. And maintaining its position as a destination of choice for people, local and overseas alike to travel to. I think we have a lot of common ground.'

Hannah noticed he deliberately only looked at Susan.

'Susan, please, Jackson. There isn't anything formal about our meeting. And indeed, you are correct, but you can never forget that this area is a local rural farming community that happens to have a natural wonder in its midst. I have no doubt you'll agree that there is a fine balancing act in protecting what needs protection for the future and ensuring a thriving and bustling economy that serves everyone.'

Hannah sat back, happy to be a spectator in this event. She spread her legs out under the table to get comfortable and her foot bumped Jackson's. He glanced in her direction, and she instantly trawled them back under her chair. Her father remained silent throughout the exchange.

'But before we can discuss anything I need to be appraised of what you would like to propose to do here at *Boondaburra* in an ideal world.'

Hannah loved how Susan personalised the resort.

'Yes,' Jackson agreed. 'So perhaps we start there, and I can answer any questions that you might have. These plans have changed slightly since last time, so I'll take everyone through them.'

Jackson held the floor for the next ten minutes. Despite her desire to hate every word he muttered; Hannah was enthralled. His passion sure was contagious and she could see her father listening intently. Hannah's stomach swooped with the dreaded realisation she was battling both Jackson and most likely her father. They hadn't discussed any development since the fire, but it was clear he remained interested in the Infinity plans. Gazing at her father, she realised with unsettling reality, how much he'd aged. His hair was more balding that she could recall, but she didn't often see him without a hat; his eyes sunken like someone more advanced than his years; his face pale with deep crevices lining both his eyes and mouth. He held his head in his hand.

Surely, she didn't have to battle her own father to save their home?

Jackson coughed, bringing her back to the present and he

took a sip of water. Despite what she might think of him, his plans were simply ludicrous. What he was proposing would fundamentally change the location from a simple bush camp to a five-star luxury resort. Should she speak up now? She sighed with relief when Susan did instead.

'What your company proposes is a major redevelopment that would have significant impact on the local environment.'

Jackson went to rebut but she held up her hand to silence him.

'You've had the floor, now it's my turn.' Susan Mitchell was her sort of woman. Jackson backed down.

'Even though you say it won't, you have absolutely no evidence to convince me that the local environment is protected under these plans, and that is, I might say, short-sighted and not well-thought out. The trucks and equipment required to build these multi-level buildings and restaurants and pool would have an impact before you've started construction. But I think we are getting ahead of ourselves. Before we can talk of such matters, it hasn't been confirmed by Robert that he is interested in either selling or working with you to develop his land to this scale.' Susan glanced at her father who still hadn't made any comment. He remained silent. What was wrong with him?

'Let me be clear from the government point of view before anything else. At this preliminary stage I would strongly oppose any such major construction to this level. Therefore, you're going to find it difficult to gain the necessary approval for the work. I wouldn't support it, but of course, I am not the sole decision-maker.' She looked at Hannah now. 'I understand that the bush resort has been a fabulous attraction for visitors to the Gorge for many years. I'm also quite up to date with environmental measures and I'm confident there are many steps that could be taken to improve the environmental efficiency of the resort and to claim its status as an eco-resort and that alone is a tourist magnet. People will travel simply to stay in a place that endorses and embraces the natural environment and does nothing to further damage to it but rather its agenda is to improve the world around it. People feel better about themselves when they are making a difference. And I can advise there are a number of grants you can apply for to assist make those positive changes to the current infrastructure. That is certainly another option and my party, and the local government is very supportive of those types of applications and grants.'

Hannah's first reaction was to defend her home. She'd worked tirelessly to recycle, ban single plastic bottle use, limit the damage to the surrounding forest and land, and minimise tourist footprint. But had she done enough?

She hadn't been aware of a push to create places of environmental significance and call them an attraction. A tingle raced up her spine.

'In fact, what I'd suggest is that both of you visit one of these types of resorts and see what they are doing, how they operate and developed their own sites to claim the status as an eco-resort.'

'You're suggesting that Hannah and I visit one of these resorts together?' Jackson spluttered, incredulous.

Ow, that hurt. Clearly spending anytime with her was repulsive to him. That was mean. Well, she didn't want to be with him either, the inner child in her wanted to respond.

'Susan, I think you misunderstand. I'm in the business of taking sites and making them great. Usually, no expense spared and creating something big, bold and incredible that people talk about and visit from all over the world. The destination is an experience in itself. What we could do here would be phenomenal. Imagine people travelling for hours and arriving at an oasis in the middle of nowhere and being pampered in luxury while gazing out their air-conditioned window at the sandstone gorge.'

Hannah could not keep quiet any longer. 'The beauty of here is the Gorge, not luxuriating in a claw-foot bath from inside a palatial suite while looking at natural beauty. The experience is getting in amongst it; walking on the tracks, hearing the sounds, feeling the ambience, observing wildlife, breathing in the fresh air and all that the Gorge has to offer. You've done it, how can you not see it?'

Jackson sat forward and prepared to pounce in reply.

Susan held up her hands. 'This isn't a sales pitch. I'm telling you Jackson that Infinity will not get over the line with this proposal. You need to amend before I'll take it further within government. And I recommend you need to seriously consider what else can be done.'

'I agree.' Her father's words were loud and reverberated around the small room.

What? He chooses to speak now. 'Both of you should travel to one of these eco places and observe and see what they are doing successfully. We need to make changes around here to make it great, viable and sustainable. It's been a long slog to make ends meet and things need to change for the future. Hannah, you cannot continue this resort as it has been. I don't want that for your future. It's too hard.' His voice cracked, and a cavern opened up inside Hannah's chest where emotions swam in. She reached out and placed a hand to his arm.

'Great. I'm not prepared to meet with either of you again until you've done your homework. I know someone at the *Outback Eco-Villa*. They were successful in obtaining a grant and what they've done to their place is amazing. I'll inform them you're coming on a research trip and then advise my office when we should schedule the next meeting. I look forward to it.' Susan rose, patted Dad on the back and left. Her father rose too, leaving Hannah and Jackson gobsmacked and alone.

3 JANUARY 2002

I can hear them talking about me, they don't know I'm listening, but I am. All I want to do is sleep. Not have visitors in and out and talking in whispers and tiptoeing around, sneaking peeks around doorways and delivering things I don't want.

I want them to leave. To be left alone with Robbie, and Hannah and baby, David.

They think I'm sad about little Davey. That he is abnormal, different, impaired. They are wrong. He's a wonderful baby, happy despite his colic, and clever, I can tell. Those smiles light up my dark days and the singsong sounds he makes.

I love him. I don't care how he looks or how he'll grow or the person he'll be…He'll be Davey.

Sometimes my hands shake near him. Sometimes, I'm just tired. Another rest and I'll feel better. Be more motivated. He's crying again, I must go to him.

CHAPTER 18

*H*annah stormed out.

Jackson followed and rushed to catch her. 'Susan's a hard arse,' he said, his tone light.

'She's a fantastic advocate for the environment and much better than that slimy character of Howard.'

Okay, that didn't work.

Jackson considered his next move. This wasn't a debate about politics. As he saw it, they'd both been trumped this morning and were in a pickle.

'Susan wants you to consider alternatives as well, not just me,' he pointed out, but it felt more like point-scoring.

'Yes, she does. But we're the owners and cannot be compelled to do anything we don't want to.'

'Yes, but someone of her knowledge and calibre can see you need to improve the resort and one way to do that is to get on this eco-nature bandwagon.' If Hannah liked this woman, her opinion must matter.

'Same old argument we've had a dozen times now.'

Jackson tried to formulate his reply, but he was stuck.

Hannah got in before him like she usually did anyway. 'Let's do this as soon as possible and get it over with.'

'This?' he queried.

She waved one hand around wildly in front of her. 'This, this road trip. Weekend away. Research. Work conference. Whatever the hell it is.' As if her brain couldn't quite keep up with her words, she stalled suddenly and turned swiftly to face him, blocking his path. Her body only inches from his. 'Unless you think we can get out of it…'

That possibility fizzed between them and they were both momentarily lost to their own thoughts.

But it was then he realised the opportunity he'd been handed. Time alone with Hannah. Just the two of them. At a resort. A strange dizzying feeling passed over him then and he made the mistake of looking at her.

Her face was set, hard and cold. She stood close, but her eyes were focused on the distance, across the park. He watched as her brain ticked over, he could see the potential scenarios flicking through her mind, except, he was sure, she'd be thinking of plans to avoid spending time with him.

Now that he turned his attention to the idea, Jackson wanted nothing more than to be forced into a sabbatical with Hannah. And he wasn't thinking about work. *Work*. Shit. He'd been too easily distracted. Bloody Hannah. His mind needed to stay clearly on task. Any feeling of victory at being forced to spend time with her dissolved like soap bubbles.

The boss was not going to be happy. He'd had one chance already and now there was further delay. If only they'd sealed the deal before the state election, and before, well, the bloody fire. *Damn it*, he cursed.

But something shifted within and he didn't feel the

previous urgency he had about the deal. The sour taste at the back of his throat was more about losing his job. The boss had been direct. If he didn't return successful, and Infinity Developments the new owners of *Boondaburra*, he'd be out of a job. It wasn't stated quite so clearly, but Cyril had reminded him how well they'd supported him during his recuperation and time away from work. There was a further reminder that he'd already had one chance with a full team of support and now it was up to him.

Okay, yeah, maybe he did feel sick. How could he provide for his mother and siblings without his job? No, that was defeatist talk and Jackson Kelly wasn't defeated. He'd seal this deal; he knew he could, and he would.

Robert approached and placed his arm across Hannah's shoulders.

'This is a great chance to check out what other resorts are doing. This could be our answer. We can adopt more green measures with the help of a grant and make this place great again,' Robert said to Hannah.

Hannah's shoulders slumped and Jackson didn't think it was from the weight of her father's arm. She nodded at him silently, the closest she might come to agreement.

'Dad, who's that?' She pointed over to Davey who was talking with a young girl.

Jackson followed the direction and sure enough Davey had a female friend. The young kid stood with his hands behind his back and his head bowed, popping up sporadically to either respond to a question or perhaps ask one. The girl facing him was short in stature with her own broad face and offered Davey a wide smile.

Hannah and her father shared a look and turned back to check what was going on. Susan approached and spoke to

Davey and the girl. Susan pulled the teenager close by embracing her around the middle and she rested her head on Susan's shoulder.

Father and daughter watched as the girl walked away with Susan but turned her head back at least twice on the short walk to the car park and waved to Davey.

As soon as the car door had slammed, Davey skipped across to them and bounced up and down on his feet as he spoke.

'That girl is just like me. Like *me*!' he emphasised.

'What's her name?' Hannah asked.

'Rosie. Isn't that a nice name? And isn't she pretty? Her mother is that woman you met with. She's important, I think. Her mum said she might talk to you Dad, about us hanging out. Can you say yes please if she rings? Please, Dad.'

Robert's mouth dropped open and Hannah too, looked uncertain, her eyes wide in astonishment. First time for everything he guessed. But for Jackson, a wave of happiness spread across his chest at Davey's joy.

'How unreal, mate, that you've met a new friend!' Jackson slapped Davey on the back in congratulation.

'A new friend! A new friend.' Davey repeated and this was enough to draw Robert and Hannah back into the present.

Robert grasped Davey's hand and together they walked back to their home, Davey talking animatedly all the way.

Hannah turned to him then. 'Okay, let's get this over with. My father is clearly on board with this stupid idea. I'll never hear the end of it if we don't go. Let's do it. Now? Can you be ready in fifteen minutes?'

Jackson nodded but she strode away not waiting for his response. This was going to be fun, or perhaps not.

~

'How much fuel does this clunker use?'

'I'd say about as much as your twenty-year-old ute,' Jackson retorted.

'Nice one,' she said.

'True though, right? These new cars are much more fuel efficient.'

Suddenly the seven-hour drive toward the coast might take a lifetime. Jackson was still stoked to be in the car with her though, prickly or not.

They drove for fifteen minutes in silence. The atmosphere in the car was electric, but Jackson didn't want to fill it with meaningless small talk. As he wracked his mind for conversation topics that wouldn't get him into trouble, Hannah reached into her pack and extracted a notebook and thick text and opened to commence reading.

'What's that?' Jackson asked before she'd read one line of the text.

'These are my uni books.'

'What?' He turned in his seat to gaze at her directly. 'What do mean uni? Really?'

'Yes. Why do you sound so surprised? Is it that astonishing?'

'Well, yes. You said you didn't have any ambition to do anything with your life other than run the park and care for your family.'

'I'm sure I never used the words *no ambition*.' She indicated in the air with her fingers to simulate inverted commas. 'Those are definitely your words and I think you might've accused me of lacking drive. And you know I wanted to study originally, right?' She glanced out the passenger window now. 'The fire changed things. And then Monroe came to visit me. Did you know about that?'

'Yeah, she mentioned.'

'She thanked me, which was completely unnecessary. But here was this beautiful young woman with bung hands and her whole life ahead of her and she was so positive and full of energy. I felt a bit lazy to be honest after her visit. I was restless. Questioned what I was really doing. Here I was bemoaning the ruination of our natural world, but I wasn't doing anything worthwhile...'

'I don't know about that...'

'Anyway, I thought it was time to learn, educate myself. So, I've enrolled into a course about conservation but also about business and management. I'm hoping I can learn about running a business but also sustainability, conservation and the environment. All I know I've learned from picking up bits of information and reading and listening to locals talk. I figure I might actually achieve more this way. Do you think so?' Her voice wobbled with uncertainty.

'That's unreal.' He reached across and placed his hand on her leg. 'That's the best news I've heard. I'm stoked for you, Hannah. I understand it was a big step. Any education and learning is a good thing, right? So, you're doing it online?'

Hannah's cheeks flushed at the praise. Jackson guessed she mightn't receive many compliments. It was clear her father loved her, but he wasn't perhaps the most emotional man, unlike Jackson's mother who expressed her love and pride in Jackson at every opportunity. Any of his own shortcomings was not from the lack of love from his only parent.

'Yeah, online. Which is great but also sucks because as you know the internet connection is patchy at best in the bush. Some days it's great, other days really average, and I have to travel to an internet cafe to attend online class sometimes.'

'But you're committed. Well done, I'm so happy for you.'

She was silent for a moment before she spoke again. 'But that's what this trip is about right? Hopefully learning something new. We both might. You, about more environmental approaches to building and construction and me about how to provide fantastic services within a natural environment.' She stared at him hard across the console of the car, but her voice was soft with an under hint of steel. 'I'll keep an open mind if you will?'

'Deal.' The tension in the car defused and they were friends again.

'Tell me about what you're learning at the moment.'

'I never thought it would be so interesting.' Her voice bubbled with excitement. 'This subject is about the connection between politics and the environment. So, me, right? But essentially, it's about the ability of contemporary governments to generate adequate responses to the issues of climate change, population growth, and resources amongst others.'

'And what do they say the answer is?' Jackson settled in for the remainder of the ride, content to listen to Hannah talk about her course.

CHAPTER 19

'Hannah. Hannah,' Jackson nudged her shoulder. 'We're here.'

Opening her eyes, her neck spasmed as she moved from her curled up position.

'I hope you had a good rest. You've been asleep for a while.'

She cricked her neck, easing the ache and smiled, but her lips were tight. Hannah collected the pile of books from her lap and secured them in her bag before she took in their surrounds.

They were in the middle of a green plateau. Tall and lean light pistachio gums and mint willows, low lying shrubs with dark-coloured moss leaves with dainty flowers in bloom and small bursts of red and blue berries. The resort was silhouetted by majestic mountain ranges creating dark shadows on the horizon, but standing to attention as if they were protecting all within its valley.

In front of Jackson's four-wheel drive was a sweeping plain

of trimmed lawn. Cabins lined the perimeter forming a perfect V a few hundred metres into the distance. Through the middle was a path delineated with low-lying lights to guide the way.

'Oh boy,' Hannah muttered as she got out of the car. They'd arrived somewhere special: the architecture, design, location and setting. But it was more than that. The detail, outlook and attention to minor aspects of the ascetic look of the place. It was special standing here. Is this how guests felt when they arrived at *Boondaburra*? Deep down Hannah knew the answer.

Jackson met her at the front of the vehicle.

'Look at the sunset,' he said. childish excitement had returned to his voice. She'd missed it. In front of them, sitting far across wide open plains, the sun was an orange orb of colour, only a whisper away from sinking to meet the horizon. The glare was so bright she squinted. The rays no longer held any heat and a gentle breeze skittered across her skin raising goosebumps and bringing with it the slightest scent of salt. They'd arrived in the Sunshine Coast hinterland and the ocean was behind those majestic mountains.

'It's incredible,' she said in a breathy voice.

A door slammed to their left and a couple headed towards them down a paved path lined with hard-wearing succulent plants and more bulbed lights. This place was like a fairy wonderland.

'You're here.' The woman, with grey curly hair was short and round and jolly. Her voice held enthusiasm as she leaned in and kissed first Hannah, and then Jackson on the cheek. 'Welcome to *Outback Eco-Villa*. We're so pleased to have you visit. I'm Rhonda and this is Fred. Susan told us you were coming. She's a fabulous friend of ours and we're happy to help. And you, hopefully. How was the drive?'

The woman stopped talking but jigged on the spot as if she was keen to get moving.

They engaged in pleasantries while Hannah and Jackson grabbed their gear and followed the couple inside.

'Now we're fully booked, but we've managed to shuffle things around and give you one of our best canopy tents. As you know there's a range of accommodation options, but I thought you might like to experience our most popular choice.' Rhonda leaned in conspiratorially. 'City folk like to think they're roughing it in the country, but they don't actually want to camp and get their feet dirty, so this accommodation is attractive to those wanting something different.'

Hannah offered Jackson a pointed stare. Isn't that what she was offering her guests? But she hadn't seen these tents yet, so she'd hold her judgement.

'Are these the tents you're talking about?' Hannah pointed behind them to her first glimpse at the resort.

'Uh, huh. Here's my first tip. I wish we'd built more of them. What we tried to do was offer different accommodation options, but mostly we have spare cabins because everyone wants to *glamp*.'

Glamp? What the? But she nudged Jackson with her elbow. 'They look the same as our tents.'

Without pretending to agree, he replied. 'They look nothing like what you offer.' *Ouch.*

Rhonda continued, oblivious, 'We need you to experience the best we've got and understand why everyone is dying to stay here.'

Yes, Hannah wanted the answer to that question and moreover, she hoped it was obvious. As she was about to thank them, Rhonda shushed her, and Fred spoke.

'It's our pleasure. And plus, we're so proud of what we've

achieved, we want to show it off and demonstrate what's possible. Hannah, this used to be a caravan park with tent sites both powered and unpowered. And well, look around, it isn't anymore, but we do cater to all types of visitors. Susan mentioned something about that being important to you. But one thing we don't provide is camping facilities with the communal bathroom and pitching your own tents and the like. We thought hard about it, but we wanted to launch ourselves into a different market and well, it's worked. But I understand there's a place for both.'

Rhonda beamed at them. 'Fred will show you to your accommodation and I'll see you at the bar in a jiffy for cocktail hour.' She waved them off.

They lugged their own gear, so it wasn't so fancy that there was a valet service. Phew. She could never agree to that get up and the expense to employ someone to carry bags!

They walked past three or four tents where couples sat enjoying the view. Fred waved to each in turn before they arrived at their canopy. Their tent was located exactly in the apex of the V, sitting front and centre, and overlooking the others.

From what Hannah could tell the tents were identical. She'd check later. Fred didn't talk as much as Rhonda. He simply showed them the basics, said he'd answer their questions over a drink later, and issued a hearty cheerio.

Dusk had fallen and the moon had commenced its ascent in a sky beginning to sparkle with stars. That was one thing both resorts had in common – a jewelled backdrop.

Okay, first surprise. No door. If Jackson had been standing beside her, she would have elbowed him again.

'Jackson,' she said. 'At least we have doors.' These canopy

tents lived up to their name with a zipped netting system simulating a real tent.

He grunted.

Hannah was like a kid unwrapping a birthday present. 'Can you believe this lighting?' There was a bright exterior light and the indoor was further illuminated. It was so bright, there'd be no squinting inside. No shop-bought bulbs in sight. The light fittings were chandelier-like with dangling glass shards and there were bedside tables and lamps. *Boondaburra* cabins had quite dull simple fittings and only one light per room and an additional in the en suite for those cabins that had the luxury option.

Oh, and holy shit, there was a king-sized bed. One bed.

Hannah glanced over at Jackson, but he wasn't paying attention. Hannah was like a shaken bottle of champagne, ready to pop. It was a beautiful bed–no bunks in sight– with plump cushions of bright yellow to compliment the cream bed coverings. She slid her hand across the smooth top and looked underneath the structure. Ah, they were two single beds pushed together. The realisation caused both relief and disappointment to surge through her.

Worry about that later, Hannah.

Jackson was worked up for other reasons. 'Hannah, this is incredible. They've taken a simple design and turned it into something magnificent…'

'I wouldn't quite say magnificent…' she interrupted.

He ignored her comment. 'It is exactly as Rhonda said. You've tried to emulate this but haven't been successful.'

Another ouch.

Is this what the weekend would entail? Jackson delivering back-handed insults?

'They've kept the simple canvas structure of a normal tent.

But glamorised it. There isn't a door', so he was listening, 'but the netting creates a romantic, indoor-outdoor effect and the interior is kitted out properly. Purely for comfort. There's timber decking running from outside in and a beautiful rug covering so the texture is different on your bare feet. A fully functional bed but inviting with good-quality linen. The fit out is exquisite.'

Okay.

Hannah stopped and carefully looked around her with a non-critical eye. That's how she'd been viewing it so far, with a view to critique it. As a guest, how did she feel? To be honest, she wanted to dive into that bed that appeared so soft and comfortable, or at the very least lay there with a good book and wile away many hours. There was an antique timber box at the base of the bed for their belongings; a vase of wild-flowers on the round table to the left of the bed and fluffy white hotel robes hanging in the corner crease of the tent. A his and hers set.

'Hang on,' Hannah spun on the spot. 'Where's the bathroom?'

Jackson gestured with his hand, and she followed. Behind the bed was a partition and they walked into the most luxurious bathroom she'd certainly ever been in. Modern black tiles surrounded a deep white porcelain tub and a dual shower with matching basins all in the starkest shade of white.

'There's no door,' she squeaked.

Jackson didn't answer because he'd left the bathroom already. Coming back out into the main space, he sat on one side of the bed. Hannah sat on the other.

'This place is stunning.'

Hannah had to agree and fought to swallow the lump that had formed in her throat.

Happy hour was held at the bar. The large timber structure housed Fred and Rhonda's private living quarters out the back, along with a communal kitchen, dining area and lounge with a roaring open fire and settees and chairs scattered about the space. With its vibrant floor coverings and free-standing lamps and dark furniture, the space was warm and inviting. The bar lined the far wall and seemed to be well-stocked with a wide variety of alcohol.

'All that luxury and no kitchens in the tents,' she murmured more to herself than anyone else as she stood at one end of the bar.

Fred stood close and heard her. 'But that's the point, love. People want the luxury but not necessarily the work. I understand it's ironic. But it's key. Once you understand that fundamental point, you can provide a place that people will flock to. As long as your price is right. But here, we provide the modern kitchen with the necessary conveniences for those families who wish to cook for their group but also those who simply wish to have the night off. Through that door there,' he pointed with his index finger, 'is the restaurant. It's taken a bit to get the menu right, but I think we've got the balance. The families don't want to cook each night but when they don't, they don't want to be paying five-star prices. We've adopted a broad menu that we hope appeals to most budgets. If you want your $45 rump steak, it's available. If your child wants a cheese-burger and fries, we've got that too.'

Hannah soaked up the information. Such a setup would require a professional chef. That she was not. 'You'll get to try the restaurant later when we dine together. You're with us tonight.'

Another guest approached Fred and engaged him in conversation about the walk they wanted to tackle the next day. He waved and strode across the room chatting with them.

A waiter appeared and offered Hannah what appeared to be a flute of champagne, but she was informed it was a Kir Royale. Tentatively she took a delicate sip of the red-toned drink. Hmm, so good she took another straight away. On a good night out at the pub she'd usually enjoy a rum and coke. She'd Google the recipe later and add it to their drink list.

Jackson approached, his eyes roaming the high and exposed beams that were a feature of the ceiling. 'They've kept everything in line with the natural environment but with stunning results.' He turned to her to ensure she was listening. 'Do you see Hannah? This building is entirely timber and I suspect recycled timber, but I'll confirm that…'

She cut him off. 'Actually, I can't see anything that makes this place eco and actually in support of the environment? Can you?'

Fred and Rhonda stood in front of the small group gathered; Hannah estimated thirty or so people, and Fred tapped a glass with a pen to gain everyone's attention. She looked across at Jackson. Did he forget she conducted information sessions and welcome events every single night at *Boondaburra*? He'd been there for one for goodness' sake. Okay, so theirs was held in an outdoor beer garden with cheap metal tables and chairs and grass underfoot, but the beer was cold, wasn't it?

Crossing her arms against her chest, she swelled forward with the crowd to hear their hosts better. Jackson flinched in front of her and she instinctively reached for him and checked he was okay. The group had moved him into position in front of the fire. It was miniature as far as fires went and completely contained in a designer fireplace and custom-built chimney, but even Hannah stepped back at the flicker of heat licking and caressing her bare skin. Jackson's gaze remained fixed on the flames. He hadn't noticed her touch his arm.

'Jackson,' she said softly at first, but he didn't respond. 'Jackson,' she repeated and this time she tugged his arm. 'Let's move over here where there's more room.' Thankfully, he followed without complaint and Hannah chose a spot where the flickering shadow of the flames didn't reach them, nor the enveloping warmth it generated.

As a waiter brushed past, Jackson swiped a cold beer and skulled it. A spike of alarm shot through her and Hannah frowned.

Fred and Rhonda had commenced their welcome talk and were explaining how each and every one of them as a guest of the Villa were supporting the environment. Hannah did her best not to frown. Helping the natural world would be not building upon the land and tramping along it with a thousand footsteps each day. But, hey, she couldn't talk. Their business was the Gorge walk and they encouraged it. At least they monitored the numbers in an attempt to minimise the damage.

'But how are we actually different?' Rhonda asked. 'Well, this is how we do it. We have a hybrid solar power station that replaces the use of diesel; we have water desalination with the usage of grey water for irrigation and absolute ban on disposable water bottles. We only use low-water toilets. We do not allow domestic pets and we recycle and reuse, and have our own vegetable patch. But it's not just a patch, it's a fully-fledged garden that provides our produce for the kitchen. Whatever we can't produce we source locally. Wherever we can, we have a commitment to minimising our footprints and soil erosion and damage to the bush. We replant and regenerate. Our cabins are built from recycled or selectively logged local timber…' Jackson nodded in her direction.

'We only host a small capacity of guests to limit the impact of tourism and, oh what else, Fred?'

'We use minimum packaging and nothing plastic within the Villa. And loads more. Our commitment to environmentalism and our natural world is always on our mind. These aren't just words. We live this lifestyle,' said Fred.

Okay, that had Hannah's attention. Passion and commitment were two things she enormously admired, plus hard work. A bit like herself. Shit, this place was pretty special. A glass of white wine was offered, and she readily accepted.

On her fingers she tried to count how *Boondaburra* matched this incredible place. One, they did not allow disposable water bottles. Bugger, they had a diesel generator. She was embarrassed. How could they not have rectified this years ago? She grimaced and grabbed another drink. Two, they used their grey water but how on earth did you desalinate water? Three, they locally sourced their food and ingredients. There wasn't much that came out of their pathetic garden. But hey, who had time for that with everything else she had to do? Never one to admit fault, she didn't want to accept that there was a shitload more the resort could adopt. It all cost money, of course.

Rhonda and Fred answered a few questions, but the crowd dispersed into smaller groups.

'What brings you to the Villa?' Jackson asked a middle-aged couple.

'Well, a weekend away within easy reach of Brisbane where we live. But as it's only a weekend we didn't want to lug the camping gear but still be outside in nature.'

The wife interrupted. 'And I want a break from cooking

and this place allows us to have our own breakfasts here in the kitchen and lunches too, but we can eat at the restaurant at night. They do a great pizza delivery to the tent, so last night we didn't even have to venture out.'

'Plus, there's a bar to relax and have a drink. I guess you could say it has all of the pleasantries of being away in the country and we can enjoy ourselves,' her husband added. A couple of children raced over to them and asked for lemonade.

'So, is it the luxury aspect you're attracted to or the location?' Hannah asked.

'Um, I don't think it's that luxurious. It's certainly nice. The tents make us feel outdoors but are comfortable and have our own bathroom which is important to my wife and yet we can mix in with other families too. The best of everything.'

Hannah's heart sank. If this wasn't luxury, well, um, her resort wouldn't rate two stars. Maybe they did attract a different audience and were completely alienating a whole group of the market.

Damn it Jackson, you might be right.

Rhonda approached, 'Hi, Susie and Rob, sorry to interrupt. But the restaurant is ready for us, Jackson and Hannah, let's head on through.'

CHAPTER 20

'*J*'m so excited to see what your chef can deliver. I love good food and wine,' Jackson said as he sat down at their allocated table in the restaurant. The deep red mahogany theme continued into the dining room with thick-legged tables and matching chairs and like everywhere else in the lodge, a warm and welcoming atmosphere surrounded them. Cosy. Another open fireplace roared in the corner keeping them toasty warm.

'Of course, you are,' Hannah muttered under her breath as she sat next to him and gave him a saccharine grin. She examined the menu and wine list with care until Fred took it out of her hands.

'Tonight, we're offering you a bit of everything, so you can taste everything we offer. Our chef, Alastair, is one of the best.' He smiled. 'But first, every good meal must be accompanied by fine wine, and this is one of our best bottles of red.' He held it up like a trophy. 'We've thought about employing a sommelier but didn't think that was the right fit for us. We want good food and wine, but having an expert on wine really takes you to another level.'

'Do you have anyone on staff who advises about wine?' Fred asked her.

Hannah spluttered out the water she'd been sipping. She apologised and dabbed her face and the table with her cloth napkin. 'I'm so sorry. But you obviously haven't been to *Boond-aburra*. Essentially, we are a nice and functional caravan park. And I don't mean that facetiously. I love our bush resort and I think we do a great job, but we aren't in any way luxurious. I have to be honest; I thought we were a bit 'bush fancy' because we have cabins and some of them include bathrooms.' Her laugh was nervous. 'But I'm listening to what you say about market. We've definitely pitched to the lower end of the demographic. Well, to be honest, I'm not sure we've pitched at all, but if we did it was to the more rustic style of traveller offering facilities for camping but with a communal kitchen rather than your bush stove and full facilities if you don't want a creek wash. Plus, our added bonus has always been the canopy cabins. I'm not entirely convinced that isn't a market of its own, but I'm hearing that there are different needs and perhaps rather than just catering to one category, we can diversify and broaden our services. Particularly when we are the only resort close to the Gorge. We have an attraction working to our favour.'

Jackson's chest puffed out listening to Hannah dissect her home and business. He sensed a change, finally, because the woman was listening, albeit not to him.

'I love, love, love your environmental slant,' she continued. 'But please assure me it isn't a gimmick, is it? You actually do it because you should and it's important?'

'Absolutely. If we could, we'd live one with the natural

world but what we've created here, we hope is the next best thing. Enjoying nature while preserving it.'

That evoked another broad smile from Hannah that made his heart swell. He reached over and touched her arm and grasped her fingers in his. Fingers atop the table, he left them there, together, touching, connecting. Not only was Hannah getting on board, but he was learning a lot too. But what he learned troubled him. It went against the ethos of his employer. Of course, it wasn't his job to destroy the environment. However, he knew Infinity would do whatever it took to create a fabulous design and if that meant losing a tree or two, it would happen without a second thought. He took another sip of the deep red wine and pushed those thoughts aside.

'What do you think?' Fred asked as he held up his own glass.

Jackson swirled the liquid in his glass and made an exaggerated motion of smelling the contents before announcing, 'definitely cherry and pepper and perhaps a dash of citrus.'

A flash of humour crossed Hannah's face.

'You're a natural,' Fred gushed.

'It's superb.' Jackson said, enjoying the moment. His body loosened and relaxed, his muscles less tight. Was it the alcohol? He could usually put away a few before it affected him. The company? Fred and Rhonda were a hoot. The location? You couldn't beat it.

Hannah.

His foot brushed hers under the table and she glanced up sharply. Her glare was stern before quickly softening, and she rubbed her foot against his in return while maintaining eye contact.

'Do you have any other questions for us? About the Villa,

our eco-status, anything,' Rhonda asked as Fred topped up the glasses already.

'Do you source your wines locally and is that a selling point?' Jackson kept a tight hold on Hannah's hand and foot even though she inched away, increasing the distance.

'Again, it's about option and choice and market,' Fred said. 'Some people only want the best. It's important to have one or two in stock. Most people want middle of the range and some, well, they'll always want a drink at the lowest cost possible. We have something for everyone.' And he detailed the wine they were drinking.

When he'd finished, Hannah said, 'Yes, I do have a question. Can you explain water desalination to me?'

Fred leaned in and explained to Hannah. Jackson listened too. He knew what it was, but not how it operated at the Villa.

As Fred outlined the process, plates of delicacies were delivered to the table. The waiter identified spanner crab, barramundi, duck and rump steak, small portions for sharing.

'Did I answer your question, Hannah?' he asked her.

She nodded. 'Good enough for now, thank you.'

'We have a set menu for sharing, it's eight courses.'

Hannah's eyes went wide like saucers. 'I've heard of that. It's degustation, right?'

While Hannah might have been incredulous, the aroma had Jackson's mouth watering.

A member of the wait staff arrived at Fred's left and whispered to him. He looked over to Rhonda. 'There's an issue we need to attend to, dear. Let's leave this lovely couple to enjoy their meal and we'll check back in later.'

Then they were alone.

Jackson cut off a small portion of steak and offered it to Hannah. She went to take the fork, but he pulled his hand away. Her eyes sparkled in amusement as she looked at him and eventually, cautiously, slowly, she opened her mouth and he offered her the piece. Closing her mouth around the meat, she watched him with hooded eyes as she chewed, savouring the taste.

Watching her eat sent hot shivers of biting lust straight to his core.

Licking her lips, she said, 'Oh man, that is so good.'

Jackson took his own bite and agreed. 'Let's try one of each.'

After a delectable morsel of crab from Jackson, Hannah said, 'This is so delicious. The menu is tops and the wine great. This place is special, isn't it?' Her head was in her hand and supported by her elbow on the table.

Jackson paused, thinking carefully about his reply. 'It is. Can you see the potential? This place is incredible. It's so much more than buildings and a resort. It's an ethos for living.'

'How much have you had to drink? It's the expensive wine going to your head. But I do agree, it's something else, but it's not *Boondaburra*.' Her lips turned down as she took another sip.

Jackson wiped his mouth with the serviette and placed it carefully on the table. 'Of course, it's not. *Boondaburra* is unique and original and its own. No one is suggesting that you simply emulate this. What you need to do is create your own unique resort.'

'By copying their ideas?'

'No. For a start, the Gorge is a completely different natural environment to this area. So that's distinct.' He paused and offered her a forkful of barramundi that she accepted. Jackson used the same fork in the knowledge that Hannah's lips had surrounded the prongs. His joy was not from the mouth-water-ingly delicious fish.

'But that's where we come in. Infinity creates individual, unique and differentiates from other similar resorts.'

'Is that right?'

He nodded but his eyes closed as the taste of the spanner crab overwhelmed him. 'I'm a terrible cook. What about you?' he asked opening his eyes.

'Can I cook? Yeah, didn't you have the roast pork special I made at camp during your stay? I'm famous for it.'

'Roast pork, hey.' He mocked her with his innocuous smirk.

'Yep, and I can do roast beef too.'

'Much else in your repertoire?'

Hannah took a long sip of her wine and placed the glass back on the table. 'I was only eight when Mum left and I had to learn to cook real fast, otherwise Dad and I would have starved. I became a master at baked beans on toast, but I've improved over the years. Nothing fancy. I do a mean spaghetti bolognaise, but most people can, can't they?'

'Nah. Not me.' He shrugged.

'Your mummy cooked for you instead?'

'Yes, she enjoys it.'

'Does she still deliver meals to you like a helpless bachelor?'

'Sometimes,' Jackson avoided her gaze.

'That's pathetic. But I guess she wants to fatten you up.'

Jackson threw a tiny crumb of bread at her.

'How is your mum? Have you been able to contact her out here?' she asked.

'Yeah, she's good. I spoke to her in the car on the way out while you were asleep.'

A waiter came to the table and filled their water glasses. A sign? Perhaps, and she agreed by taking a drink.

Jackson devoured another couple of mouthfuls. 'She was worried about me, you know, before, but now that I'm okay, she's well.'

'She must have been frantic, and your siblings, as you're all so close.'

'Yeah, they were. But it's all good now.' Jackson concentrated on eating. 'How's your dad?' he asked and inched his chair slightly closer to her so that their bodies touched.

'I haven't spoken to him.'

Jackson didn't question it.

'He's a big guy and can look after himself,' Hannah continued.

Jackson sipped more wine.

'I never have a break from Dad and Davey, so it's good to be apart, right?'

'Yeah, sometimes,' he agreed.

Hannah looked across the restaurant and seemed contemplative. 'Plus, I'm mad at him.'

'What for?'

'I've mentioned my Mum?' Her voice dropped to a whisper.

'Yeah, not much. I know she left, and it's cut you up a fair bit.'

'I guess you could say that. But a while back, not long after the fire I found a letter inside a jewellery case. It was from my Mum.' Her fingers lifted to touch the base of her throat as if to fondle a necklace that wasn't there.

'What did it say?' Jackson put his fork down and placed his arm on the table, focusing solely on her.

'Some words were faded. But it gave me the impression that she loved me but was unhappy and that's why she had to leave.' Hannah turned in her seat then, animated. 'Firstly, she left a gift of a necklace. That says heaps. I always thought she didn't care and up and left without so much as giving me and Davey a second thought. But to find a present with a hand-written letter specially to me, well, it's changed things.'

'Look, I don't know your mother's circumstances. But I think I know enough to understand that no mother would make the decision to leave her two children lightly. No parent would. That would have been heartbreaking. And I'm sure there was a reason.'

'I want to know that reason.'

'"What does your dad say?'

'Well, that's why I'm angry. He's always maintained that she couldn't cope—you know basically with life and kids and the resort. So, she left. Sounds quite simple, doesn't it? But I agree with you. There must be a reason. The letter was the first glimpse I've had of any explanation. She said she loved me. She did love me. But Dad, other than the same story over and over again, gives me nothing. In fact, I've raised it so often, he now refuses to talk about it. I remember bits of back then, though. He was severely cut up. But I don't know if that was because he was a man with two small children and a full-time job. Or was he heartbroken? Devastated that the love of his love had left him? He's never answered that question.'

Jackson inched closer so that he could feel her body warmth; vulnerability oozed from her. In that moment, he wanted her to protect her, comfort her, make everything all right. His need was overwhelming.

His mobile phone trilled in his pocket he retrieved it and checked the screen. *Shit.*

His boss.

CHAPTER 21

*H*annah watched Jackson's expression harden as he read the caller ID. He had been more relaxed than she'd ever seen him during their day together, and particularly tonight at dinner. But now, looking at the phone, his forehead creased and his eyes lost their sparkle.

Her interest in the caller was piqued. Hannah frowned as he raked one hand through his hair.

'I've got to take this,' he said as the phoned belted out the Rocky theme song. *Interesting choice.* Pulling the back of his chair out from under him, he rose and left the dining room.

Hannah took the opportunity to check out the surrounds. Couples enjoyed romantic dinners, larger groups drank and laughed, families appeared relaxed with empty plates in front of them and children were happily colouring-in sheets of Australian wildlife. It was an eclectic group. She glanced down at her own table and noticed one portion of the barramundi remained and she reached for it. The white meat was creamy and smooth and delectable; she sighed in appreciation. Fred and Rhonda were right, their chef was incredible.

A hand settled on her back, and she peered over her shoulder.

'We can't have you all alone. Where's Jackson?' Fred asked as he slipped into the adjoining chair. Without his formal dinner jacket, Fred appeared younger than she'd first thought. It was probably Rhonda's grey hair that made her think they were older, whereas Fred was probably only in his early fifties. Fred was tall and lithe and appeared fit; the opposite to Rhonda who Hannah would describe as an earth mother. Even now she could hear Rhonda's laughter across the spacious dining room. Watching her interact, Hannah thought she was perfect for this role and made a wonderful house-keeper and hostess. Whereas Fred looked like the type to be out regularly walking the trails surrounding the Villa, and no doubt, taking guests with him.

Fred still waited for her answer. 'He had to take a call, but I'm fine by myself. Enjoying some quiet time. I feel so relaxed.'

Fred signalled to the waiter. 'Ah, well, thank you, that's the greatest compliment. If people can forget about their troubles if for only a little while and unwind here, rest and what's that saying? Regroup? If they leave here feeling better than when they arrived, our goal is realised.'

It's not a health retreat. Hannah held back her thoughts. She *was* on track to feeling rejuvenated herself and that was without any of those fancy benefits of a health spa. But the weekend was still young. Her gaze wandered in the direction of the entry, again, checking for Jackson's return. No sign yet.

'I'm going to send you back to your room with another one of our locally sourced and popular bottles of wine that will go beautifully with a smorgasbord of delicate petite fours.'

'More food!' She smiled and patted her tummy.

'Trust me, it's worth it. We source them from a French pastry chef, and these delicacies are the best. Plus, they're only small.'

Fred waved to Rhonda as she rushed past. The waiter arrived and he made the arrangements and said it would only take minutes to be delivered to their tent.

'Sleep well.' Fred tapped her arm in farewell before striding over to join his wife whom he cuddled from behind.

Watching them, Hannah's body flooded with warmth and a light fluttering commenced in her chest. Was this sensation similar to Jackson's heart palpitations? She didn't know. But her physiological response was longing; yearning, pining for what Rhonda and Fred had. For the girl who pushed everyone away, protected her heart so fiercely she never let anyone near it, the realisation hit her hard like a knock to her chest, making those damn flutters disperse like dandelions in the breeze.

Is this what her mother desired but couldn't achieve with her father? Is that why she left? Or did she feel it and Dad didn't return her love? A tingle raced up Hannah's spine making her shiver.

There were too many questions and not enough answers.

She'd never looked at happy couples and felt this way before. Perhaps it was the wine making her melancholy or perhaps the warm welcome and the relaxed day they'd had. Whatever the cause, she wanted to see Jackson.

Wiping her mouth with the cloth napkin one last time and collecting her bag, Hannah glanced around before heading for the exit.

The lodge was packed with guests at the bar, in the lounge area and the dining room at capacity. Humans really did crave company, didn't they? All this analysis had her reminiscing of their own ramshackle beer garden she'd never thought twice about before. It matched the best outback pubs, but was that what they wanted?

No, not her, was that what her guests looked for? Their outdoor seating area was nothing like this place and the communal kitchen had the stainless-steel long benches and tables meant for the outdoors, not for lounging around with a good wine and enjoying a chat with your nearest neighbour. Their resort didn't provide a comfortable and welcoming space for socialising but their guests did linger over meals and talked while washing up at the sink.

Outside a full and bright moon greeted her accompanied by swirls of steel-grey clouds and between them, the brightest of sparkling stars. The scene reminded her of the Van Gogh print hanging in the reception area at the resort. While she didn't mind Impressionism, it became suddenly clear to her that they needed to emphasise the natural environment around them, as a way of advertising. Their office and the reception should be filled with real photographs of the flora and fauna. She wasn't brilliant at photography, but she bet Davey would enjoy having a go at capturing the beauty of the Gorge. The idea seemed so obvious to her it was ridiculous that they hadn't done it already. She added that to her mental to-do list.

She relished the cool night air sweeping across her cheeks and cooling her body as she headed for their accommodation.

Jackson paced in front of the tent and she quickened her steps. He glanced up as she approached and ended his call. She crossed her arms in front of her chest.

'Hey.'

'Hey.'

The waiter was behind her and placed a tray on their outdoor table on the raised deck to the tent.

'Thank you,' she said.

Together they ascended the two short steps and crossed the outdoor area. Once inside, Jackson zipped them up. With the 'door' to the tent fastened, they were protected from bugs but still in the outdoor compartment of the tent. Indoors yet out. She loved it.

Jackson inspected the delivery. 'What's this then?'

'Fred has arranged a plate of their finest petite fours to be accompanied by another locally sourced wine that he recommends.'

'It feels like we're on holiday, doesn't it?'

Hannah paused, glanced at him. He smiled, but his lips were tight and the fake joviality didn't reach his eyes either. His shoulders were slightly slumped, as he examined the goodies on the table. He was quiet, whereas most of the day he hadn't shut up.

'Is everything okay?'

'Oh, yeah. Just work stuff.'

'Oh.'

'I mean, let's not talk about that now, but we can't forget it's why we're here, right?'

Hannah nodded, feeling the happy mood slipping away. She reached for the wine to open it. 'Want to guess the flavour again?'

He sat down on one of the white timber deck chairs. 'Sure.'

'So, this is a rosé from a Stanthorpe winery.' She poured the crystal pink liquid into two glasses and offered one to Jackson. 'I love the colour. I'd drink it based on that alone.'

An easy smile played at the corners of his lips. 'And here I was thinking you weren't a girly girl.'

She teased him with her own smile. 'It's so fragrant.'

'That's not going to cut it. Most wines are fragrant.'

'Okay, smarty-pants. I mean floral…'

He swirled the liquid in his long-stemmed glass. 'Yeah, you might be right. I detect rose and spice.' Jackson took his first sip. 'It's so good when it's cold and crisp.'

'Isn't it better to drink red wine when it's cold?'

He sat back and laughed, and Hannah relaxed.

'No, I mean the wine is cold. But yeah, traditionally red wine is warmer and deeper and richer and better sitting around a raging fire.' Jackson went quiet as if he realised what he'd said.

'Well, thankfully we don't have a fire and we're drinking rose.'

His first glass was gone in a wink. Hannah didn't comment but quickly sipped the remainder of hers —she wasn't going to be left behind—and refilled their glasses.

'Perhaps we should enjoy a treat.' She passed him the plate to choose. There was a selection of mini-chocolate eclairs—who could ever resist—a citrus tart, raspberry cheesecake and a lemon tea cake. Her mouth watered.

'I make apple crumble most nights to go with the roast dinner. People scoff it down.'

'That puts a very unattractive image in my mind.'

'It's easy to make in large quantities.' She shrugged and popped an éclair into her mouth. 'This is divine!'

Jackson joined in with the tea cake and they were silent while they savoured the sugary sensations.

'Tell me what the bottle says about the wine,' he asked.

'Okay.' She held it up to the light. 'This wine exhibits a perfumed bouquet accompanied with red fruit flavours and spice and rose petals. Hmm, exquisite. Too good to drink.' Despite that she took another large gulp.

'That's exactly what I would've said!' Jackson took the cheesecake and ate it in one bite.

'Hey, I wanted that one!'

'Too late,' he said as he finished chewing and taking more wine.

'You've got a bit of cheesecake on your lip, in the corner.'

Jackson wiped at his mouth in all the wrong spots. Hannah leaned over him in the chair and with one finger found the spot and collected the speck. Without thinking she placed that finger in her mouth and licked the remnants of the crumb. Her lips opened and closed, and she flicked her tongue across her lips chasing more of the delicious flavour. Jackson's smile disappeared and he stared at her hard and reached out and grasped her wrist and tugged gently.

He propelled her forward until she sat on his lap. His sudden closeness, his warmth, the feel of him had all the blood in her body rushing to her groin. Hannah took the last sip of her wine and placed the glass down and shifted forward jerkily until their middles touched. Her legs were wide open, and she could feel him.

Leaning down, he lifted his head to meet her and they kissed. He tasted of berries and sweetness and her body instinctively swivelled closer. Jackson groaned and held the back of her neck increasing the pressure of their mouths. He claimed her lips again, crushing her to him while their tongues licked at each other until they couldn't breathe. Jackson pulled away and placed a trail of kisses down her neck and along her jaw until reaching her parted lips once more.

Her erect nipples rubbed against his chest and he pulled her closer. The cool air kissed their skin, but Hannah was hot. Her body temperature rose so quickly she wanted to remove his clothes and feel his bare skin against hers, and quickly.

'We'd better move inside,' he mumbled as she reached for her T-shirt.

'Shit. Yes.' They were after all, still outside. Once inside nobody passing would see them, particularly because they were the last tent in the row.

Thank you, Rhonda and Fred.

Hannah rose first and pulled him up in the same motion. He was taller and she gazed up at him, her eyes landing on his pink and swollen lips. She wanted to kiss them again, but instead, they stood together. His chest rose and fell, close enough, she could tell he was turned on. Man, so was she.

With their hands by their sides, she twisted one finger around one of his and he returned the pressure and clasped her hand. With that hand she led him one step at a time inside. On the way he grabbed the bottle of wine and took a drink straight out of it.

Dutch courage?

Inside he discarded the wine bottle and rolled the zipper shut, locking out the world. The sliding of the zip was loud and echoed around the tent. He turned back and faced her, but he was too far away. They both simultaneously stepped closer and his erection brushed her hip. She couldn't resist and she moved her hand down to the spot in his jeans and rubbed the long and hard bulge. They kissed as she touched him. No longer slow and sensual, it became hard and fast and heavy.

Hannah pulled Jackson's shirt out of his pants and trailed her hands across his chest under the fabric. His body was hard, except for the soft ridging of his scar. Jackson paused and lifted his shirt over his head tousling his long hair as he did. His fringe fell across his eyes. She thought about moving the hair out of the way, but her eyes were locked on his bare chest. Transfixed, she wanted to touch every inch of it.

Between his nipples, across his hard six-pack and down the slim sides of his torso. Her mouth itched to caress him there too.

Instead, she traced one finger down the length of his scar with the lightest of touches, scared it might hurt, then she circled one nipple. He tossed his head back, his mouth wide open. He let her play, but his fingers went to the hem of her shirt and lifted. It came over her head effortlessly and she stood before him in her bra.

His nearness was overwhelming, she wanted to touch him, crawl into his skin, leave no distance between them. Hannah tugged down her pants and then did the same for him. He wrapped his arms around her midriff and pulled her inwards, their skin kissing. Her leg crept up and circled him, resting on the back of his knee. His skin was smooth and soft.

She heard echoes of people talking in the distance and their voices dumped her back into reality. Hannah opened her eyes and was dazzled by the lights that still blazed. Yes, the tent flap was secured but, there might be gaps where people could see. Who knew? But Jackson found her lips once more and all thoughts evaporated from her mind, except for him. He lowered her onto the bed and lay on top of her. Her hands were on the tight muscles of his back, down his legs and feeling every contour of his body. He nudged her legs apart and she opened them willingly.

Pressing her hands to grasp his bottom, a hot tide of passion surged through her and her body sang.

He lifted his shoulders slightly and his hair fell over his eyes again. A wonderful sensation welled up inside of her at his cuteness, his innocence and yet how much she wanted him. With one hand she traced the strands of his fringe and slid it off his forehead only for it to fall back onto his face. He offered her a gentle, shy smile as their desire simmered, their bodies alert.

Taking the pressure of his body off her, he leaned on one elbow. His other hand found her breast and fondled the soft flesh through the fabric of her bra. His finger dipped inside and found her nipple and flicked gently. Hannah's back arched. She wasn't sure how much longer she could wait.

'Condom?' she asked, her voice husky.

He nodded without uttering any words and rolled away from her.

'I'll just duck to the bathroom,' she said as he rifled through his belongings that he hadn't unpacked yet. At the sight of his erection escaping the confines of his underwear, a fresh wave of desire washed over her. She'd slip away first.

Remembering the bathroom had no door, she went to the toilet, and then had a quick drink. She heard the tinkle of a glass. Jackson was having more wine. She glanced in the mirror. Her hair was always unruly, but now it was sideways across her scalp and the curls flattened at the back where they'd lain. It stood out at every angle. She raked her fingers through it and patted down the fly-away strands on top. Her bare skin was cooling. She pinched her cheeks until they turned pink and sniffed her armpits.

Okay, she was ready. But she paused again. Should she go out naked or still wearing her bra and panties? Would he have undressed? She deliberated, unsure. Well, they were going to come off anyway and she undid the strap and the bra dropped to the floor. Her panties followed. She left them where they fell.

Hannah stepped back towards the bed, her heart fluttering again and her nerve endings tingling. She rounded the corner and saw Jackson's feet hanging from the end. On his side, he lay facing away from her. Gently she lowered herself onto the bed and approached him from behind. He held the condom packet in his hand laying on the bedcover. She aligned her body with his and held him tight, rocking slightly, excited to have him close once more. Hannah kissed the fair skin across his shoulders ignoring the rippled skin that formed there, and Jackson stirred. Touching one shoulder she attempted to roll him onto his back, but he was like a dead weight.

'Jackson,' she whispered and leaned over to see his eyes were shut and he was asleep.

CHAPTER 22

*J*ackson was rock hard.

And that hard part of him was resting against Hannah's soft back. One of his arms lumbered over her middle, hand resting on the linen sheets while the rest of his body spooned her. Their legs were in perfect alignment, their feet crossed over each other.

Memories of last night flooded back: lots of delicious kissing and touching and Hannah wearing little clothes.

His erection jerked.

Yep, and that was exactly the reason he was awake with a hardon. He crumpled up his face. How could he have fallen asleep? What a schmuck. No bloke ever fell asleep on a beautiful half-naked woman!

Snuggling closer, he buried his face deep in her wild, curly hair. When the sun shone upon it, Hannah's hair was strawberry blonde, other times, a light shade of copper but, now with his face crushed in amongst it, he could smell the scent of cherry and vanilla.

A strand tickled his nose and Jackson swallowed to squash the sneeze. Argh, God, his mouth was as parched as the desert. That's when the dull pulsing at his temples racked up a notch.

Great.

Then his full bladder caught his attention.

Double great.

He didn't want to move; he wanted to stay close, keep her near, have her body wrapped around his and enjoy her every curve.

But needs must.

The arm lying under him was asleep and pins and needles shot through it.

Jackson wiggled his toes to see if it would disturb Hannah. Nothing. Her chest rose and fell in a gentle rhythm and he heard her shallow intake of breath indicating she was sound asleep.First step, he lifted his fingers from the bed. Then his hand, and when she still didn't react, the heavy weight of his arm. If Hannah didn't wake at the movement, he might be all right. He sat for a millisecond with his arm half-raised and untwisted his foot. This allowed him to roll over and to the far side of the wide, king-sized bed. Last test would be his weight shifting off the mattress. He inched over and urged on by his need to pee, rolled off quickly.

His head spun as he stood and the ache in his head worsened to a beating throb.

The need to empty his bladder lessened the blood flowing to his groin, and by the time he stumbled his way to the bathroom, he was good to go.

Hannah's toothbrush perched in a glass, and he snatched it out and drank water from the tap greedily.

Gulping down his second cup, his heart started racing too fast. Doubled over at the middle, Jackson gripped the sides of the basin with both hands and breathed in and out. The beats were erratic and shooting pains criss-crossed his chest. Damn these palpitations and their random arrival. But he knew it would pass, it always did. He spied a washer on the bench and he placed it under the cold gushing tap. Once saturated, he wrung it out and placed it at the base of his neck so he could keep it bowed. The relief was instant.

Sure enough, his chest settled, and he stood up tall, the wet washer fell, skirting his bare legs on the way to the floor. He remained only in his underwear. With baby steps he made his way out of the bathroom and searched for his phone. It was on the side table. The light illuminated the room as it opened at his face recognition. *Shit.* 2.12am. No wonder the world outside was black.

And then he remembered.

Work.

Before he and Hannah had got all hot and heavy, he'd spoken to his boss. That was why he'd drunk the entire bottle of rosé and that was after the red wine with dinner and the cocktails. Sheesh, no wonder he was hungover.

The most glorious cool breeze wafted in through the open canvas windows. Usually, it would be inviting and cool, a natural air-conditioner. Now, without his clothes, and guilty thoughts, he felt exposed and vulnerable. Using his phone for a light, he reefed through his overnight bag and found a T-shirt and boxers. He dressed quietly. Hannah hadn't moved. Then he took his phone, a spare bottle of water he swiped and stepped outside. By now, he was pretty confident Hannah wouldn't wake so he unzipped the inner wall.

Being outdoors provided instant relief; a lessening of the claustrophobia that was closing in on him inside the canopy. Now he welcomed the cool air. Jackson sat in the outdoor chair, remembering Hannah draped over him. She'd felt so good. And he was ecstatic that he'd finally cracked her steely exterior. His boy bits stirred again, but it didn't last. The moment was gone now; he was wide awake and other more serious issues pressed down upon him.

Cyril, his boss had always been a good bloke. The first to shout drinks at the pub on a Friday night, to offer time off and a slap on the back for a job well-done. But they hadn't crossed words before. Each of Jackson's projects had run smoothly and according to brief. Better than directed in fact, perfect. The results in his previous developments were worthy of praise. The briefs had never been difficult before. Develop a five-star apartment complex. Remodel an out-dated hotel. Take a corporate space into the twenty-first century. Properties Infinity purchased were easier. There was no brief and open slather on design and product. Well, to the extent they could double their money and profit, of course.

It had all sounded so easy when he'd been assigned this project. The groundwork had been done. Scouting had occurred on remote rural locations that they could take from ordinary to magnificent. And *Boondaburra* had stood out. Its location certainly, but also the potential. That's how Infinity worked: potential equalled money. And when the company decided they wanted something, they made it happen. Because usually money talked. That was somewhat the problem now. Cyril, owner, operator, and founder didn't accept defeat and Jackson was worried generous offers wouldn't cut it with the Wallace family.

Cyril firmly reminded Jackson that the deal was taking too long, there had been too much delay, each extra day was lost profit. He was a patient man, he said, but Cyril wanted the deal done, *now*.

A small part of Jackson had thought Cyril would entertain the new fandangle idea of an eco-resort. Honestly, their industry loved fads and the newest best thing, how was this any different? But his head must have been filled with fluff—he'd forgotten the most important thing—money. These fabulous initiatives here at the Villa were not the cheapest option of construction. That was the way of the modern life—want to eat healthier: eat organic fruit and vegetables at double the price. Want to save wildlife: foster an animal or buy beauty products that aren't tested on animals and are chemical free, but it will cost more. Want to build a resort that works as one with the natural environment and your costs soared. High overheads meant less profit. Basic 101.

He had clearly let the situation get on top of him. Or perhaps it was the enraging character of Hannah Wallace with her morals and ethics, and her outback charm who had deflected him.

Jackson had tested the waters with Cyril and floated the idea of desalination, recycled timber, and that's as far as he'd got. Cyril was fast to ridicule; that was a first. Again, he was reminded, stick to the brief. And worse, Cyril had intimated his greatest fear: if he couldn't pull off this deal, there would be no promotion, and they would have to rethink his position. His boss had spoken the words this time; the message was clear.

At the recollection of their conversation, his heart skipped a beat and another crack of pain shot across his chest.

His body had an amazing ability of crashing him back down to earth fast.

But gazing up at the expansive night sky coloured a glorious shade of midnight blue and scattered with luminous and twinkling stars, his troubles faded fast. It was that transcendental time of night where there was total silence, not the whisper of a cicada or bug or bird.

He wracked his brain for when his next open-heart surgery might be required. But that was like choosing the winning gold lotto numbers. Who knew? Who could predict the future? It had been a few years now, so crossed fingers, he had a while yet. Would he be lucky enough to get another six out of this valve? The uncertainty was something he struggled with and therefore, he always needed to be prepared, sorta like a boy scout, except he'd already proven he wasn't the outdoors type. A smile curled at his lips, but it was autopilot and disappeared quickly.

He needed to work to earn money: for himself; for any extended sick leave he might require and to assist his mother and siblings. Jackson Kelly could not be unemployed. That had to be avoided at all costs, no matter what.

So, he found himself back where he started; on the path he should have remained. It was easy, really. He had to convince Hannah that this fancy eco-stuff wasn't for their resort and that they needed the superior ideas of Infinity to make *Boond-aburra* the success it could be.

Easy-peasy. Then why did he feel sick in his guts? Deception didn't sit well with him, nor being a fraud. But he wasn't a liar. He'd always been honest with Hannah about his intentions. And he'd never lied about his attraction to her, that was real too, but unfortunate. Despite that desire, he was grateful he hadn't done the deed with Hannah last night. Imagine the consequences, the emotional fallout. It would have made his untenable position even worse.

Jackson had lost focus and what he needed to expedite now was securing the deal over *Boondaburra* and trying to avoid Hannah hating him in the process.

Hannah woke and knew instantly Jackson was gone.

She faced the canvas wall of the tent and felt with her hand toward the other side of the bed to discover the sheets were cold.

Doing her best, she tried to ignore the sinking disappointment that hit her in the chest. She was the last person to know what to expect from men. She'd never had a relationship that lasted so how would she know? But she knew how she felt as a woman and waking up next to him, seeing his lips curl into a lazy smile, maybe an arm draped across her and holding her tight, would have been nice. Having a chat and a cup of tea in bed and watching the activity around them increase as the world awoke, would have been nice.

Perhaps that was the stuff of romance movies?

But what the heck was she thinking? Those were the activities of a boyfriend and girlfriend, together in a committed relationship. That wasn't what Hannah Wallace did, nor was it what she had with Jackson. Something shifted within and she couldn't identify the sensation.

These thoughts were stupid anyway. Jackson didn't owe her anything and nor she him. It was kind of weird, though, to kiss so passionately and caress bare skin and stand naked before each other to then move on and pretend it never happened.

Okay, that was a bit rich.

Usually, she was the one to sneak away in the early hours of the morning, the one to search for pieces of strewn clothing in the dark. But hey, this was different, they were spending the weekend together.

And Jackson was different, wasn't he?

Laying back in the spacious bed she heard the birds calling

and was reluctant to move. Rarely did she have the luxury. At home, Davey would be rushing around doing not only his own chores but hers too: covering reception, dealing with complaints, emptying bins, cleaning the communal kitchen… the list was endless. He'd be adept at it too, but a frisson of guilt twisted her gut. She should be helping, but she was always there. And this was research for the future. Hopefully Dad would step up.

One last stretch and she rose languorously. It was hard not to think about Jackson's body in front of her, his smooth skin, and taunt muscles. Remembering those kisses gave her goose bumps. Would they kiss again?

Hannah peeked her head out of the tent and saw children racing up and down the green area and parents scoffing into bowls of cereal on their covered decks and other people with boots on and walking poles at the ready.

Spying the empty water bottle–reusable of course–she realised how thirsty she was. Collecting it, she refilled and drank the entire contents. Dressing in simple shorts and T-shirt she headed for the lodge.

The blades of grass edging the path was still crisp with frost. The temperatures overnight must have dipped but there was no tell-tale sign of that now with the sun rising and creeping through the tall eucalypt trees.

While outside was slowly coming to life, inside the lodge was bustling. There was no fancy buffet for breakfast, of that she was grateful. What a waste of food and something she didn't imagine Rhonda and Fred would tolerate.

Unlike last night when the rooms had a dark and moody atmosphere, this morning the large drapes were pulled open letting the outside in and streaming the room with light. It still welcomed her with open arms.

Across the room Jackson sat with Rhonda and Fred. Fred spotted her and waved.

'Good morning, love. Did you sleep well?'

Before responding, she snatched a glance at Jackson who kept his head bowed. A knot entwined in her tummy.

'Like a log. Best sleep I've had in ages.'

He chuckled, and a glint entered his eyes. Fred slapped Jackson on the arm and said, 'Glad to hear it.'

Hannah wasn't always wonderful at nuances and picking up social cues, but she knew Fred was imitating a romantic night spent together. That was the plan, she wanted to say.

'Morning, Jackson.' She too placed a hand on his arm in greeting.

He flinched, recovered himself in a second, and raised his head to offer a tight smile. It was as if he'd slapped her.

'Again, we're going to offer you a selection of our breakfast menu. But coffee first?'

Hannah nodded and Fred took over making the arrangements with the staff.

HANNAH PLACED HER HANDS TO HER CHEEKS. 'THESE ARE luxurious.' She looked at each person in the group, suddenly unsure. 'They are, aren't they? Or am I out of touch?'

'Yeah, they are love. But within certain limitations. There are always going to be guests who only want the best and even this accommodation isn't good enough. But this is the top of our range.'

Jackson walked around the cabin looking into each cranny and opening doors. His lips moved and Hannah knew he was taking calculations and measurements in his head.

These cabins were set well back from the canvas tents, in the bush behind. They sat on the incline, on high stilts and seemed to mould into the rise. The one they toured was three levels–three levels! –but there were both one and two storey versions as well. This was a three-bedroom cabin, used mostly by families, Rhonda said. The master held best spot at the top, living amongst the tips of the trees. It had its own bathroom and was such a large room there was space for a chaise lounge chair and a beauty mirror with an additional chair.

Hannah held her breath. The middle level housed a compact kitchen and living area and the lower level, the remaining two bedrooms. There was carpet, and simple, but elegant furnishings in a muted shade of green. Pastels cushions, bedcovers and those prints often found in housing stores– the ones easy on the eye and pretty to look at but weren't pictures of anything distinctive.

Again, Hannah came back to the prints of wildlife idea. Wouldn't it be fabulous to have their own prints of the local area in each cabin? Whoa, she was getting ahead of herself. These were super fancy, and she could only imagine the cost of building such luxury.

Standing in the middle of what she would call the living area, she brought herself back to earth. It was luxury to her, but nothing was elaborate or over the top. It was beautiful but simple. That seemed to be the key. But then Fred opened the closed curtains to reveal a timber deck that again had you eating in the trees, and there sat a hot tub.

Her head swivelled pretty quick. 'Is that...?' She couldn't finish the sentence.

Rhonda laughed. 'Yes. Remember, this is our top accommodation. Trying to give the people who want it a fine experience.'

Hannah stared at the tub. 'But how do you sell the environmental slant when you have outdoor spas in this level of accommodation?'

'That's a great question. And we have the answer. It's all linked to our water system and its reusable grey water. Not safe to drink but we advise of that, but safe to use with bubbles.'

'And Rhonda, let's show Hannah the bathroom. One of the main features is the provision of shampoo and soap. You know how in rated hotels you will receive the plastic bottles of conditioner?'

Hannah nodded.

'One of our keys to conservation and reduced wastage is providing these,' and Fred opened the door and pointed to containers fixed to the wall. 'See these — these are refillable shower gel, shampoo, soap and conditioner. That way we don't use those nasty throw away plastic tubes, there's reduced waste and we refill from the top when necessary. Pretty clever, huh?'

Hannah agreed. They didn't provide any such extras. But she imagined this was something reasonably priced they could think about and definitely not the throwaway type.

She couldn't help the smile that crept across her face. 'You guys have thought of everything.'

Hannah looked across at Jackson. As if he felt her hard gaze, he moved away and didn't respond.

Cold. Civil. Polite. Stranger.

That's how he was acting today. As if she'd never rescued him from a blazing fire and kissed him along his collarbone and made him shiver. It was easy to call him a bastard. But that's what she'd expected anyway. Perhaps it was the romance of the location, but she'd forgotten her fundamental rule— always run before they do, or better, avoid getting close in the first place. Jackson had beaten her to that realisation and she'd let that happen. Stupid.

Hannah would not make the same mistake again.

'Okay, so we'll take you to the other cabins. They're all similarly furnished with less rooms and no tub. Smaller, of course, but still as beautiful.'

'Can I ask how much you charge for these cabins?' and Hannah waved her hands behind her indicating where they'd come.

Rhonda told her and Hannah blushed. Or maybe that was Jackson accidentally backing into her and their bodies connecting.

Hannah paused on the path. 'I want to see the simpler cabin.'

'Of course, love. We'll show you. So, you've seen the best, but for the more budget conscious, the cheapest accommodation we offer, is a similar version of these cabins but less elaborate,' Rhonda said and smiled. 'But as I've said the most popular choice is the canopy tent. People love them. The standard cabins are popular too. And when I say standard, I mean comfortable and always clean with electricity and their own amenities.'

Hannah couldn't stop glancing at Jackson. But she needed to stop. He was paying her zero attention and making few comments.

This place was huge. No getting around it and well above their scale. No denying it. But it was the possibility of options and that's why she was here. Plus, of course, the environmental initiatives they could also employ. However, it was obvious this was a serious business.

Boondaburra wasn't, but is this where she wanted to take it?

6 JULY 2002

I love Davey.

I love Hannah.

Robbie is angry with me. He says I should feel better now, less tired, that I don't care for the baby...

I am not sure I can do this anymore.

CHAPTER 23

*J*ackson was impressed. The Eco-Villa was a well-thought out, environmentally friendly, and a classy joint. It was hard to criticise. If he was pushed, he'd say it wasn't as luxurious as some of the developments they were involved in. But as the brochure promised, it did deliver, catering to families to singles to serious hikers. A one-stop-shop for this part of the world.

It didn't matter if he was impressed, though, none of it mattered. Infinity Developments wasn't an eco-warrior. In fact, it had no policy on the environment at all. He agreed that wasn't great, but not their demographic. And not his brief.

Throughout the day he'd been wracking his brain about what to do. Such wasted energy. There weren't options—only one, and that involved Robert, the weak link. Hannah's father was worn out, ready to give in and be released from the ongoing pressure and stress of running the bush resort, whereas Hannah was headstrong and determined to make it work. Robert was the key to success and to speak with him he had to head back to *Boondaburra*.

Soon.

Hannah cast yet another furtive glance at him again. Man, he was a prick and that wasn't his usual style. Jackson Kelly wasn't mean, but he was torn in two directions and regardless of his burning attraction to her, he couldn't lead her on. That was wrong and unfair.

God damnit.

Every time he looked at her, he imagined her naked. His desire wasn't dampening despite the shit situation he found himself in. He wished it would. Then he could get on with his job; the project that meant there could never be a Hannah and Jackson.

After touring the vast accommodation options, Rhonda and Fred surprised them with wine tasting at a local vineyard. The setting was idyllic and romantic and exactly what he didn't want right now. No denying the spot was glorious, and he'd love to send his mother for a small break. She could relax and rejuvenate in a place of sweeping valleys and short walks and fantastic food and wine.

Lucky they'd had a tour with the owner and operator of the winery and the sommelier and there'd been no time to be alone with Hannah.

Except for now.

Back at the villa, and to finish the day, they'd been sent along a walking track and told to stop when they reached a pool. The gurgling water rushed towards them as they walked. The sun had lost its heat, was slowing sinking to kiss the horizon and the temperature was pleasant.

More romantic conditions, the world was not helping him right now. Only twenty-four hours ago he might have reached for Hannah's hand, laughed softly into her ear, and smiled seductively at her.

Now, he turned off any such thoughts. The future made him sweat and he forced himself to remain focused.

Rhonda and Fred had left them to assist with dinner prep. They continued to be fully booked and all hands were needed on deck. The couple worked hard and Jackson admired them. To be sentimental about it, they'd had a dream and built it. And it worked. From an observer's point of view, business was booming with happy customers.

Hannah walked ahead with cicada song filling the silence between them. Instead of watching her petite and cute backside move as she walked, he stared at the ground. Miniature frogs occasionally hopped across the path. They were the smallest creatures he'd ever seen. Not knowing anything about wildlife he didn't know whether they were friend or foe? A friendly green frog or a nasty cane toad variety? Hannah would know, and he opened his mouth to ask, then shut it again.

In only a few short minutes they were walking beside a crystal-clear creek that flowed easily around tree stumps and mangroves. Before long they'd reached a picnic area that surrounded a larger pool in the creek bed. Hannah paused in front of him. He moved to stand next to her and realised she'd stopped in front of a picnic rug laid with a variety of snacks and lit by fire-safe camping lamps. Jackson had noticed the path they'd walked had low-set lights to guide the way. No risk of not finding their way back then.

"This is beautiful. They sure do have a great touch," Hannah mused, and Jackson winced at the whimsy in her words. She deserved to be here with a man that adored her and would feed her chocolate-dipped strawberries and pour her glasses of bubbly.

Focus.

He waved away the pesky mosquitos and jiggled his leg to shove off the march flies that tended to land on him. Only a few short months ago he would have probably squealed like a girl and danced a jig at the bugs.

'It's all about creating their brand and they do a fantastic job. Marketing is important.'

Hannah looked at him and he felt pierced by the barbed rays shooting from her eyes.

'I actually think they live it rather than it being a commercially trained advantage.'

'I agree, they do, but it's all designed for giving their customers the ultimate experience while they stay here. They don't rely upon one attraction to ensure a person's stay is ideal.'

Hannah sat on the rug and smoothed out the non-existent creases in her shorts. She picked up a cracker and took her time to lather it with cheese and add a slice of salami.

'You don't think this place is incredible and a destination that people will rave about? The fine accommodation, the walks, the food, the beauty…' Her voice drifted away.

'I think this place is phenomenal. They've done a fantastic job. It's definitely a destination.'

'You sound like a travel brochure.'

Jackson still stood and he moved to sit at the opposite edge of the blanket to Hannah with the food spread between them. Around them the sun was sinking and the sky filtering through the branches of the trees varied between bright orange and fading to muted pink and purple.

'I don't think what they do here suits your bush resort.'

'What?' Hannah's head jerked up.

'I don't think you can achieve what they've done.'

She continued to stare at him hard, one hand halfway to her mouth with a handful of grapes. 'Why?'

'Developing this sort of resort takes money. Everything environmentally-friendly and eco adds significant cost.'

She cut him off. 'But is a fundamentally better option for the environment, the world and everyone in it.'

Jackson sighed. 'Of course, that can't be denied. But when there isn't an excess of money available, the cost of this resort is prohibitive.'

'But that's where you come in, right? Infinity designs, drafts, arranges and makes it possible.'

'We can't do the impossible.'

'Well, that's where the government grants come in.'

Shit, she'd thought about this. He sighed.

'Those grants will help you build a desalination plant. Or install solar panelling. They will not go anywhere near assisting you build lodges with recycled timber and built to maximise cool air to avoid the need for air-conditioning which you'll be opposed to. Or canvas tents when the original variety are half the price. Or a lagoon pool. Or a day spa. Or…'

Hannah sat up straighter and held up her hand. 'Enough. Just so I'm clear, tell me exactly what you're saying.'

'Infinity will not be involved in making *Boondaburra* the next best eco-friendly resort. That is not what we do. We will take the cabins and make them luxurious and install an air-con unit in each with an en suite with modern conveniences and do so in the cheapest way possible and without any regard to the environment.'

What was wrong with him? He was saying too much. But it was true, and he felt sick saying those words out loud. He wouldn't say that they'd trample over the earth to get the prime spots for those same cabins and most likely not take any regard to the wildlife or the flora in its path.

Hannah was shaking her head. 'What are you doing here then?'

He couldn't look at her. 'The same as you. I am researching and wanted to know and understand possible options. But now I'm here I understand that this is not a development that I can endorse to my boss. Those weren't the terms.' He bent his head and studied his hands before stealing a glance at her. And immediately wished he hadn't. 'Isn't it time to give up? Your father is tired, Hannah. He's had enough. He wants to live a quieter life. If you keep going like you are, it will lead to your ruin and I don't know how bad things are, but maybe bankruptcy.'

'You know nothing about my father or our resort,' she hissed the words through a clenched jaw. 'Why can't this be something that your fancy company does? You've been rabbiting on about fads and the fashion of things and doing the right thing, developing to the market. Tell your boss there's a role for this sort of development and there's money in it.'

Jackson was shaking his head in refusal before she'd even finished speaking. 'It's all about money, you don't understand. I've told you that to build something like this would cost a fortune. Yes, Infinity takes the ordinary and makes it magnificent, but it's a business and its business is making a profit. If the outlay is greater than the return, it's a bad investment.'

'Jackson are you proud that you work for a company that has no regard to design that might improve the world but only design that achieves the best possible result for the least amount of money that improves their bottom line?'

The question obviously didn't require an answer. Hannah

stood, swiped the bottle of wine into her hand and stormed off.

∼

HANNAH SLAMMED THE PASSENGER DOOR WITH SUCH FORCE, Jackson thought it would fling off its hinges.

She stormed off, across the way to the reception of *Boondaburra* but then stopped, head down, turned and came back and stood at the rear of the four-wheel drive.

Jackson pushed the button for the boot to open and watched as she shuffled around for her gear, apparently desperate to be as far away from him as quickly as possible.

The journey from the Eco-Villa to the Gorge had been like travelling in an icebox. Silent and cold. Clearly, they were both as stubborn as the other as neither tried to thaw the chilly atmosphere.

It had been a long trip, but he had one last thing to do.

The glass sliding door opened and Rosie and Davey rushed onto the timber deck and down the stairs to the car, holding hands. Hannah dropped the bag she held and Davey embraced her and in return she squeezed him extra tight and held on for a long time. Rosie stepped forward shyly and after the slightest motion of agreement from Hannah, did the same.

Then Davey launched at Jackson. He understood Hannah's reaction when Davey was in his arms. It felt good, like home. And as always when Davey was around, he thought of his brother. He missed his sibling and couldn't wait to get home and see his family.

Not yet.

'Did you have a good time? Did you learn lots? Tell us,'

Davey danced up and down on his toes and Rosie matched his moves.

For the first time in the last twenty-four hours, Hannah's stance softened. Davey had that effect.

'You would have loved this place, Davey,' she said. 'They have these amazing tents that are super fancy and a creek that runs straight through the park. It was pretty and so green.'

'So pretty,' Davey repeated.

Hannah didn't move and Jackson remained at the rear of the vehicle. 'Have you two been hanging out together?' she asked, her voice lighter, gentle.

'Yes, lots,' Davey said. 'We are in love.'

Hannah must have had a moment of weakness at the gesture because she glanced at him, and they exchanged a smile. She quickly looked away, remembering he was the enemy. Habits were hard to break, he guessed. Davey and Rosie bridged the gap between where they stood and held hands again and swung their entwined fingers forward and back like a pendulum.

'That's fantastic, mate,' Jackson came forward and slapped him on the back. Davey kept grinning like the Cheshire Cat. He chanced a glance back at Hannah. Her lips were turned up imitating a smile that was lopsided and forced. She was frozen and unsure and stood watching her brother.

It made him remember one of their previous conversations. She'd cited Davey as one of the reasons she could never leave. Davey, and her father, needed her. Hannah's reaction, he could tell, was one of seeing a future she thought was set in place, slipping away. Jackson looked down at the ground, away, up into the trees, as his stomach twisted into knots. Add to her feelings about the weekend, and he knew she'd be feeling frail, knocked about and uncertain.

His chest tightened, and he shuffled his feet to relieve the sensation. He hated that he'd contributed to whatever she was feeling. Shame washed over him and worse, he knew his mother would be ashamed of him too.

Robert came out shortly after and broke up the scene. He kissed Hannah on the cheek and shook Jackson's hand. In contrast to Hannah, Robert's face was full of expectation. He kept scanning between them but stopped once he picked up the vibe. They were metres apart, both standing stiffly with feet separated. Neither looked at the other. Robert placed his hands on his hips and observed the gravel under their feet too. It sure was an interesting patch of dirt.

No time to prevaricate. Moving to the rear of the vehicle, he went to the backseat and extracted an envelope from a pile of papers and folders.

'Robert. Infinity will not be able to assist with the sort of eco-resort that operates at the Villa. I have to say I was very impressed with what they're doing out there, it's incredible and a wonderful place to stay and it's doing well. The owners, Rhonda and Fred, were accommodating and so generous in sharing their knowledge. But that style of resort is a whole different level and not something that Infinity has entertained before. It's not what we specialise in.'

Robert didn't respond but continued to listen. Jackson didn't detect any aggression from him, but Jackson moved his feet and the gravel shuffled. Suddenly the heat was bearing down on his bare neck. He wished he'd retrieved his hat but instead rubbed the spot where the sun bit.

'I have instructions to proceed with an offer.' Jackson handed over the envelope. 'It's generous and won't be repeated, not by us, and most likely not by anyone else, either. It's a one-off…'

Robert held up the envelope and flapped it about. 'This is an offer to buy our resort?'

Jackson nodded. 'That's correct.'

'And if you purchase the resort, your intention is to develop it into a fancy place with improved accommodation and a lodge and a pool and all of that?'

Jackson nodded again. 'That's also correct.'

Hannah stepped forward but Robert held up his hand. 'Not now, Hannah.'

And not only to his surprise, but to her father's, she didn't say what she was clearly desperate to express. He'd cop it later, Jackson had no doubt.

He slapped at the mozzies biting his legs and waved his hand around his head to shoo the flies.

Speaking to the ground, Jackson continued. 'I got distracted by talk of eco-friendly resorts and saving the world. That is not something my company can offer.'

'What about the opposition you'll experience from the local government?'

Out of the corner of his eye, Hannah nodded her head vigorously in agreement.

'In my experience, money can solve any problem.' He winced; knowing he sounded like an absolute twat. Who had he turned into? Pushing that to the side, he had to push on with the negotiations.

'This investigation has taken too long. I'm getting pressure from my boss.'

Hannah snorted at this.

'So, we need an answer within twenty-four hours. If you don't accept, we'll move onto our next project. But we are committed to this one and want it to proceed. We can make this bush resort fantastic. I believe in it.'

Hannah snorted louder now. 'Dad, rip it up and throw it in his face. That's what he and that offer deserve. Don't read it.'

A pause, and Robert didn't respond.

She stepped forward. 'Here, give it to me. I'll do it.'

Robert held fast and spoke to him instead. 'I'll have a look at it and let you know.'

'What? No! Dad…'

Ignoring her, head down, Robert turned away and returned inside. Davey and Rosie gazed at each other oblivious to the war waging. His life had become a whole pile more complicated; when did that happen? But he knew. When he met Hannah Wallace and her high moral ground with her saving the world ethics and doing what's right. All those months ago he would never have guessed that his trip to the country would have seen him injured, on road journeys discovering new places and least of all, meeting a woman that stood her ground and was not intimidated, kept her heart under lock and key and one that had dazzled him, so much so, he'd lost focus.

A fly buzzed around Hannah's ear, and she didn't flinch. Her face was screwed up in fury and she breathed heavily, her chest heaving. He prepared himself for the vomit of vitriol, but she didn't speak, instead she raised her hand and slapped him hard on the cheek.

Shit.

He hadn't expected that. Her vicious tongue, yes, but ouch, his cheek stung. And worse, he probably deserved it. She turned and stormed away, again.

'Jackson.' Davey rushed to his side and placed his palm against his cheek that was no doubt pink. 'Are you okay? Hannah is mean.'

Davey was being kind to the man who was trying to take

away his home and livelihood. It was wrong and he didn't deserve the compassion. Jackson placed his own palm on top of the young man's while Rosie stood by in support.

'I'm okay, Davey. Hannah and I are disagreeing.' He pulled the two of them in close. 'Can you promise me something?'

They both nodded enthusiastically, happy for him to impart a secret. 'Can you promise to take care of one another and Hannah, too?'

Davey smiled like it was the easiest request in the world. 'Of course, Jackson. I'll love Rosie and look after Hannah.'

CHAPTER 24

*H*annah sat cross-legged on her single bed and fondled the necklace. It needed a good polish as the trinket was still tarnished and dirty. She rubbed it on her T-shirt but to no avail.

It was so tiny, the book only fit between her fingers and was but a speck in her palm. Not knowing anything about jewellery she wondered if it was an antique. It certainly wasn't like anything she'd seen before. Was it solid gold? Along with getting it cleaned she could have it valued. But the monetary worth of it was irrelevant to her. This necklace held sentimental value.

She traced her fingers along the loops in the chain. This same cord may have once adorned her mother's throat and tingles raced up her spine. Did her mother fondle it as it sat at the nape of her throat? Did she finger it when concentrating? Did she adore it?

A single tear escaped and rolled down Hannah's cheek. Regardless, she would treasure it forever. Undoing the clasp, she placed it around her neck and fastened it. Worried about ruining it she hadn't been wearing it, but now she did, she might never take it off. More importantly, would her father even acknowledge it?

With it now securely clipped in place, her fingers roamed the edge of the old velvet box. The letter was contained within and while desperate to read it once more, she was loathe to cause further ruin to the delicate paper. Unable to resist, she extracted the fragile sheaf.

...filled with despair at leaving you...

Reading those few words was enough to do her in but she couldn't let the water of her tears blur the words any further. Hannah fell back onto her fluffy pillow. There was no need to read the letter anyway, she'd memorised it and thought about its meaning a million times. With the letter safe, sobs formed and now fat tears rolled sideways down her cheeks causing tracks in her grimy face.

There had to be further evidence of her mother here at *Boondaburra*. She felt confirmation deep in her gut. Her mother would have done the same for Davey. Her thoughts went crazy at both the possibility of what it might be and where it was hidden.

Her mind was roaming every nook and cranny of the park when there was a light knock to her door.

'Hannah, can I come in?'

Her traitorous father was the last person she wanted to see right now, but he entered anyway after the obligatory and polite pause.

She sat up and as quickly as she could she flicked the necklace under her T-shirt collar and gently placed the letter and box behind her. God knows why she was protecting her father from further hurt. He didn't have the same agenda with his daughter.

Robert noticed her tears and motioned to place his thumb to one cheek and wipe them away. Hannah jerked back swiftly not allowing him anywhere near her. Robert bit down on the corner of one lip and swallowed so his Adam's Apple bobbed too many times. Good, let him be wounded. He was hurting her.

'I understand you're upset…'

She cut him off, 'Are you accepting the offer?'

In response he simply stared. That told her the answer, but she wouldn't accept it until he said the words.

'I'm thinking about it.'

'Bullshit, Dad. We've always been honest with each other. Tell me, are you going to take it?'

'Yes,' he said but lowered his eyes.

The coward.

Hannah jumped off the bed and paced the small bedroom, her fists clenched. Luckily, she wasn't violent otherwise she'd grab the vase on her nightstand and throw it against the wall or at Dad's head. She clenched her hands harder giving fuel to the thought. She'd loved to see the glass smash against the cheap gyprock wall and explode.

'How can you?' she screamed, more tears coming unbidden and moisture trickling out of her nose. She paused pacing and stood her ground. 'This is my home, Davey's home. How can you do this to us?'

Her father was calm to her storm. He addressed her floral bedspread, the one she'd had since she was eight years old and never changed. That was the bedcover her mother had chosen. 'I am thinking of you and me. I can't do it anymore. This place has been struggling for years. We barely make ends meet. It's pathetic to keep going. Sometimes it's important to admit defeat. The offer is generous. We can set ourselves up in a new life, a new business. There are endless opportunities.'

'I don't want a new life. I like the one I have. I'm committed not only to the resort but to the environment that we are protecting. And what about my study? I'm learning how to improve business and about marketing strategies and learning to understand more about the importance of politics. It'll all help. You haven't given me the chance to fix it.'

'It's not your problem to fix.'

'It's our home.' Her voice cracked, and she sat with a thump on the bed. 'I know! I'll buy it from you. You don't have to bear the burden or responsibility anymore. I understand you haven't enjoyed running this place in recent years. But I'm young and keen and I'll get a loan.' For the first time in the fog of despair a spark of hope sprang.

But her father was shaking his head. 'I can't let you do that. I could never put you in that position. How would you manage by yourself? You can't afford to employ staff. This place is us; we are *Boondaburra*...'

'Exactly!' Hannah fist-pumped the air.

'I don't mean that in a positive way. We don't pay ourselves a wage because there's nothing left over. Other people will not work for free.'

'Davey will help me.' She sat up taller.

'Davey wants to marry Rosie.'

'What? What do you mean? Davey can't marry Rosie, that's ridiculous. He lives here, with me, with us.' Her voice lowered.

'Well, he wants to and it's something we'll have to discuss. He's an adult. There isn't any reason he can't.'

Davey marry Rosie and potentially leave the bush resort?

The wind knocked right out of her and she struggled to breathe. This was as bad as her father selling their home to a major developer who was going to ruin it and turn it into modern accommodation.

But Davey?

She glanced across at her father and his face was filled with sorrow. Or fatigue. Every time she looked at her father, he seemed tired. Bone-weary tired, something a good night's sleep didn't help. His eyes were hooded with dark grey bruising shadows underneath. His hair was dishevelled, and he'd lost weight.

Hannah's body slumped. Her will was seeping away like the rainfall into the hard, dry ground. She couldn't give up.

'You still can't sell. I won't let you.'

'It'll take time to get used to the idea. You've never lived anywhere else. I understand it's unsettling.'

Hannah wanted to scream and beat her closed fists against his chest, but he continued.

'But it can be an exciting change. A new beginning. You've missed out on a lot of things being stuck out here in the middle of nowhere with your old man and brother. It's time for you to live a little. Have a think about the things you can do. I think once you've gotten used to the idea, you'll realise it's a wonderful opportunity for all of us.'

Her father's smile was weak and pathetic. He left the room and shut the door.

'I will never get used to the idea,' Hannah vowed to his departing back.

⌒

EVERYTHING WAS QUIET AROUND HER NOW. OUT HER WINDOW the world had turned dark and a full moon shone bright in the ink-black sky. That'd be right, she thought. A full moon! Blasted superstition. As usual the temperature had dipped with the loss of the sun and a gentle breeze entered through the open flyscreen.

Her tummy rumbled because she'd skipped dinner, ignoring Davey's pleas. She'd lain on the bed for hours, twiddling the necklace, thinking, crying, not wanting to move. Nor face up to reality. Everything had gone to shit.

After all the damage they'd caused, Infinity was still going to win, get what they wanted.

The forest was an amazing place and already, sharp, green shoots were sprouting up amongst the charred and darkened landscape. It looked so promising, but those shoots were mainly resilient ferns and low-lying green shrubs. The trees were desecrated and hollow stumps that gave an eerie feeling to the top of the Gorge. Like the place has lost its soul and its livelihood. What had once been welcoming and a sight to behold, now made her shudder. She should be thankful she guessed, the damage was limited and only to the top section of the Gorge near Gadds. The deep, lower walk with its lush rainforest and creeks had not been affected. That section was briefly shut to visitors, but soon the Big Walk would re-open too.

Once more she contemplated what moron lit a campfire when they were clearly forbidden? That information formed a large part of her welcome and introductory talk, plus signs were everywhere. You had to have complete disregard for the environment to plead ignorance. Surely, Hudson had understood, and acted recklessly and belligerently? He wasn't an idiot. Hitting the bed with her hand and causing dust mites to rise, she realised of course he'd been arrogant, he was an employee of Infinity Developments. Monsters, all of them…

The melodic sounds of the singing breeze and the nocturnal animals coming to life, familiar noises of her home, of the bush, drifted in from outside her open window. Closing her eyes, she listened, and felt calm for the first time in hours. Her heart rate slowed, and she breathed easier.

Until, she sat bolt upright, eyes wide open, alert.

Hudson had caused the fire and ensuing devastation. He was employed by Infinity, the same company destroying her family. At the time, her father had refused to report the incident, agitate for a prosecution. But what occurred was criminal. Hudson was culpable for the damage and the stupidity and contempt he and his company had shown. The ramifications were huge.

Unlike the calm of moments before, thoughts ricocheted around her head so fast she couldn't capture them. Could she really? Did she dare?

Hell yes, she did.

Turning on the light, it blinded her, and she squeezed her eyes shut for a moment and searched for her mobile phone. Hannah lifted the covers of the bed and looked under the rug, on the pile of clothes on the floor, but found it on her desk. Please let there be a couple of bars she prayed as she lifted her face to the screen. She was in luck. Rolleston or Injune Police Station? Injune, she decided, as it was bigger. Decision made she punched in the number and received a recorded message when it answered.

Argh! Twisting her wrist, she checked the time.

Idiot.

Both police stations were shut and were only manned half the time anyway. Living in the bush was a bloody nuisance sometimes. Okay, her adrenaline was spiking but there wasn't anything she could do until tomorrow. And should she be contacting Queensland Parks and Wildlife Service instead? QPWS would probably investigate jointly with the police but as she understood, it was the police who had to lay the charges. Yes, police first thing tomorrow. She Googled opening times and would be ready at 8.30am. Maybe she should drive in and report in person, they might take her more seriously then. If she made a trip of it, she could collect supplies on her return.

There were consequences for actions. Just like her father selling their business and home. And for Hudson lighting an illegal campfire. Hudson needed to accept his role in the devastating bushfire his actions had started. Not to mention the injuries suffered by Jackson and Monroe. Not that that was her motivation. If she had to be turfed out of her home because of them, they should face the consequences too.

CHAPTER 25

*J*ackson walked out of the Infinity headquarters
and felt… nothing. Not unbridled happiness or
satisfaction, nor a flicker of chest pain.

His heart was always his organ to behave unexpectedly,
and usually his symptoms flared at overexertion, but often also
at times of high emotion. Clearly, he was numb.

Most of his adult life, since working for Infinity certainly,
he'd craved promotion, reward, and recognition. There were
times when such thoughts consumed him lying awake at night
imagining running the company and making the high-level
decisions and importantly, raking in the big dollars. Today he'd
achieved this dream and he should be racing out to buy top
shelf champagne, but he wasn't.

He turned back and peered up at the building. One of
their finest that had won prestigious awards in architecture. A
modern design with curved steel and tinted windows with so
much glass his eyes blurred from the glare in the morning sun.
The structure was tall and narrow and a neutral grey-blue and

one that he'd always loved entering before. In fact, he recalled many times his breath had caught at his pure luck at working at the company and its headquarters being in one of the most superior buildings in Brisbane.

Had he always been deluded?

Jackson inhaled deeply and smelled, well, nothing. Or perhaps the slightest hint of smog and car exhaust. The main highway of the city was close by and he could hear the rumble of cars driving too fast and trucks braking and horns beeping. Closer by in the atrium of the building, talking and laughter and the rustle of paper reached him as people consumed their morning coffee with a muffin from the cafe. The specialty café provided by the firm. Only the best for their staff. There was the blast of noise from the overworked coffee machine and the tinkle of glasses and cutlery from within.

Noticeably, Jackson didn't need to wave his hand about his face because there were no flies or pesky bugs buzzing in his ears. The sun was hot, but not the suffocating heat of the outback. He was back wearing his corporate gear of long suit pants with the hard crease down each leg and collared business shirt. His feet were still adorned in his R.M Williams leather boots that carried the dust that he hadn't yet wiped away from his rural adventure.

You're an up-and-coming star of this firm and we welcome you to the position of partner. Those were words he'd longed to hear, but now the claps and cheers bellowed in his ears.

Cyril had given a brief speech about Jackson's rise to fame, outlining his career highlights. It was a story of rags to riches; of change from dungarees and work boots, to suits and leather shoes.

Jackson had worked damn hard, and it had paid off, but at

what cost? Reality was, he'd succeeded at the expense of the *Boondaburra Bush Resort* and Hannah's vehement opposition.

An unpleasant sensation swept through him thinking of her. What on earth was she going to do without the resort to manage and nurture and love? He couldn't think about it. If he did, the pains in his chest would start, he was sure.

He should be doing cartwheels, celebrating…he'd done it, achieved the promotion he dreamed of, instead he dissected his career. Never had he questioned his job, his goals or ambition. He had produced aesthetically beautiful work and had improved the lives of many people over the years. Pride and guilt mixed in together. He recognised semantics when he heard them, even spruiking from his own mind. He hadn't saved Hannah, but he'd saved his job. That dichotomy sat uncomfortably, like a rock on his chest.

He needed to shake it off and four days away from the office, his reward for promotion, was just what he needed.

He longed to see his mum and brothers and sisters, and that's where he was headed. That provided comfort. The normalcy of home and hearing Sienna's latest school results; academic and hardworking, she had a bright future. Or Georgia, who was the star member of her aerobics team and had recently performed at a competition. Jackson didn't know how her team had placed. And of course, Sam, who would no doubt have an amazing fact to share with him. He often became obsessed with something and had gone through several phases: stars and astronomy, the human body and once dinosaurs but that was when he was young. What young boy didn't love dinosaurs? Yep, he quickened his step wanting to feel the embrace of his mother. Seeing them would make everything better.

His mobile rang and he checked the screen. A number he

didn't recognise but the intelligence of the phone suggested it might be the *Outback Eco-Villa*. Odd. He couldn't imagine why they'd be ringing him.

'Hello, Jackson Kelly speaking.'

He listened to the reply on the other end and the familiar voice.

'I'm great, Fred. How are you? This is unexpected.' They exchanged polite pleasantries before getting to the purpose of Fred's call.

'Sorry, you're breaking up. Did you say you want me to come out and give you advice?'

Jackson paused under the shade of one of the many trees in the concrete jungle leading to the Infinity building. They'd been planted after the firm had conducted research on the value of green and clean air and how people were attracted to gardens in urban areas. It sure as hell wasn't because Cyril liked Jacaranda trees. Jackson knew he hated the purple petals that landed on the ground and had to be scraped off the pavers like gum.

He nodded, listening to Fred. 'Are you serious? I'd love to come out and advise on the development of a pool complex. Yeah, yeah, I get it. I understand completely, it has to fit within the structures and environment you've got with the most minimal of damage to what exists. I'm on a few days off so the timing is perfect but today I need to see my family. I might head up tomorrow if that suits your schedule.'

Jackson rang off. Now his heart was pumping blood through his arteries at its usual fast pace and his whole chest tightened. He'd just secured an elusive partnership position at one of the best development companies in the city and his pulse hadn't fluttered. But having been asked to consult on an exciting project out at the Villa and adrenalin was surging through his body. Viscerally, it tingled.

In amongst thoughts of what he might suggest to Fred and Rhonda about their eco-pool design, he wondered whether he should pick up French patisseries for his family or ingredients for a barbecue lunch. Damn it, he'd get both.

THE SMALL GROUP OF FOUR WALKED AMONGST THE LEAFY shrubs and bushes and beautifully lined gardens on what was currently a flattened terrace area at the eco-villa. If the design plans came to fruition, Fred and Rhonda hoped the beauty of the area would be enhanced with an oasis of glistening clear water and pools with natural shade from advanced trees. Jackson imagined it as a sanctuary of escape for the guests; a place of relaxation and rejuvenation that replicated a rain-forest or at least a flowing creek in the Australian bush. He pictured a pond nearby to the eco-swimming pool that housed wildlife and fish and snails and water lilies. It would be beautiful.

Yeah, he was getting carried away because he hadn't yet worked out the logistics of no chemicals and natural heating. These elements were key and at this point in time, outside of his knowledge base. He'd learn though, and advise.

The ideas were endless, and he bubbled with excitement.

Samuel trailed along behind him, literally like a lost puppy dog. He wasn't disruptive, noisy or intrusive and Jackson wondered why he'd never thought to have his brother tag along before. While Sam mightn't say much, Jackson knew he was listening and digesting the information. Most likely, later, he'd reveal his view of the design of the pool complex and add other complimentary ideas. Then he'd research environmentally safe practices to ensure it adhered to an eco-approach. He could be a fabulous sidekick of fresh ideas and at the very least, Jackson enjoyed his quiet intensity.

With a jolt of shock, Jackson realised he didn't know if Sam enjoyed the outdoors or not. At a glance, his brother seemed comfortable. Due to his own medical condition, Jackson worried that he'd set the scene and had forced his siblings to an indoors lifestyle. What a cruel twist of fate. He hoped his health hadn't prevented his brother and sisters from learning the joy of outdoor sport or activities.

After all this time, he still played catch up. Too late he thought, to suddenly became an expert cricketer or soccer player, but he'd adapted. And with further clarity, he realised more recently he enjoyed the natural world. Jackson shook his head; at the moment he wasn't sure who he was. Everything that was once certain, seemed topsy-turvy and upside down.

Plus, spending time with Sam gave his saint of a mother a break for a few days. Sam was a young man now and more independent than ever, but their mother still cared for him as if he was a child. Briefly, the worry of his future made Jackson pause. But those weren't issues to resolve today.

Ideas kept forming and Jackson couldn't keep up with his thoughts. He took copious photographs of the site and bounced around ideas with Fred and Rhonda who were as excited as he was. They had strong opinions, of course, having run a resort so committed to working with the natural environment for so long. He was beyond chuffed to be involved in the innovative stage. He wouldn't reveal that he hadn't designed a pool complex before because of course, there'd been many a swimming pool at Infinity modern unit complexes and ergonomic office spaces. All of them paled in comparison to the images of this place in his head.

In the middle of taking notes, it took him a moment to realise his phone was ringing. He finished writing his sentence and answered without looking at the caller ID.

Cyril's voice boomed down the line. The vitriol caused Jackson to pause and hold up a hand to the others indicating he needed a moment. Head bowed, he walked to the edge of the green area.

The torrent of abuse continued, and Jackson couldn't get a word in. Not that he'd have much to say if he could interrupt, what he heard was unbelievable.

The saga that was the *Boondaburra Bush Resort* continued. Only two days ago the firm had been celebrating, now he was being treated like the lowest level of imbecile and it was his fault that things were going pear-shaped, again. In his professional life, the earth was constantly shifting under his feet, and it made traction hard.

It had to be Hannah. Cyril had never met her. It was easy to underestimate someone you'd never spent time with, but Jackson knew deep down in his gut that she was responsible. And he wasn't disappointed, instead it provided him with a rush of relief. Excepting it was his mate in the firing line, but Hudson, had done the wrong thing.

He thought back to immediately after the fire. Robert had been understanding and reluctant to pursue any formal charges. He could have; the resort had been threatened and it may have been destroyed in the fire. But Robert was a calm man, much to Hannah's disgust.

After the passage of time, someone must have instigated the investigation.

Hannah.

A curl played at his lips, but he should be cursing her. Damn woman. She was like a pesky mosquito that kept buzzing in your ear and refused to be squashed.

Cyril screamed his final words and he had to hold the phone away from his ear. The message was clear. Fix it. If he didn't, again his job was in jeopardy. The persons who instigated the investigation had to retract the accusation, or the deal was off. Cyril was ordering him back to the resort. The pool of suspects was small, he agreed, but Robert would never place the sale at risk, would he? Jackson thought Hannah's father was a weak man, but he'd shown enormous courage in the face of animosity from Hannah to agree to the sale. Jackson couldn't accept that it was him, not after indicating his acceptance and being lured by the big dollars. It was only a matter of time until his signature was on the dotted line.

Shit.

He and Sam were about to make a trip to *Boondaburra*.

Jackson was only certain of one thing: he wouldn't be welcome by the young unruly and curly-haired fireball who was Hannah Wallace. Her vitriol might be as bad as his boss. He could handle Cyril, but could he handle Hannah?

CHAPTER 26

*H*annah would know the deep rumble of that car engine anywhere. The sound sent her body on high alert and her hands and feet tingled. God damn her body betraying her. Her feet should be stomping over to his fancy and ridiculous 4WD and kicking his tyres. That was the welcome he deserved.

What was Jackson Kelly doing back at the resort?

The quivers slowly evaporated, and dread settled like a rock in her tummy. He knew.

Did that mean her father knew?

It didn't matter anyways, soon enough everyone would know that Hudson was being charged with illegally lighting a campfire in a protected national park. No doubt the country grapevine would be running hot with the latest gossip.

The car skidded to a stop sending pebbles flying. Did he never learn?

Jackson slipped out of the car effortlessly, his ash-blonde hair blown back by the air conditioning vents blowing too hard in the heat, no doubt. His fringe sat in a strange wave across his forehead. As always, he was neatly dressed with his collared shirt and dress jeans. He looked darn fine, perfect and her heart lurched. Hannah watched, fixated.

He stood, stretching out after his long journey. His arms lifted above his head and the sinew in his forearms flexed and the muscles in his back filled his shirt. She did an intake of breath and blood rushed straight to her erogenous zones. Regardless of his behaviour, the man was damn hot. She doubted it was absence making her heart grow fonder and all that Hallmark Valentine's Day stuff, because she still wanted to kick him in the shins, but there was no denying he was one fine-strapping bloke. Still too slim though. Hannah took comfort in the criticism.

But then the passenger door slammed, and a young man sauntered around the front of the vehicle towards Jackson. They exchanged a few words and Jackson placed his hand on the boy's shoulder. It was intimate; they knew each other well. Jackson's face lit up at the interaction and his body was soft and not the often, tense stance.

Her body sagged too. Icicles dripped from her cold heart. She wiped her forearm across her brow. It was the heat. The morning sun was out in force, only to get hotter. Now mid-October and summer was upon them with daily temperatures rising to well in the high thirty degrees Celsius, keeping everyone except the rare grey-nomad and occasional backpacker from the area. No one else was brave enough to venture to the outback at this time of year.

Hannah realised she'd stopped still to gawp. Having cleaned the toilet block, she held the bucket of cleaning products in her hands and was on her way to the storeroom. Bending her head, she leaned as close as possible to her armpits hoping she didn't stink. Seemed okay but she hadn't washed her hands. Quickly discarding the gear, she turned her back away from Jackson and washed her hands thoroughly at the basin in the common area. At least the fragrant smell of the soap might disguise any lingering toilet smell.

The reception door opened and shut, and Hannah heard the distinct shuffle of Davey's feet across the timber decking. It followed quickly by another pair of shoes. Rosie. Those two were inseparable.

Hannah finished rinsing and stood at the basin, letting her hands drip dry. Davey hugged Jackson fiercely like a long-lost friend. She often wished she could act like him, with such little inhibition. His heart on his sleeve that kid. More icicles dripped away as Jackson embraced him just as tightly. The young boy with him stood back. Being released Davey went to lunge for him too, but the boy jumped back and flinched. Jackson held up his hands, gesturing warmly to Davey not to be alarmed and also reassuring the boy. Jackson pulled the boy closer and appeared to introduce them. Jackson coaxed him to shake hands and reluctantly, he did. Davey wasn't able to restrain himself though and held onto his arm too tightly and too closely. The boy didn't flinch this time but looked to Jackson for reassurance.

His brother! The boy had to be his brother. His brother on the spectrum which explained his social interactions and reluctance to embrace new people. She didn't blame him; she never enjoyed being over-friendly with people she didn't know.

Hannah continued to watch on as Davey re-introduced Rosie and Jackson kissed her on the cheek much to her delight as she burst into a fit of giggles. The young boy relaxed, and he smiled brightly at them for the first time.

They were all so lucky; this free and easy exchange they

shared. Hannah's feet were rooted to the spot, but she desperately wanted to race over to Jackson too, and draw him in close, smell his hair and feel his body against her. She remembered the heat of him with all her being.

But she wouldn't.

Stubborn wasn't her middle name for nothing. He didn't deserve it even if she wanted it. Some needs just couldn't be met.

As if his ears burned, he scrutinised his surroundings until his gaze landed on her and their eyes connected. The sun blazed in his and he squinted. Good, he was unable to see her properly. God knows what her expression was giving away.

Uh-oh, not for long. He said something to the trio and walked towards her. She stood tall, both hands in her back pockets. That way they were safe and wouldn't do anything to betray her, either romantic or mean.

She recovered herself in his few short steps. Her heart thudding with the rage building. 'You've got a nerve turning up here again.'

'Nice to see you too, glad to see you haven't changed.' Jackson paused. 'And soon, Infinity can turn up here whenever it likes.'

'Yeah, well, all thanks to you.'

He was so close she could hear his intake of breath and see the swell of his chest. His right eye twitched at the edges, was he nervous?

Good.

Words wanted to burst out of her mouth but she'd lost the ability to speak. She looked down, scuffed her feet and swallowed. Eventually, she found her voice, but she didn't like the sound of it when she spoke. 'What do you want?'

Jackson took a small step forward so that their bodies were

almost touching. She saw him take a breath, release it and open his mouth. Those lips were pink and moist and inviting. He shifted his gaze between her eyes and her own mouth where her tongue tried to lick the dryness away. She willed him to kiss her but knew if he did, she'd slap his cheek so hard she'd leave a mark. Bloody hell, she didn't know what she wanted.

'Jackson.' Her father's voice came from behind them.

Jackson's lids shut briefly, in relief or annoyance she couldn't tell, then he turned.

'Robert. Nice to see you.' He held out his hand to shake. Like gentlemen do, except neither of them was.

Trailing behind her father were the trio of young people, chatting and now seemingly firm friends.

'Hannah.' Jackson turned briefly, but still didn't meet her eye, 'Robert, this is my brother, Samuel.' He turned to the boy then and gestured for him to step forward. 'Sam, this is Robert, he owns the resort and his daughter, Hannah.'

Davey pushed in front of them and said, 'Hannah and Davey are brother and sister, and Rosie is my girlfriend. Hannah and Jackson are friends too.' His smile was so wide Hannah's heart ached.

Friends, funny word for their relationship. Did friends betray each other? But just because she was bitter and twisted at her young age, didn't mean she would inflict that upon Davey and least of all, Jackson's brother. From previous conversations she knew Jackson was protective of his brother and from the way Samuel looked at him, he clearly adored his older sibling, too. That was precious and she wouldn't ruin it. She wasn't a completely heartless bitch.

Jackson stepped forward. 'Davey, do you think you and Rosie can show Sam around? Show him any kangaroos that might be out or offer him a cold drink? I need to talk to your dad.'

Shit. It must be serious if he was sending them away. Surely, he wasn't here about the charges? Surely? But suddenly Hannah wasn't so confident. Dad glanced in her direction, but she avoided his gaze.

The three young people wandered off and when out of earshot her father suggested they head to the deck and have a cold drink. Too civil for her liking, but she followed suit and kept her mouth shut. For the time being.

HANNAH SAT LIKE A TIMEBOMB WAITING FOR THE INEVITABLE explosion and sure enough it came and didn't take long.

Her father stood, seemed to keep his cool and paced only a short, few steps, before swivelling sharply, placing two flat palms on the table, and peering into her face before bellowing, 'What have you done?' She sat back at the shock of the volume, but she wouldn't cower. One day she'd come asunder from her actions, but today wasn't that day.

'Someone had to be held responsible for the devastation of our natural environment, *the Gorge*,' she emphasised the words, 'and our livelihood.'

Robert stood his ground over her. Hannah would not be intimidated. 'We agreed that we would take no action after the event. We talked about this.' Spittle formed at the corners of his lips and Hannah found it repulsive.

'Yes, we did talk about it, and you decided that you wouldn't take any action...'

He cut her off, 'No, we decided, together, as a team. As the team that has always run this place and operated on equal terms.'

Hannah's temples throbbed and she was sure her veins would burst. 'That's just it isn't it, Father, we have always been a team, excepting when you decided to make decisions about future ownership of our home, of our business and didn't include me or my wishes. So that's when you made it abundantly clear that we were no longer a team, and I think, um, how did you put it, I needed to think about my own future. Well, I did and decided that ignorance of the law and complete and utter stupidity should not go without punishment.'

She sat back at the conclusion of her soliloquy and caught her breath and held her hands that shook violently.

Jackson had remained quiet until now. 'Okay, I'm sorry that this is causing disagreement between you.' He cautiously ran his eyes over both of them. 'However, I'm sure you can appreciate that Infinity cannot proceed with the deal when the seller is pursuing legal action against the purchaser.'

'The action isn't against Infinity, it's against Hudson as an individual and it's not *Boondaburra* taking the charge. He's broken a law; it's a criminal offence and he'll be prosecuted by the state.' Hannah spoke in a sneering tone that assumed Jackson was stupid.

He responded in like. 'Oh, c'mon, Hannah you aren't stupid, please. Hudson was here on business and the incident occurred whilst he was performing his duties for Infinity. Of course, the company is implicated and moreover, it will assist him to vigorously defend the charges.'

Hannah stood up too quickly and the outdoor chair fell backwards with a clang.

'Are you kidding? He does something stupid, irresponsible

and your boss is going to bail him out? He should be charged and plead guilty and pay compensation for what he's done. That would be the proper and right thing to do.'

Jackson paused and hung his head. 'I have a message from the CEO of Infinity and it's twofold. The first is that the firm will be responsible for his legal representation and the charges will be fought by the most expensive and best counsel in this country. No expense will be spared.'

'The evidence is overwhelming. There's not a chance he can get out of this.' Her voice was soft now, the doubt creeping in.

Bastard. At least she detected sorrow in his eyes that drooped at the corners. She could read that expression. Hannah understood he was the messenger but still, selling your soul and all that.

He'd lost his spark too, because when he replied, his voice was lower, regretful and she had to crane forward to hear him. 'I can assure you that Infinity will take whatever steps it needs to have this matter thrown out, quashed, withdrawn, whatever the legal words are, and they will pay anything, and,' he paused and stared directly at her, 'anyone to do it.'

It was like he jabbed a sharp knife directly into her chest, the pain was so acute.

'What does this mean for the deal? You'll still deliver the contract?' Robert's mind was clearly on one issue only. Watching him her anger spiked again, at his patheticness.

Jackson shook his head. 'If the request for the matter to be investigated and subsequent criminal charges are not dropped, then the deal is off.'

Hannah was too scared to look at her father. He slammed his fist on the glass top table and one solitary crack appeared and traced its way across the circumference.

'Hannah, you need to fix this.' Her father's eyes pleaded with her.

'I can't,' she said but her voice was croaky, too dry. She needed a drink; she rose and went over to the refrigerator. Still facing the other direction, she cracked open the water bottle and chugged, taking longer than necessary. She turned, wandered back, faking nonchalance. 'When I lodged the complaint, they advised once it is investigated and filed by Queensland Police and the wildlife department, it no longer becomes a decision for me. It becomes their decision to prosecute based on the evidence. Clearly, like I've been saying, there's sufficient evidence to back up the claim and they're running with it.'

Her father's face cleared of scorn and anger, his eyes open and round, presenting as calm. That composure was more alarming to Hannah than his anger. That she could match.

'Just so I'm clear, Jackson. You confirm, do you, that if the prosecution proceeds and it appears as if it is, and Hudson is charged for these offences, Infinity will withdraw their offer and our deal is off even though we've verbally agreed to proceed?'

'Robert, your understanding is correct, and I guess, given what Hannah has said, you can take it as confirmation that our verbal contract is rescinded.'

CHAPTER 27

*J*ackson wanted to puke. Yes, he was doing as instructed; yes, he was the messenger but the rift this was causing between Hannah and her father was unforgiveable. The actions of Infinity were unforgivable; using their power and influence to pay their way out of this mess.

Robert had stormed away, slamming the door. Hannah sat seated with her head down. Davey and Sam stomped back up the short set of stairs.

But Jackson had his own problems.

He was unemployed. It made him break out in a sweat. But he'd hold it together until he was alone, then well, who knew.

'It's too far to travel back tonight. Is it okay if Sam and I stay the night?'

Hannah looked up at him then and their worlds collided with both wills seemingly broken.

'Of course. Should I charge it to the account we hold?'

Jackson was quick to shake his head. 'No, I'll pay for this one.' He rose as the boys arrived. They bounced on their feet and talked over one another.

'Jackson, I saw kangaroos. And there were lizards…'

Davey interjected, 'Goannas.'

'Yeah, that's right, goannas and they were really long. Plus there's a lookout and Davey took me up there and we could see the creek. Can I run down to the creek?'

'Great, mate,' and Jackson slapped him on the back. 'It's beautiful, isn't it? Let's get ourselves a cabin and get our gear from the car and then we'll meet Davey at the creek. How does that sound?'

The boys nodded and grinned. When Jackson looked around, Hannah was gone.

In the end, Davey checked them in and escorted them to a cabin with en suite. To Sam the whole place was incredible: a cabin in the bush with bunk beds, an outdoor kitchen and wildlife wandering past your door. Being with his brother was refreshing and Jackson pulled in a deep sigh and tried to remember the simple and small things that mattered.

He changed into his swimmers too, but was not at all convinced that he'd take a dip. 'Hey, Davey, can you swim in this creek, the one that runs near the camp?'

'Oh, yeah, Jackson, of course.'

Of course. Well, it wasn't so long ago that he'd been in trouble for swimming in sacred waters. God forbid he made the same mistake again. But if Davey said it was okay…

Not convinced, Jackson picked up his laptop and diary and headed out behind the boys. Rosie was getting changed and would meet them there.

The boy raced ahead like they were firm friends. Sam didn't make friends easily, but Davey had such little inhibition it was easy to get swept away with his enthusiasm and kindness.

It was a narrow creek and he had to admit he hadn't noticed it before. It snaked along the edge of the resort to one side, hidden behind copses of tress and a slight decline. A memory flashed back of a half-naked woman reclining on a rock. Ah, he had seen it before but only from a distance and perhaps at that time he'd been distracted by the glimpses of the wild-haired raven.

The bush met the creek, there was no genteel and soft sand lining its edges. Boulders dotted up in the shallower parts of the water and Rosie perched on one of the larger ones while the boys splashed like they were at the local public pool.

'Oh, that's cold,' he said as he dipped his toes in.

'It's not cold!' Davey scolded. 'Hop in.'

Jackson shook his head and set himself up with a camping chair and rested his computer on his lap. At each bird chirping, or twig cracking, he turned, secretly hoping that Hannah would join them.

Ah, well, there was work to do anyway.

Ants crawled over his now-thonged feet, and he rubbed them viciously away. Flies swarmed but at least the mozzies weren't out yet. He was more comfortable in the outdoors now, but the bugs were still super-annoying.

Without hesitation, he shot off an email to Cyril advising of the fallout and then formalised his resignation. Could he rely on the fact his boss might be bluffing—surely Cyril wouldn't follow through on his ultimatum? But the more he mulled it over, Jackson realised Cyril would continue to engage those tactics whenever it suited him. He'd used threats of terminating his employment twice now. If he didn't sack him this time, there'd be other times, wouldn't there?

Job security was of utmost importance to Jackson, but he couldn't live like that because he needed the job; needed the money and the security it provided. And, ethics and morals were important, right? Hannah had taught him that. Plus, Infinity's reaction to the charges was off. Wouldn't it have been better PR to apologise for the reckless actions of Hudson and make a hefty donation to rejuvenating the forest, rather than defending the charges?

So, in the end he had no choice.

He hit send. Surprisingly, the sky didn't cave in, time didn't stop and more importantly, he didn't keel over with a heart attack. Jackson would be lying if he wasn't counting his savings in his head and working out the maths on how long it might last. His mother had always said he was overly generous with his family; so, a few cutbacks might be necessary. They'd understand. Plus, he knew if anyone missed out, it'd be him.

It was a strange feeling that settled over him then. Relief, he realised. A nervous knot dissolved in his stomach; it was temporary he understood. When the reality of no work on Monday morning hit, it would return with a vengeance.

Until then, he'd try to enjoy it. Shutting down his emails, he closed the lid of his laptop and used it as a bench to place his paper and pens. With a rough hand, he sketched the Eco-Villa pool complex of his dreams. No budget, no limitations. It would be the best environmentally friendly pool in the world. A boy could dream.

What he thought would be a rough sketch, turned into a few pages of finer tuning and then a meticulous colour-shaded design to scale. With his pencil poised an idea came to him. Could he do it?

Plucking out his phone, he rang Fred but damnit, there was no reception. He flung the phone onto the ground. He didn't want the idea to cool so he flipped open the laptop again and shot off an email to the Eco-Villa.

Jackson was unemployed. Fred and Rhonda had asked for his advice about their pool complex. Was it crazy to think they might employ him to design, and project manage its build? The more he thought about it—maybe it was, but he sure as hell was going to ask anyway. It'd be a bit of cash to tide him over.

But as the words appeared on the screen, something bigger, something grander and wild formed in his head.

THE SOUNDS OF THE OUTBACK WOKE HIM. IN HIS SLEEPY DREAM state it comforted him like a lullaby and his mind floated along with the trance-like rhythm. Jackson lay in bed with his eyes shut, listening until suddenly it stopped and he heard the usual morning cackle of hens and felt the bite of cool morning air upon his arms.

It was as if the Gorge spoke to him, and he knew without a doubt that he had to see it again. There was no time for the Big Walk, but he could do a shorter trail, the one most hikers chose. Yes, that's what he'd do today.

Sam snored quietly in the lower bunk bed and Jackson looked around him. Yeah, he still hated these cabins. Compared to the Eco-Villa, these were places you'd stay on a school camp with the absolute bare basics, not a creature comfort in sight. The green linoleum floor, black steel bedheads and rails, timber shelves plonked in the corner that looked like they'd fall over in a slight breeze. Yep, it was bad. Sorry Hannah, but true.

He pondered all nature of ideas until Sam stirred and they

dressed and headed to the office shop. Not having intended to stay, or lack of preparation really, they didn't have any food.

After their fill of a breakfast his mother would frown at, Jackson collected snacks and sparkling water for his walk and shoved them in his small daypack. No heavy hiking rucksacks today.

'Are you sure you'll be okay hanging around with Davey today?' he asked Sam for the tenth time. Deservedly, his brother rolled his eyes and answered positively.

'I'm going to follow him around and work at the resort like he does. We've got cleaning to do and manning of the shop and reception cover. It'll be hard work.'

Jackson smiled at the use of the lingo he'd picked up and slung his arm across the boy's shoulders, pulling him close. The best cuddle he'd get.

He approached Robert. 'Are you sure it's okay leaving Sam here with you?'

Robert looked up from his seat behind the desk in the office. A pile of paperwork lay in front of him, untouched.

'Yes, of course,' but his shoulders were hunched, and his posture sagged. A man defeated. Had he done this? Had Infinity? But he knew that wasn't the case. The deal falling through was his last stroke of bad luck. This was long-term exhaustion and a man with the world on his shoulders. Did Hannah see it and realise? Where was she anyway?

Usually, you couldn't walk two metres in this place without colliding with her. Oddly, he hadn't seen her since yesterday.

Davey and Sam were collecting buckets and trollies and he left them to their work. Jackson decided he was walking from the bush resort even though he'd since learned that you could drive to the entrance of the Gorge. He thought back to that day when Hannah had insisted they walk from the reception of the resort to the track. Right from the beginning she'd been trying to teach them a lesson.

Today he chose to walk.

WARD'S CANYON WAS ONE SIDE TRACK THEY HADN'T EXPLORED last time. He honestly couldn't remember why, perhaps they were saving it for the return journey that never happened.

To reach the canyon was almost six kilometres, a good solid walk, and with the return journey, a respectable day's trek. Of course, it was steamy, hot and humid, nothing like he'd experienced back in June. There was a reason the Gorge was not a popular hiking destination in the Australian summer. But hey, there were still a handful of people walking the track. Mostly, grey nomads for whom time didn't exist or young people, well, probably the same, who had nothing better to do and didn't care about the stinking hot summer in Outback Queensland.

But walking the short path off the main gorge track was like entering another world of diverse flora. The temperature dipped and the sweat making his shirt wet, cooled against his skin. There was nothing strenuous about this side path; it was a timber walkway until you reached the main section of the Canyon. There he put down his pack and continued along moist algae-covered and narrow rocks following the sound of trickling water.

Ferns were everywhere, clinging to tree branches, along the moist ground and sprouting from the most inconceivable of spots. Everything about Ward's Canyon was wet, a haven for the plant. Unlike the tinder-dry and now greying and heat-tinged Gorge, the Canyon provided lush bright green vegetation. Jackson followed the trail as far as it went and paused and listened, breathed in the clean air before walking back the way he came.

Upon reaching his pack, he sat and drank from his water bottle and enjoyed the serene environment. This random trip to Carnarvon Gorge had opened an entire new world to him, not only of a natural world he knew little about, but also of his own abilities and that he could be an outdoors person. He could match it with anyone his age, sure, he wasn't about to run a marathon, but if he wanted to, he could give it a go.

But in the beatific and cool environment sitting amongst the ferns, Jackson knew that he was strong, fit and healthy. Yes, he had a heart condition that was heavily managed and unfortunately, would require treatment in the future. But the future would also inevitably hold advanced technologies. Could he dream that one day his replacement valve surgery might be keyhole? It would be fabulous to avoid the saw cutting his ribcage apart to reach his heart, and the recovery thereafter.

Enough dwelling on that. He had other things to think about. The walk had been the perfect quiet environment to indulge in his idea and his mind was bursting.

Voices drifted towards him on his right. He wasn't alone. The gentle stomping of feet upon the timber path reached him and as they drew closer, the heavy breathing of those who'd walked a fair distance.

It was a small group of five women and leading them was Hannah. She was chatting to the women behind her and it sounded like information about the Canyon. He noticed the moment she spotted him because her words faltered, and she took a misstep. At least he still had an affect upon her.

He stayed where he was and watched as she pointed to the top ridge of the walk, advising them of where to go and to mind their step on the slippery rocks. The women wandered off and she made her way to him.

Laying down her pack, she extracted her water bottle and then carefully chose a rock to sit upon, and one not directly next to him. 'You still here?'

'You have such a way with words.'

'I don't have time for small talk, nor do I enjoy it. Why don't people say what they mean?'

Typical Hannah, never one to mince her words. 'Indeed. I agree and yes, I'm still here. I had the urge to come back and see the Gorge again.'

'And?'

If he could throttle Hannah Wallace, he would, she was so frustrating. 'I'm loving it more than the first time. Except it's bloody hot.'

She grinned from ear to ear and said, 'Do you have enough sparkling water?'

He laughed, 'Yes, Hannah, I have plenty and a few snacks too. Would you like to check?'

'I'm just ensuring you're okay.'

'You've done that right from the start even when you wanted nothing to do with me or my team.' He wasn't jesting now, and she stared at him, holding his gaze.

The women in her group wandered back one at a time, and Hannah and Jackson stopped talking. Hannah cared for them and their needs. Jackson admired the group of older women for having the fitness to undertake the main gorge walk at their age.

Hannah explained it was now simply a matter of traversing back in the direction they'd come. Obviously, they weren't walking any further today. She said they could take their time as a group but stick together within a reasonable distance. Like a dutiful tour guide she checked their water supplies too and ensured blisters were under control and no one was too hot.

Jackson loved watching her in action. This tough country woman with her sharp edges and tongue had the softest heart and truly cared for others. And the environment. He had to respect her for that. Her conviction was like nothing he'd ever seen. To be that passionate, it was both courageous and stubborn.

He hoped that his developing idea might become his passion. It certainly evoked that endless sense of excitement that bubbled away inside; thinking about it and a bolt of pleasure shot through his body.

He'd rested long enough and commenced to repack his bag and tidy up his rubbish before standing.

'You heading straight back to camp?' Hannah asked as she rose too.

'Yep.'

'We are too, you're welcome to walk with us.'

He wanted to rebuke with a joke, that she thought he was too hopeless to walk alone; that he'd come a cropper twisting his ankle or with a snakebite or some such thing, but he didn't. He was momentarily stunned, but willed himself to not read into the situation. She was doing her job, being the proper tour guide and responsible local.

Hannah didn't wait for his reply but rounded up the women and advised them she'd walk behind with her *friend*.

Jackson smiled and watched the group pass and head toward the main track. Hannah hung back and they walked in single file until reaching the main track once more, less than five hundred metres.

'Is your dad okay?' he asked when the group was well ahead.

She turned to look at him, as if checking his intention. 'Um, he's hardly speaking to me, but that's not unusual. He'll get over it. We've disagreed over *Boondaburra* a million times over the years. Perhaps we'll never agree.'

'He wants out, Hannah, can't you see that?'

She spiralled towards him before he could blink. 'Is this another sales pitch with you trying to rescue your deal? Because if it is, I'm not interested in hearing it.'

'Whoa, back up. There's no sales pitch. I'm telling you what I see. The man is exhausted with bearing the weight of this place.'

'Do you think that's how my mum felt?'

The change of direction caught him off guard. He expected Hannah to bite his head off for interfering, to yell and tell him to mind his own business, but not this. 'I don't know,' he replied honestly. 'Maybe. But they were much younger then, more enthusiastic, I'm sure. And the resort might have been doing better?'

Hannah shrugged and took off unexpectedly and he had to increase his pace to catch up.

'I don't know the answer, but I can see that Robert isn't enjoying himself anymore. You can see it, right?' He tried to engage her again.

'Yeah,' she said almost undiscernibly, but nodded too. 'I get now that the offer was his escape.' She held up her hand, 'I don't agree with it, but I've come to learn that his heart isn't in it anymore. I mean, he's not young and he's been doing this for a long time. I told him I'd run it, take responsibility...'

'And what did he say?'

'He said it was a ridiculous idea. As if he'd let his daughter take on the mountain of debt and a resort that wasn't making any money.'

'That's because he loves you.'

'Yes, but he's also raised me and Davey here. It's all we know and want and what he's trying to do now is snatch it away from us without our agreement.'

Jackson didn't miss the use of the royal "we". 'Well, I agree his heart is no longer in it, but it's his. The deal is off, there's no more persuasion coming from me. And there won't be from Infinity. They are done.'

'Why are you talking like you aren't part of them?'

Whether it was the question, or he simply wasn't paying attention, he tripped over a boulder rising out of the path and Hannah reached out to steady him. He liked the feel of her warm hand on him and he stared at it until she noticed and pulled away.

'I no longer work for Infinity Developments. I am officially unemployed.' The words didn't slide easily off his tongue, and something washed through him: disgust, disappointment, despair, he didn't know.

Hannah stopped again. At this rate, they'd never get back. 'Holy shit, Jackson. Did you lose your job because of me?'

'Well.' He stumbled on his words. 'Yes, the answer is yes. It's been a disaster from day one. In hindsight we should have walked away much earlier. But like a dog with a bone, we kept going. In the end, though, I resigned before I was sacked.'

'Shit! I'm really sorry. I'm such a bull at a gate sometimes, I know that.' She held up a flat palm again, admitting defeat. 'But honestly it was never my intention that you lose your job or that the deal would fall through because of my actions.'

'I know you didn't mean it, but actions do have consequences. You can't put up roadblocks preventing something without thinking there is going to be fallout.'

'I know, I know. And I'm supposed to be feeling smug and successful right now, but I actually don't. I hope you believe that. I feel sick when I look at Dad, but I'll confess, also a tiny bit pleased. I'm not about to be turfed out of my home, but to see his sadness, it kills me. And now, to be told you've lost your job. And while, again, I don't agree with the projects Infinity develops, I knew it was important to you and that you needed the job to help your family. So, on that level, I'm sorry.'

'You are complex, you know that, right? All that you say, they're opposing positions and you have to work out that you can't have both. But you're committed and passionate and those are your best qualities, even if you're a bit off sometimes.'

They were walking again, and she offered him a tight smile. It felt like a truce.

'But you resigned, wow. That's huge!'

CHAPTER 28

*H*annah's world tilted sideways.

'I've got this idea. Can I tell you about it?' Jackson said with a sparkle in his eyes, that wonderment she'd seen when showing him the beauty of the Gorge for the first time. The excitement of discovery.

Jackson talked nonstop the remainder of the walk; his passion was palpable. A few times Hannah answered a query from one of the walkers or tended to an issue, but as soon as she'd finished, Jackson launched back into his train of thought, as if they'd not been interrupted. And for once, Hannah didn't interject.

She was impressed. And proud of him, of the person standing next to her, of the person waving away the flies and bugs without complaint. Sweat saturated his shirt and he didn't flinch. Where the sun beat down on the pale skin of his neck he said nothing but applied further sunscreen. He had his own supplies and never ran out and carried a sensible pack and appropriate walking shoes. She was proud of his every action.

They were on the home stretch where the track narrowed, the bush dried and became sparser and the sun flickered through the treetops. She sang out to her group, 'Almost there, keep going!' They waved back in response and kept walking, a few holding their backs in support or wiping a handkerchief across their brows.

'Do you think I can help you redevelop *Boondaburra* into the eco-resort that you'd like it to be?' Jackson hadn't stopped talking. 'It would be excellent advertising and publicity for me and my new company. It's hard to attract clients if you haven't got any previous projects to show them. *Boondaburra* could be a fantastic example of the great work I can do, of my commitment to this sort of building and co-existence with nature. You could write a testimonial for me...we could take before and after photographs.'

'I'm sorry?' she said sure that she'd misheard him. He repeated the question.

Hannah formed her words. The last thing she wanted was to burst his bubble of excitement. 'Jackson, we have no money. We can't afford to hire you as part of your fabulous new eco-development company. You get that right? As much as I'd love to, we simply don't have the funds. If we win Lotto.' She shrugged.

She expected him to be crestfallen; to be faced with one of the first roadblocks in his grand plans might be depressing. But his smile didn't falter and his eyes kept their ebullience.

'What if I fund it?'

'What! Absolutely not. No.'

Jackson laughed. 'Okay, that's probably a good thing. I don't know how successful I'd be obtaining a loan when unemployed and with no collateral. Wishful thinking, I guess.'

They walked in silence for a few minutes. Up ahead, was

the short path across the creek signifying the welcome return to the Gorge entrance and the Information Centre. Her heart sank lower in her chest; she didn't want the walk to end, she wanted to chat with Jackson for hours more. Particularly when they hadn't argued for the last hour! Her lips curved into a smile. She was also sure it wouldn't last.

'I have been thinking about this a lot...'

'Yes, I can tell. You've worked out so many details.' She touched his arm in a gesture of solidarity, of trying to communicate as best as Hannah could, that he'd done great.

'Yeah, so many ideas and thoughts. But in seriousness, remember the grants that Susan talked about?'

He waited for Hannah to nod. She was conscious they were only a few steps away from the end.

'Well, I don't know anything about them or what they offer. But I think that's the first thing to investigate. What will they pay for and how much? We could then develop a plan, or a staged design to achieve the work that the grants will pay for and then, ideally, if business improves, continue to develop as permitted.'

All Hannah heard was the use of the word *we*. Jackson talked as if this was a joint project, a joint commitment. Her heart squeezed in her chest as if it was being held too tight. She stumbled over her own feet and her head felt light.

'Okay, we're here. Gee, that walk seemed like it took five minutes, not an hour,' he echoed, oblivious to her reaction. 'I understand you'll need to sort out your group. Do you want to meet at my cabin in half an hour and we can talk more?'

All Hannah could do was nod again.

~

Jackson had a quick shower and checked on Sam and Davey. They weren't hard to locate; Jackson followed the singing. As he turned the corner of the toilet block, Davey sang into the handle of a mop in the communal dining area and was encouraging Sam to join in on the chorus. Sam stood next to a small child in tears standing over a spilled drink. He leaned down to the child's level, trying to comfort him. The scene was a surprise to him on many levels. Sam being empathetic to someone else in distress and touching them! With Davey in the background singing his lungs out to a pretend microphone, Jackson couldn't help but chuckle. He wondered what his mother would make of the scene.

Clearly, there was little reason to worry, and he left the boys to it, saying he'd be in the cabin if they needed him.

Inside his room he rifled through his gear locating his paper and pens, hoping he'd have enough left to tinker with a few plans for the resort, when a soft knock landed on the screen door.

Hannah entered and the door banged shut behind her. She'd freshened up too, and her hair hung wet down her back in perfect waves. Putting down the stuff he held, he walked towards her and touched the tips of her tresses.

'The only time my hair is tamed, is when its wet,' she said, her voice husky.

Jackson moved from the more golden tips to the copper strands that fanned her face, a couple clinging to her skin and he moved them to the side. He smelled cherry and vanilla shampoo, mixed in with fresh soap. She wore a tank top and denim shorts and thongs, not her usual work boots.

Jackson placed his hand to her lower back and pulled her towards him. There was no resistance and she fell into his arms, their eyes never breaking contact. A hot tide of passion raged through him. Burning desire for her, her touch, her bare skin against his. Her breasts rested against his chest and moved as she breathed.

Hannah reached up and stroked his cheek and he was hypnotised. Every muscle in his body tensed as heat pulsed to his core, the unsated need building. With shut eyes she placed her hand to his neck and pulled him down and claimed his lips. He succumbed to a kiss that was deep, hot and demanding. His hand explored the soft lines of her waist, over her hips until he reached one breast. At the first touch of skin through her shirt, his body burned hotter. Hannah tugged at his clothes and in seconds there was a discarded pile on the floor.

'Lock the door.' Those were the last words she said for quite a while.

HAD SHE DONE IT AGAIN? FALLEN INTO OLD HABITS AND SLEPT with someone, well, not just anyone, with Jackson, and would he now up sticks and leave? Great sex but see ya later? Because if anyone was running, it would be her, but problem was, this wasn't like any other time.

Making love to Jackson had taken her to a new level of passion she'd not experienced before, dare she say it was the best sex she'd had, but Hannah was in trouble. In trouble because she'd enjoyed it too much. Had been driven wild by Jackson's touch, his kisses that had trailed a line over her body and felt their connection deep down inside of her. A part of her, that before now, had never come alive.

It was intimate and she crossed lines and released barriers she'd never let down before. She'd never let herself truly feel before; to enjoy the sensation, the sensuality of baring yourself fully to someone else, of being truly uninhibited and free. And caring desperately how they felt and whether they enjoyed it, too.

Was this what it was supposed to be like when you slept with someone…oh man, what? Someone you loved? She shivered as they lay on the double bed, naked atop the sheets. 'Can we have a play around with designs? I'm busting to see what a dream resort would look like, not restricted by money or possibilities, but an image of exactly how you'd like *Boondaburra* to look,' he said as his fingers danced down her bare back.

'That would be fun,' Hannah said, but forced the words out and they fell flat. She searched the cabin for her strewn clothes, the post-coital glow wearing off quickly.

'It's just dreaming and then we can be more serious later. Do you think you can speak to Susan and find out more about the grants?'

Hannah was quiet.

'Hey, what's wrong?' Jackson said and kept stroking. The sensation was both annoying and tantalising. Her fingers itched to shake off his touch, ironically what she needed was answers. Confusion reigned deep and for perhaps the first time ever, she needed to know where she stood. Desperately. What the heck was happening to her?

'I agree talking about the resort is super fun and exciting. But, what's this?' and she waved her hand across the bed indicating their naked bodies, their legs still entwined. 'I admit I'm the first one to avoid talking about serious stuff, but I can't discuss future plans for the resort, without, I guess, knowing what's going on.'

She barely dared to look into his eyes. Would it be now that he said, it had all been wonderful, but he was off and thanks very much? Hannah held her breath.

'What do you want it to be?'

'Not fair. When I ask the question that means I want answers not further questions.'

Jackson looked away and out the window and Hannah's stomach swooped.

'Look, I'll be honest. I don't know what this is. I'm unemployed, looking to start my own business—I've never worked for myself before—and that worries me. I have a few things on my mind.'

Hannah's stomach did loops.

'But, I don't know, Hannah. I like you. I've liked you since that first time you dumped me in the bar...'

She swatted him on the arm. 'I didn't dump you! You chose to answer your phone over getting lucky with me.'

'It was my mother!'

'I know that now and do not begrudge you from answering given how important your mother is to you. At the time it looked like perfect excuse material.' She lowered her voice. 'I would do the same if I still had my mum.' A knife dug into her heart.

He smiled. 'You know I reckon it would have ruined everything if we'd slept together that night. No doubt it would have been great, but for the wrong reasons. Think of what we've achieved and learned about one another since then. We're different people.'

He likes me! Her heart sang.

'I'm going to be hanging around now that I've got this gig at the Eco-Resort...'

'Wait what?' He was throwing her curveballs.

He smashed his flat palm against his forehead. 'Oh, sorry. I forgot to tell you. That's right, the moment you entered my cabin, my brain turned to mush, and I forgot about it. I was distracted by you,' he said and again touched her loose strands of hair. 'But yes, Fred and Rhonda have agreed to let me design and project manage the development of their pool complex. It's an absolute scoop and I'm stoked. That'll be my first project under my new banner—whatever that banner is—and I can then use it in my advertising. It'll be all I've got!'

Hannah sat up. 'That's fantastic news. But you do realise the Eco-Villa is hours away, so you won't be exactly hanging around.'

'Seven hours is like running out to get milk, isn't it, to you country folk?'

'Fair play. Almost, a grocery run is a six-hour round trip. Not for the fainthearted.'

'When I'm not working at the Villa, I can stay here. With you.' The words hung in the air.

'Is that what you want? After what I've done, ruining your business deal, and causing you to lose your job. I seem to have a habit of wrecking things and especially acting before thinking.' She collected the sheet and covered her naked chest; she couldn't bear to be exposed at this moment.

'That is exactly what I love about you the most. You're feisty, opinionated, determined and oh so passionate about everything you do but especially the environment and making this place work. Those are incredible qualities and I admire them. You. It's courageous to stand up for issues you believe in, and hard. You aren't always the most popular person when you do and it's easy to give in when faced with opposition. Plus, you are incredibly loyal to your family and those you love. You and your dad have hit a rough patch, but you'll recover because you love each other. And Davey, well, you've been here for him his entire life putting your wishes on hold for him. That's gutsy.'

Hang on, did he say love?

But the other words caught up and Hannah was shaking her head. 'You're wrong. I'm not courageous or gutsy, I take the easy option. The comfortable option and only pursue issues I know about. And plus, I've never left the Gorge! There's nothing amazing about what I do.'

'You're wrong and hopefully you'll realise it one day. But until then, I want to get to know you and set up my new business with your help from what you're learning in your course. You could be my, like, what, I don't know, executive assistant?' He shrugged.

Hannah lifted the pillow and launched it at his head. 'In your dreams, I'm no secretary.'

'Ain't that the truth,' Jackson laughed. 'But while I treasure honesty, I can't say to you that we'll get married and live happily ever after. I'm not going to make promises I can't keep.'

Hannah's eyes pooled with tears, and they bubbled over and streamed down her cheeks. Blimey, she was crossing those boundary lines she worked so hard to maintain; at this rate they were tumbling down around her. But how could a girl not blubber, faced with that sentiment and the naked handsome guy in front of her?

Honesty was important, she agreed, but Hannah couldn't return the sentiments, not yet, and perhaps not ever. She'd see. The test was whether he hung around.

After having said so much, Jackson pulled her in close, squeezed tight and rubbed her back, up and down methodically. Now it was calming. It was the best thing he could have done and again, also the worst. So intimate, so familiar and too much. In response she stiffened as if his touch repulsed her when in fact it was the opposite.

The guy was pretty intuitive. 'You're getting twitchy and want to hightail it out of here. That's okay. I get it, I'm getting to know how you operate. How about we get dressed and sit like normal civilised people and get back to my dreams of turning this place into the most amazing and fancy bush resort ever.'

She nodded into his shoulder but was quick to retort. 'A bit less of the fancy, hey? But yes, let's do it.'

He released her so that they faced each other, and Hannah experienced all the emotions at once. Her heart raced, her adrenaline spiked, she was excited, she was scared and most of all, he was right, she wanted to run away, and fast. But then his lips touched hers and she closed her eyes and got swept away with the velvety warmth of them and the way he paused to kiss away the moisture from her cheeks and lingering on her lashes. Yes, she was totally in trouble and she didn't know what the hell she was going to do.

CHAPTER 29

'What's the time?' Hannah asked as she shrugged on her T-shirt.

''Bout five o'clock.' Jackson stood in his naked glory. She was momentarily distracted by his narrow, but defined chest and the muscles in his legs that led to…

'Did you say five?'

'Yep,' he said after checking his watch again.

'Shit. We've got a special group of grey nomads in, and I've agreed to hold an info night. I've gotta go.'

He pulled on his jeans. 'No problem. I'll come with you and bring my pens and paper and have a beer until you're finished. And then we can eat?'

Jackson was so relaxed. They'd had sex! She understood the act itself relaxed most people, but she wasn't most people. Her world was shifting and sending her off-kilter, but he took everything in his stride. He saw her staring with a blank face, no doubt. He'd think her a weirdo if she didn't snap out of it soon. Instead, he offered his lazy smile and wandered over, his chest still bare. Most of the time now, she didn't notice his scar. She placed flat palms to his skin and looked up at him, probably resembling a dreamy teenager. They didn't waste time on smiling, he leaned down and kissed her again, his lips covering hers and his hands on her bottom. They pulled apart naturally and he continued dressing. How many times would they kiss and her heart hammer out of her chest or a deep longing tug in her groin?

Leaving the cabin, Jackson reached for her hand but that was a step too far for her and she moved away to increase the gap between them. He didn't comment and they walked the remainder of the way in silence.

Davey and Sam stood behind the counter at the open-air bar chatting amiably with an elderly couple who sipped a red cocktail she didn't recognise. Hannah went to pour Jackson an icy cold beer straight from the tap, but Davey gently slapped her hand away and pushed Sam in front to take control.

Hannah turned to Jackson with wide eyes. Jackson smiled and happily accepted a pint of beer with not too much head. Davey slapped Sam on the back while Hannah embraced Davey around the shoulders and addressed them both. 'Thanks you guys! You're doing a brilliant job and I'm really appreciative of your help.' Having those two around had lessened her workload and she was grateful that Sam could keep Davey company too, someone his own age and with things in common. Boy, she hoped Sam liked music.

Sam asked if she'd like a drink, but she only accepted water in preparation for her talk.

∼

Jackson settled into one of the worn outdoor tables to the far right of the green area not wanting to steal any of the oldie's glory. They were an inquisitive bunch and before Hannah had finished her usual spiel, they were shouting plenty of questions.

He'd intended to get work done, but once Hannah started talking, he was entranced. She commanded the audience, answered their questions, crazy and otherwise, added additional information and in such a manner that everyone was captivated. This woman was not only smart, she was beautiful. That glorious head of curly hair was big and bold and framed her delicate face perfectly. But it had never been about looks with Hannah. Right from the beginning, he'd been drawn to her as a person: her quick wit, passion and staunch beliefs. The intrigue of her tough exterior but knowing, inside, she felt deeply. He understood now, led by her complexities, her past hurts but also her stubbornness and determination, it was an incredible combination.

In some ways Hannah reminded him of his mother. His mother had never been conventional so perhaps, unlike others, he didn't shy away from uniqueness. His mother had strong opinions and a level of self-confidence he rarely encountered. And despite always searching for love, was not scared of being alone.

Hannah smiled in response to a comment from a man in front, and her face lit up. Her hair glowed chestnut in the dusk light and her almond eyes were full of warmth.

Robert sat in a chair across the way and drank his own beer. Jackson shared his awe as Robert watched his daughter. He hoped Robert and Hannah could patch things up and see a future for the resort with his help. Occasionally, Robert's eyes flicked to the bar and Davey, and Jackson registered the same look. One of admiration and pride; Robert Wallace loved his kids.

Eventually, Jackson pulled his eyes away from Hannah and doodled on his sketch pad. Shapes formed with intertwining letters and then for some reason a footprint. Hannah had referred to visitors not leaving their human mark on the environment, behaving as if they'd never been on the trail and leaving nothing behind but a footprint. His mind buzzed with a name for his company. His thoughts rushed through footprints, leaves, wreaths, logos, symbols and his hand sped around the page in a number of scrawls. Hannah continued, but now he zeroed out.

Eventually she pulled up a chair beside him and took a large sip from a glass of white wine.

'That was fantastic. The group loved it, well done,' he said.

She beamed at him and then looked down at the table. 'What's this?'

'I got distracted listening to you talk about the environment. Images came to me. Is this ridiculous?' and he held up a rough leaf crown with one bare left foot in the middle. The words *Eco Footprint Developments* were scribbled across the top in a swirly script.

'Is this a name for your business?'

He nodded, waiting on her reaction.

'I love it. Imagine those leaves a shade of green with a nude-coloured footprint in the middle and that same colour matching the lettering?' she enthused staring at the paper with consideration.

'It was when you talked about visitors leaving nothing behind but their footprint that the idea came to me. And that is exactly the type of impact I'm trying to achieve–build amazing places but co-existing with the environment while nurturing it and reducing impact. Seems to fit, right?'

'Absolutely, it's brilliant. I could never have come up with that!'

'I've never run a business, what else do you think I need to do?'

See my accountant, he wrote on a growing list.

'We've covered this in my course. It teaches us about the business side of the environment, along with politics and lobbying and whatnot. Let me think.' Hannah rattled off ideas and Jackson furiously wrote them down.

'I have to complete an assignment on the operation of a business. A case study I think, but I can use you and these beginning steps as my example. And as I move through the process we can learn together and get feedback too.'

The boys arrived at the table with steaming plates of spaghetti. They both looked up in surprise, but Jackson spoke first. 'Did you make this, Sam?'

His brother nodded and grinned from ear to ear. Davey nudged him and Sam said, 'And Davey helped too.'

Hannah took her first mouthful and exclaimed, 'This is delicious. Did you make a plate for dad?'

'Of course,' Davey replied, and they both bowed and steered away.

'This is fabulous. I can't remember the last time I haven't had to run around, perform the talk, make dinner, and check guests and, well, do everything. I've had a real break today and it's been,' she paused, her voice a whisper, 'wonderful.'

Jackson pushed aside the papers and concentrated only on Hannah.

～

'I WANT TO STAY,' SAM SAID AND STAMPED HIS FOOT TO emphasise his point.

Jackson looked at Hannah and Hannah looked at him and the pause lingered.

'Mate, I have to work at the Eco-Villa and it's hours away. I can't stay here with you and I don't think you should stay without me. It's time to go home and see Mum, she misses you.'

'I want to stay here with Davey and work like he does. I'm really good, ask him.'

Hannah's heart ached. She turned to Jackson. 'This is a surprise, and we haven't had a chance to discuss it, and I don't know what your mum will think, but he is welcome to stay. He's been an enormous help and is such a good friend to Davey…'

Jackson soaked in the words. He continued to look at Sam who stared back with a pouty look of defiance. Mellow, but determined. Jackson turned to her and reached for her hand. 'Are you sure it's all right? You're not just saying that?'

'No, it's seriously A-okay with me.' She turned to address Sam. 'I'm being honest, Sam, you've been such a great help. However, if you stay, I'll feel bad about not paying you. But we can certainly offer room and board and we'll feed you well.'

Sam's face went from blank to ecstatic in a second. But Jackson held up his hand, 'First I have to speak to Mum. If she agrees, then well, I guess I'll see you back here in a week or so.'

Jackson walked away and pulled out his phone. The two boys danced on the spot and sang a few bars of *Staying Alive*. Davey was teaching Sam all sorts of things.

'I do need you both to help me out, right? No slacking off, okay.' Hannah didn't need the declaration because it was never Davey who slackened off, only ever their dad.

Within moments Jackson was back and smiling along with the rest of them. He wasn't even able to get the words out before the boys were screaming and had run off to celebrate.

Alone again, Jackson tugged on her waist and pulled her in close. No flinch this time, she was getting used to his constant caresses. He said over her shoulder, 'I have a feeling this is only going to get harder. He'll eventually have to go home.'

She pulled back abruptly. 'Oh my goodness, Jackson! I've had another fantastic idea. And perfect timing because we can talk to Susan about this too.'

'Go on, don't keep me in suspense,' he said before trailing kisses down her neck. 'I'm going to miss you like crazy next week. I'll be racing back here so fast…'

Hannah paused and straightened her neck that tingled from the featherlight touch of his lips. The blood rushed faster through her veins. Did he mean that? She guessed now he had to return because Sam was here. Would that be an excuse, or would he be dying to see her? Her mother had loved her, she said, and she'd left and not come back.

Jackson intervened, 'It's true.' He slapped another direct kiss on her lips, teasing her by retreating just as fast. 'Your idea?'

She relaxed and let her shoulders drop. 'We can see how hard both Davey and Sam have worked. Davey has always worked hard. I've only ever had to show him a task once or twice and then he's perfectly capable. And let's face it, nothing is difficult around here. There are issues with how people respond to him, but we deal with that on a need-to basis. And one of our problems is staff. There's three of us and we do everything and don't get paid.'

Jackson was nodding but clearly not following yet.

'I'm pretty sure there are government schemes that

subsidise the wages of disabled people. If we partnered with one of those schemes, we could hire people like Davey with Down Syndrome, for example, and be assisted with paying their wages and receive the help we need.'

Jackson reached around her middle and lifted her into the air. 'That's a fabulous idea! I know nothing about programs like that, but if it's possible, it would be an ethically wonderful thing to promote and would be a mutually satisfying business arrangement as well.' He placed her back to the ground and a swelling of emotion overtook her.

'Imagine, for example, that we're able to employ Sam and pay him and he could stay,' she gushed.

'Are you intending on moving my entire family to Carnarvon Gorge?'

She shrugged, 'It's a nice place to live.'

Susan pulled up in her vehicle and sang out hello as she approached. In a blur of pink, Rosie waved and rushed past in her hurry to see Davey. They caught a look and whispered, 'And Rosie as well?'

'That would be awesome,' Jackson concurred.

CHAPTER 30

*H*annah drank the remnants of her second cup of instant coffee and stretched her legs out under the desk in the office behind reception. The morning sun streamed through the cheap blinds giving the room a warm yellow glow. It teased her, too; her legs jiggled to be outside, to feel the sun's rays against her face. She'd even be prepared to clean the bins at this point; a job she'd delegated to the boys only half an hour ago.

Office work wasn't her forte, but she was determined, without the distraction of Jackson and his cheeky smile and long lithe legs and bare chest…oh, last night. She'd be lucky to concentrate all day. Muscles in her legs ached from being clamped around Jackson, her lips were swollen from kisses that had made her toes curl, her chin was specked with a beard rash and a light headache throbbed at her temples. Staying up most of the night and making love not once, but twice, and seeing the first glimmer of dawn approaching, might do that.

And in between the sex, there'd been sweet whisperings, making her crave him even more.

But now she needed to buckle down and commence their first grant application.

Problem was, it wasn't easy to focus. Jackson had been gone less than an hour and she either reminisced about his caress on her skin, and hot tongue, or wondered what he was up too. Had he reached the truck stop yet? Or the apple stall? She hoped his music blared to keep him awake for the drive.

In between her carnal thoughts, an internal tussle broke out, fear trying desperately to simmer to the surface and override her happiness. Would he return? But she squashed that proposition back down and refused to give it traction.

Hannah twiddled the fine chain of her mother's necklace as she gazed at the bouncing cursor on her screen. Who knew these applications were so detailed?

Yesterday's meeting with Susan had been a resounding success. You'd be hard pressed to find a more supportive local member. Quick as a whip, Susan had rattled off the appropriate grants, and the tips and tricks to being successful. Hannah's hand had ached from taking notes. Useless though, because now she couldn't read her own writing. But she'd found the Government website and the form, a good start.

A long day indoors beckoned.

After completing pages of information about their proposed program and its purpose, her eyes blurred at the screen of the PC.

Time for a break; she'd search for the additional information she needed: business and tax documents, title deed references and formal company operating names. Hannah was astounded so much financial data about viability and specifics was required and about exactly where the money would be applied, down to precise dollars and cents. The resort didn't have any money and needed help, wasn't that the point?

The documents were stored safely in the study, so she rose, stretched her arms high above her head, and headed to the loo first.

Washing her hands in the bathroom basin, Hannah noticed a pink toothbrush in the holder. Rosie. That had transpired yesterday, too. The developing relationship of Davey and Rosie. Hannah blushed for them both, these adults who had concerned parents talking about them as if they had no say in their own futures. She hoped they were doing the right thing. The relationship was moving fast, but Rosie and Davey were convinced they were in love. And weren't they allowed to try like the rest of us? If it didn't work out, well, would it be any worse than the fall-out of any other adult relationship? Emotionally it could be disastrous, but both families had agreed to let them try.

Susan was crestfallen at losing her only daughter but pleased it was to the safe hands of *Boondaburra*. Heat climbed Hannah's neck as the recollection of the sex talk Susan and Robert had forced upon Rosie and Davey. Necessary, yes, but seeing Dad's face turn beetroot-red had her hightailing out of the room real quick.

Before she'd died of embarrassment, it was agreed the young couple would move into a cabin together at the far reach of the property. Jackson had turned swiftly then and glared at her.

'You have a cabin?' he'd said. 'A real cabin with walls? You've never shown me,' he accused.

To be honest, she'd forgotten it existed. Last time she checked it was inhabitable with inch-thick dust and spider webs. Previously it had been the manager's home and after they left years ago, it hadn't been used since. A clean-up with minor repairs was required and until that was completed, the pair were bunking in the main house with them.

And Sam, as well.

After the meeting she and Jackson had agreed more cabins should be in their plans, particularly if they wished to get their scheme off the ground. Or perhaps a bigger boarding-style house? They hadn't quite worked out the details yet.

Argh, man, now she was thinking about Jackson and last night, again. Hannah squeezed her legs together blocking out the sensations and remembered the documents she needed. Her dad wasn't the best at record keeping, but usually he shoved every important piece of paper into one cabinet. Pulling open the bottom drawer she figured she'd work her way up. By the third drawer she had what she was looking for, slammed the filing cabinet shut with satisfaction and stepped back onto something on the floor.

A fluffy pink rabbit. Hannah picked it up. It was well-loved and scruffy and Rosie's special toy; perhaps she even slept with it. Walking to Davey's room she placed it safely on the bed to ensure it wasn't lost.

His room was a mess. His bed wasn't made, and books lay scattered on the floor along with discarded clothes. Out of habit she picked up the clothes and folded them on his bed next to the rabbit which lay on the pillow. She up righted the few paperback novels and placed a couple on his desk which was somewhat neater. The third book had thicker pages that sat open with a leather cover. It wasn't a novel and, intrigued, she turned it over. It was a notebook with a clasp. It was thick and bulky in her hands, and she opened it to find yellowing lined pages inside. The title page had a name written in cursive print. She leaned closer in the darkened room to read it. *Louisa Wallace.*

She dropped the book like it burned her hands and it landed on her left big toe.

'Ouch!' She bent down and retrieved it. Her heart hammered and nausea swirled in her tummy. She flipped the pages quickly, too quickly because she couldn't read them. She slowed her flicking and saw her mother's handwriting, the same expansive neat and sloping letters. Each page was filled with script. Hannah went back to the beginning of the book and clumsily opened the cover again. At the top of each page adorned a date. It was a diary!

Gripping tight to the book for dear life lest she lose it, she ran from the room, slammed open the back door and heaved in great big gulps of air. The relief was instant and she calmed. Lifting the book to her face, Hannah smelled the old leather and felt its coolness against her cheek and the old, worn grooves and tough exterior. Nausea rumbled in her tummy at the prospect of its contents and all thought of grant applications disappeared.

'No more arguments, okay, Dad?' Hannah addressed her father as she walked into the living area. Robert sat in his favourite reclining armchair and drank a cold beer straight from the can. His agreement might depend on his mood, but he acknowledged her with a simple nod.

She sat in the adjoining lounge and held up the diary. 'Have you seen this before?'

'A book?'

'Not just any book, but a diary, Mum's diary. It's not

complete and spans less than a year or so, but it's hers. I found it in Davey's room.'

'Davey's room, hey? Odd.' He held out his hand and Hannah passed it over. Turning it over from front to back, he didn't open it. 'I've never seen it before, Han.'

He hadn't said her nickname for a while. So, he'd forgiven her. She allowed herself to relax, grateful, because there was little fight left in her.

'Really? You've never seen this before? Never saw Mum writing in it?' Usually, such accusations directed at her father would be filled with venom. Not today, her tone more soft and conciliatory.

'No, really. I never knew your mother kept a diary and I haven't seen this before.' He handed it back and Hannah believed him.

She rubbed her eyes. Hours of crying had made them sore and puffy, and Robert noticed.

'Are you okay? What does it say?'

In the diary her mother had called her father, *Robbie*. There'd never been any mention of the name before, and no one ever called her father by that name.

'She called you Robbie.' It was a statement. And her father replied with a sort of lopsided smile, but his lips quivered.

'She was the only person to ever call me that.'

'Do you want to read it?' she asked and held it up again.

'I'm not sure, love. Is it that distressing?'

'Well, for me, yes, but I assume it wouldn't be a surprise to you. You realised, didn't you, that Mum was unwell?' Her large, open eyes rounded on him, and he squirmed in his seat.

Then he sighed like a worn-out old man. 'Are you talking about before she left?'

Hannah nodded.

'I knew something wasn't right and I tried to get her to see the doctor, but she refused. She said she was simply tired, but it didn't make any sense to me and day after day she wouldn't get out of bed. I was starting to lose it myself because back then I was the only one managing this place. Don't get me wrong, your mother did her share, but after you kids came along, that was her job and freed me up to manage this place. But after Davey, she couldn't handle caring for both of you and then I had to do that and my usual work. It was tough and no matter what I said or did, it didn't make any difference.'

'I think she was sick, Dad. I think today it might be called post-natal depression or something similar. Maybe it was something else, I'm guessing, but she was sad.' Hannah brushed fresh tears away. 'So sad and felt hopeless but she talks about being scared sometimes…'

'Scared?' Her father looked mortified.

'Yes, but not of you.'

He sat back and took another sip of beer. 'She may have been having thoughts about hurting Davey. It's hard to work out. Maybe hallucinations from lack of sleep. But she seemed frightened of what she might do to him and how that made her a bad a mother. Do you think that's why she left, really left, because she thought she might hurt her baby?'

'Gosh, Han,' Her father scraped his hand across his forehead and down his face. His skin sagged and he looked older. 'I don't know. All I know is that she left and didn't come back, and I never heard from her again.' Hannah stared at him hard even in the circumstances. What else did he know? The glower worked and he cracked. 'When I saw the bank account cleared out, I knew it was real and she'd gone for good.'

'She would have needed money…'

'Of course. I never begrudged her that, but it seemed final

to me. And no contact. I waited day after day in those first few weeks, thinking she was having a break like, and would come back fresher,' his voice cracked, 'but she never did. Then I started waiting on cards for birthdays and Christmas and they didn't arrive either. She well and truly disappeared.'

'Why didn't you search for her?'

'I thought about it. At the time I was flat out. Now the sole carer for a disabled baby and young girl, and owner and operator of the resort. Alone. Hannah, all alone out here. It was bloody tough. Each day I'd think about reaching out to someone to see if they'd seen her or heard from her, and at the end of each day, I came home and tended to you two and fell asleep exhausted. Sometimes I didn't sleep. Then, to be honest, the anger set in. I was so mad that I refused to find her. She abandoned us and if she didn't want to be here, well...' Her father gave a strange hiccup to disguise a sob, but Hannah let him go and didn't offer comfort. She wept too.

'She loved us. She says so.'

'Despite it all, I'm sure she did. We show love in different ways. And the truth of the matter, love, is that I blamed myself. I should have done more, helped more, listened more. Anything. I felt so guilty that I had driven her away, that I wasn't enough of a reason for her to stay.'

'Oh, Dad. It wasn't your fault. You didn't know how she felt, and she didn't seek your help. Or anyone's help. Hopefully she sought help afterwards and got better.' Hannah's heart shattered into a thousand tiny pieces. 'Why didn't she ever come back? Even later?' Hannah spoke through the tears falling freely now.

'I can't answer that, love. I don't know. It was probably wrong of me, but I never did try to find her after that. I just got on with it.'

'Do you think she's still out there somewhere?'

Robert shrugged. It was pathetic and small and insignificant.

Davey trailed in drinking a glass of milk. He looked from her to their father and back. 'Davey, you remember this?' and Hannah held up the diary.

'Uh, huh. It's Mum's.'

'Where did you get it?' she asked.

'I dunno. I've had it for years…'

Hannah broke down again. For years? All this time she'd wondered whether their mother loved them and why she left and the answers or some of them, were in Davey's bedroom, probably on his floor gathering dust? If she wasn't so upset, she'd be furious. 'Have you read it?'

He nodded, completely unperturbed about the whole thing but upset that she was crying. He came and sat on the arm of the lounge and patted her on the back. 'You okay?' he asked.

Hannah leaned in further and they snuggled. It wasn't his fault. He didn't know. In fact, it was her fault because she rarely talked to Davey about their mother as a measure of protection. In her head, she'd been the monster Louisa described herself as. The horrible mother who'd left her family within twelve months of the birth of the Down Syndrome baby but that wasn't true. She'd loved him from the first moment. It wasn't him that caused her to leave. It was her messed-up head that seemed to worsen throughout her pregnancy and further after the birth of her son. Davey was the innocent factor in the big mess. They all were.

Except her father blamed himself.

She blamed herself.

All those years of guilt and wondering…what a waste.

'She loved you, Davey,' Hannah said to him while they still cuddled.

With sudden clarify, she realised that she'd done the same to Davey as her father had done to her. Avoided the topic, refused to talk about their mother because it was too painful and of course, that had been the exact situation her mother had been in. If she'd talked about it to someone, anyone, would she still be here and be better?

Davey chuckled. 'I know, she was my mother. She went away but she loved me. And that meant Dad and you looked after me.' God, she wished she could view life so simply. To her, it seemed they all had some forgiving to do.

Hannah was completely spent and could murder her own beer. 'Let's have a drink,' she said and rose off the couch.

'I have a drink, silly,' Davey said and Hannah smiled. Davey never drank alcohol; said he didn't like the taste. She gestured to Dad and he nodded for another beer.

CHAPTER 31

*H*annah balanced up and down on her tiptoes as she surreptitiously stretched her neck, yet again, at a ridiculous angle to catch a view out of the reception glass doors. With each glance a thousand butterflies took flight in her tummy.

Jackson was due back any minute.

One week had morphed into two. He'd phoned and emailed but the days of separation were long.

Having left the Eco-Villa early this morning, and on her calculation, with a stop for fuel, coffee and the toilet, he'd be driving down the entrance to *Boondaburra* any second. A customer entered the shop whom she served with one ear peeled to the driveway.

Yes, we sell maps, they are $4.99, and whereabouts are you headed?

The small talk was killing her and how was her luck? In the heat of the December summer there were only a handful of guests. The large group of grey nomads had moved on and now a few new caravans had arrived. And the lovely lady from site number twelve chose exactly this moment to have a chat. It was probably a good thing and would prevent Hannah from carving out a path in the shop floor.

But then she heard it, the distinct rumble of a noisy jet-fuelled car that could only belong to one person. The needs of her customer disappeared as she shot out of the store, almost stumbling over her own feet. Jackson hadn't pulled to a stop when she appeared at his driver's door. Her beaming face greeted him as he alighted and jumped straight into her arms.

'You came back!' she said.

'Duh, of course, I came back.' He laughed, his head thrown back.

Davey and Sam arrived too, with Rosie trailing behind. Reluctantly Hannah released him, and he clasped hands with the boys, patted their backs, and kissed Rosie on the cheek.

Tears welled in Hannah's eyes and before anyone could spot the moisture gathering, she swatted them away. Much to her own disgust, she had an urgent need to be near him, touch him and soak up all that was Jackson. The others drifted away, and they were left staring at one another, their eyes zeroed in, intently. Then, she allowed the excitement to bubble through her; he was here!

Jackson offered his earth-shattering and dazzling smile that reached his eyes. For her, that smile caressed everywhere, into each fold of skin he'd previously kissed, across her curves, the soft moulds of her breasts, the inside of her thighs.

'Hey,' he said and pulled her in close. Did he long for her as much?

'Yes, I came back you silly bugger,' he said. 'I've been counting down the days like a lovesick teenager until I could see you again. I must confess, I'm relieved you're here to greet me. I wondered whether you'd have run... or be standing here with your hands on your hips demanding I return to the city and never talk of fancy bush resorts again. So, thank you.' He kissed her, soft and lush and inviting.

'I'm embarrassed to say I've missed you, and I can't believe I'm telling you that!' Hannah buried her head in his chest.

Jackson placed a fingertip to her chin and titled her face upwards. 'It means a lot to me to hear you say it. I'm happy to wait until you're ready. I know life is complicated at present, and that's okay. But you know what, Hannah, I'm not going anywhere, and I'll keep saying it until you believe me.' He cupped her cheek. 'There's something special between us, I can feel it and I know you can too. I can't wait to see where we go together, what we do. I can't bear the thought of leaving you.'

Hannah choked on her words but spat them out. 'I do, I do believe you and I want to spend time with you too. Plus, you need to hang around to fix the mess you've caused.' She teased him with a seductive smile, placing them back into familiar jesting territory.

He hesitated, appeared momentarily lost for words. 'I'm pretty good at fixing things.' He laughed once more, full and throaty, and they kissed again, this time longer and deeper and Hannah's insides came alive with desire.

Savouring the taste of him on her lips, she pulled back. 'Let's duck away for a minute before anyone notices.' She could feel her eyes sparkling and her nerve endings tingling at the anticipation.

He followed without question, and that pleased her more than she could express.

∽

'How did you go at the Villa?' Robert asked Jackson as they sat on the deck eating dinner that evening. Robert was at the head of the table, surrounded by his family and seemed to survey the scene with satisfaction. Was the extended group with Rosie and Sam and Jackson, the family he always longed for?

'Great. I have a couple of shots of progress so far.' He pulled out his phone and passed it around the table. 'I've learned a lot about environmentally friendly pools, that's for sure. But not only that,' he placed his hand on Hannah's knee, 'I'm seriously committed to this approach. Why would you build any other sort of pool? Crazy.' His beaming smile was returned by everyone present, his enthusiasm contagious.

'I knew I'd convert you,' Hannah joked.

'You've done more than that, I'm a complete devotee.'

Robert watched their exchange and glanced at his hand upon Hannah's leg.

'One of the positives of being at the Villa and alone,' he said to Hannah, 'was all the spare time. After I'd eaten three course meals each night with Fred and Rhonda,' he chuckled, 'there was so much time to plan. I have pages of notes and ideas for your resort.' Swivelling left to Robert, he said, 'I can't wait to hear what you think.'

Robert seemed lost to another time for a moment until he responded, 'You can show those to Hannah. She runs this place, it's about time we formalised the arrangement.'

'No, Dad. What?'

'It's time, love. I should have done it years ago. Allow me the glory of living here and on the property, but it's yours and Davey's. Do what you like with it, I hope it prospers, and I'm confident it will under your guidance. You're both so smart and enthusiastic. It'll be a ripper.'

Hannah opened and closed her mouth a few times.

Robert laughed. 'No need to say anything. You've said it yourself, I'm tired, worn out, I need a break, retirement sounds good. I had been dreaming of the beach but a tent up the back there, that'll do me just fine.'

'Don't be ridiculous,' Hannah scoffed. 'As if you're moving up there. This is your house.'

Robert shook his head and smiled. 'No, this house is now for you and Jackson. You don't want me hanging around. We'll get everyone sorted. I spoke to a few blokes at the pub the other night and they said they'd help out to fix up that cottage for Davey and Rosie and, if I offer enough beer, they'll help build something for that bonza idea of employing those other young people. Wouldn't that be grand?'

'Holy shit, Dad,' Hannah expressed, taking the words right out of Jackson's mouth. Her cutlery clanged against her china plate. 'That's incredible.'

'Holy shit, Dad,' Davey repeated.

Robert was on a roll. 'Yeah, they're coming this weekend so we'd better feed 'um some grub. You can arrange that huh?' He grinned.

'Um, sure. But are you certain about moving out?'

'No doubt.'

'I better start drafting plans for this other place, then. Do we call it a house or hostel, or employment quarters? Gosh, so much to think about,' Jackson offered. 'We can talk about that later, but the timing's perfect, isn't it, Hannah, because Susan's been in touch, hasn't she?'

'Yeah, she helped me with an application to this one particular scheme and we're waiting to hear back. Thank goodness she helped me, it's so much better than I could have prepared. But hopefully a reply won't take too long.'

'I want to work here at *Boondaburra*, too, I want to live here forever.'

The table went silent. Ready for argument, Sam held up his hand so everyone would listen. 'I know I have to speak to Mum, and I will, but I have a life, too. I do good work here and want to continue to contribute and meet people and help. I'm happy with board and living, I don't need much money.'

'You're a great help here, Sam, without a doubt. I know from my point of view, I'd love you to stay on. You could be one of our first paid employees under the scheme,' Hannah said, casting him a sidelong glance.

'I agree, you've been a fantastic addition to the team, lad,' Robert added.

As he looked at his brother, Jackson welled with emotion. Like Hannah worried for Davey, he'd always been concerned for Sam. Where would he go, what would his future look like? It was ironic; was there anything *Boondaburra* couldn't offer? He reached over and placed his hand on Sam's shoulder. 'That would be fantastic. How about we invite Mum out so she can see what goes on here? If that's okay, Robert and Hannah?'

Robert gestured to Hannah. 'Her call.'

'Of course, that'd be fantastic. I'd love to meet your family. Invite them up to spend Christmas. That's not far away.'

Everyone continued eating until Hannah piped up again. 'Actually, Sam, what would you say to being accommodated in these new premises we're building.' She placed her palm on her father's large, scaly hand. 'And, along with Davey and Rosie, be responsible for and in charge of the newbies as and when they arrive?'

Jackson offered Hannah a sly grin and then held his breath waiting for Sam's reaction. The kid didn't need words, because his face lit up, his smile extending across his already broad cheeks and his eyes glinted in the light. Davey raced around the table and man-hugged him from behind.

'You're staying. You're staying!' he chanted and then broke into the Pharrell Williams *Happy* lyrics. Everyone around the table sang along too.

CHAPTER 32

*W*eek before *Christmas*

The familiar rumble of a car engine echoed down the valley entrance. It was more evident as the park was empty for the holidays, everyone having returned home to their loved ones. It had to be Jackson's family.

Jackson splashed her with water. 'Excited?' he asked.

'Nervous.'

'Don't be. My mother will adore you.' He splashed her again.

Everyone, including her father, waded in the creek bordering the resort. It had been a dry and hot summer and the water level was low, but still cool and inviting. Davey lay tummy down on the pebbled bed, Rosie next to him as if they were joined at the hipbone. Those two never tired of their own company. Sam happily tagged along most of the time and was never left out. Hannah looked forward to employing other young people who could join in their exclusive group.

A flash of red appeared as the vehicle drove down the

long, dirt drive. She turned to Jackson. 'After all this time, have you not lectured your mother about her motor vehicle?'

He looked bashful. 'Well, that's my fault. Back before, you know my conversion to the greater good, I bought her that car. And now she loves it and won't entertain getting a new one.'

'Leave it with me, by the time she leaves *Boondaburra*, she'll be a convert too.'

The car didn't pull into the reception area but headed off track and directly towards the creek. Sam bounded out of the water, racing towards the car, shaking his dripping legs as he went.

A woman, who appeared much younger than her fifty years, hopped out of the car squealing and straight into her son's open arms. Then she proceeded to plaster his face with kisses until he ducked and dived out of her way. Two other women jumped out of the backseat and did the same; hugging and kissing their brother until he held up his hands in defeat.

Their mother's shirt was wet and plastered to her skin like glue. She laughed and did not care one iota about her blouse being saturated. Hannah took her time leaving the creek, letting her arms and legs dry naturally in the heat. Plus, Jackson strode ahead, and she didn't want to gate crash their reunion. She arrived at the group who chatted animatedly, and stood to the side, scuffing her toes in the gravel.

Jaclyn Kelly wasn't having any of that and as soon as she noticed Hannah, she pushed Jackson to the side and stepped towards her.

'So, this is the young lady who has stolen our Jackson's heart and is making him an ethical environmentalist.' She kissed her on the cheek and pulled her in for a soul-crushing hug. 'I don't know you yet, but I thank you. You helped our Jackson find his way.' She released Hannah, but leaned in close and whispered in her ear, 'Plus he adores you, so we do too.'

Hannah loved her use of the word *"our"*. It was intimate and caring without the slightest taint of ownership.

Jackson introduced his sisters, Sienna and Georgia. Despite different fathers, the children looked remarkably similar. Or it might be they their similar temperaments. The trio of women had blonde hair fairer than Jackson's and were slim, too. His mother's eyes were permanently crinkled from laughing and they sparkled like no others Hannah had seen. Jaclyn had an infectious and welcoming personality, and Hannah knew immediately why Jackson loved her so much.

Hannah was about to suggest she show them their accommodation when all three bustled around in the boot of the car and extracted their swimmers. Without any fanfare they disappeared behind the nearest tree and changed. Before Hannah could blink, they were in the creek mingling together and shrieking at the chilly gorge water. Robert and Jaclyn met and chatted comfortably.

Rosie was immediately attracted to the two beautiful young women and admired their hair and painted nails. 'So pretty,' she said.

As the afternoon headed towards dusk, Hannah snuck away to the house and made a picnic. On her return, she spread out a lavish feast and let everyone graze as they wished. The wine chilled at the edge of the creek.

Jaclyn came and sat beside her and munched on a grape. 'I'm so sorry to hear about your mum. So traumatic for all of you and for her, too, of course. If you'd ever like to talk about it, please let me know, I'm happy to listen.'

Hannah hadn't spoken about her mother to anyone, except her father, in her twenty-six years, and, of course, now

Jackson. Jaclyn discussed it as if the topic wasn't taboo. Something Hannah was slowly coming to terms with. But still, how would she struggle through the detail with someone she didn't know well?

Jaclyn patted her leg. 'Only if you want to, and after we've gotten to know each other better. But when you're ready and if you want, I have a few contacts and I might be able to help and see if you can find her.'

Hannah sat up straight, the food she'd eaten swirling in her tummy. 'What, do you think that's possible, after all these years?'

'I can't guarantee anything. Some people simply don't want to be found and others actually disappear, but if she sought help from organisations or hospitals, then we might be able to trace her. It's possible.'

'That's not something I'd considered. Of course, I wondered where she was, but I didn't think she might be traceable. Wow!'

'It's a lot to think about and only when you're ready. Until then I can't wait to get to know you better. And plus, thank you for taking care of our Sam. I can tell how much he loves it out here and how he's filled with purpose. I'm sure your mother was the same. You worry for your children and when they find themselves and have a passion and purpose, it's one of the happiest days of a parent's life.' Popping another grape into her mouth, she accepted Sam's hand to consider a bug he'd found at the creek bed.

Her mind swam with possibilities. Find her mother. It was difficult to comprehend and she was also worried about disappointment. All those years of heartache only to be further hurt if nothing eventuated. But, oh, even having the chance...

Hannah glanced at her father. He'd relaxed considerably

since announcing his retirement and had turned one of their canvas tents into his personal space. Hannah vowed they'd upgrade and make it special for him when they could. And she would. And if she was knocked back for this application, she'd keep applying until someone took her seriously and wanted to help out their humble bush resort and turn it into something great.

Because it would be great. Yes, she'd been sceptical but now she had nothing but confidence in what they could achieve, her and Jackson, together as a team. It may not happen overnight, but improvements would occur in time, and they'd attract a whole new class of clientele. Even to call them clientele, she smiled. Life was changing and she couldn't wait.

Jackson's mother laughed. It was a beautiful tinkling sound and she wondered if her mother's laugh sounded similar.

One thing she did know—she liked Jaclyn Kelly, even without her kind offer of help. She looked around at the motley crew cooling off on boulders and at the bank of the creek. Her father and Davey who she loved dearly and their new friends. Had she finally found a family? The thought gave her tingles and goosebumps erupted across her bare skin.

'Are you cold?' Jackson asked as he approached and plonked himself down with a larger than necessary splash.

'Your body isn't big enough to create such splash!' She wet him more. He grasped her hand and encouraged her to sit between his legs, with her back resting against him. 'Your mum offered to help find my mum.'

'I thought she might. I didn't ask her too, but it's sort of her line of work, well kind of.' He caressed her leg. 'Plus, that's the type of person she is.' Each stroke of her bare skin was like a hot iron straight to her core.

'Jackson,' the word was a whisper but enough for him to

lower his head until it rested on her shoulder. 'I love you,' and those words weren't a whisper. She said them loud and proud.

Jackson flipped her around to face him. 'Hannah Wallace, I love you too, since that first day I drove in here and you eyeballed me. I knew it was going to be one hell of an adventure and it has been.' And then he leaned in and kissed her.

EPILOGUE

hree years later

DAVEY STOOD AT THE HEAD OF THE MAKESHIFT RED CARPET and sang one of his favourite songs, a rendition of *Hallelujah*.

Hannah had been blubbering like a baby all day, and now this. There was no way she could hold it together and that darned painted-on makeup would go to waste. Opening her purse, she extracted a tissue. She had a few stuffed in there ready for later; no doubt she'd need them.

She blew her nose in a very unladylike fashion. As much as she tried, she couldn't be a lady, but today, admittedly she looked like one.

It was a special day. For everyone. Looking around made tears threaten harder and a lump formed in her throat, soon she'd be sobbing, again. Her outback home, *Boondaburra Bush Resort*. It was no longer a place she recognised, but simultaneously, a place she'd grown to love more, and she was the most surprised about that.

Some things would always be the same. The grass was never going to be verdant green, the heat and conditions were a daily battle, but the use of grey water, especially in the weeks building up to the wedding, had been helpful in creating a lush and inviting paradise. Now there were fewer crispy brown blades and the grass resembled a soft layer of carpet under foot. Yes, paradise. To her it had always been paradise, but she'd been biased, for too long.

Now, others thought it was a haven too, and not only because of the wedding.

The tealights along the edge of the path were new; they twinkled in the approaching dusk light creating a fairyland atmosphere. It was the week of their grand opening of the newly refurbished and recognised eco-resort, and the day of Davey and Rosie's wedding.

The crowd of friends and family were gathered in their common area, the green space connecting their shared facilities. Despite the renovations, the space had remained the same, picnic tables dotted throughout the wide, open space where the kangaroos roamed free.

Hannah had insisted that the tent and caravan sites remain. A contentious issue, Jackson had wanted a total commitment to their new direction. But she'd argued that the entire grey nomad market, which had always kept them afloat, would have less options to stay close to the Gorge. It was also her need to hang on tight to the past. Jackson knew that too.

But additionally, they were surrounded by glamping canopy tents, very different to the originals with their basic facilities. These were new, wide and glamorous open canvas tents with comfortable beds, mood lighting, cane furniture, their own en suite bathroom with porcelain tubs and luxury organic soap, and a spacious outdoor space. She'd have loved an open-air deck facing outside with none of the netting, but the harsh environment of the outback would have rendered that useless and unusable. Now the setup was similar to that they'd seen at the *Outback Eco-Villa* but there weren't any luxurious cabins in sight. The point of difference they'd opted for, and more environmentally friendly and affordable, was the canopy tents and they'd made that their specialty.

All heads in the crowd turned at the arrival of the bride but Davey did not lose his momentum. His words rang out loud and clear hitting Hannah square in the chest.

As promised, Robert's friends had carried out the necessary repairs to the cabin for Davey and Rosie. And they'd worked tirelessly to construct the new boarding house-style accommodation for the new workers. Davey and Rosie, with Sam, were officially appointed managers of that accommodation and the new staff. The boarding house, set well back from the main area of the resort was located next to their private cabin and was a grand structure made of recycled and locally sourced timber. Dad's friends had also tidied up a tent for him. Robert had been a stubborn old mule and refused any form of luxury but his home was comfortable and simple, and to be honest, it suited him. Hannah loved nothing more than seeing him sitting on his narrow and uncomplicated porch, sipping a coffee in the mornings, or a beer in the afternoons. More than that, she hadn't seen him this happy in years.

And those projects meant their successful grant monies could be funnelled into their new glamping tents and building their new café/restaurant and bar.

The crowd cheered as Rosie commenced her walk down the aisle and she lowered her head, her cheeks flushing pink with embarrassment. As the group quietened, Rosie only had eyes for Davey. Her mother, Susan, wore a beaming smile to match her colourful summer dress and walked with her daughter down the aisle. Robert looked flash in his suit with an open-necked collar and short sleeves. The dress code suited the climate and their environment, but if Davey and Rosie had insisted on formal wear, they all would have acquiesced. Anything for the couple whose relationship had blossomed. Rosie had taken to living at the resort better than Hannah could ever have imagined. Moving from town to country, even a country town, was not easy. Hannah had been nervous but she needn't have worried. It was all about Davey, and Rosie was happy wherever he was.

Also, they had an entire community of new friends with the workers living at the resort. The government scheme had ensured the park had developed and now employed six young disabled workers. Hannah planned for more. It had greatly reduced her workload; she couldn't remember the last time she emptied a bin.

Davey paused his singing, unable to continue as his bride continued her slow walk down the aisle. The silence was almost as powerful as his singing. Samuel stood to Davey's left, his best man. The two were firm friends and Hannah had grown to love him like another brother. Her shoulders shook as another sob threatened.

Where was Jaclyn? Hannah scanned the small group and found her, standing with her daughters, the trio watching with love and pride displayed on their faces, their gazes on Sam.

Perhaps Jaclyn felt the heat of Hannah's stare, and she turned and offered a wave with a slight smile. Hannah knew Jaclyn felt sorry for her. But she wasn't responsible, and she'd never blame her for delivering the crushing news.

As promised, Jaclyn had used her resources to find her mother. It hadn't been hard because she'd been hospitalised, and unwell as Hannah had suspected. It was a paper trail for sure, but with enough perseverance and time, it led to a conclusion. Closure for Hannah and Davey, an end to the sorry saga. As much as it was distressing to learn that their mother had died five years after she'd left them, at least they knew. Hannah felt ridiculous, mourning someone she'd barely known, but nonetheless, she'd taken the news like a knife to the chest. With answers came heartbreak. Her mother had continued to keep diaries and given the lack of next of kin, they'd been kept by a kind old nurse who'd cared for her. Hannah had them now, had read them from front to back and knew each painful word. There were happy memories in there, and much love, when her mother was feeling well, but mostly sadness and confusion touched the words. Whenever her mother had mentioned her family, including her beloved Robbie, there had been a sense of love. Endearment. Hannah took great comfort in the fact her mother had loved her, and would never have abandoned her if circumstances had been different.

But most of all, there was an underlying sadness that her mother had died alone. That would be harder to forget. And that is why, in the midst of her grief, Hannah had poured her heart and soul into creating a garden, a special place dedicated to her mother. They'd all pitched in: digging, planting, toiling and arranging and rearranging without a word of complaint when Hannah had asked. In the middle of the blooming wild native garden designed to last, was a bronze statue of a woman, wistful, yet happy. That is how she would remember her mother.

A hand slid into hers and she clasped it before turning to

face Jackson. The man who had hung around, who had loved her like he said he would, who had cared for her and nurtured her dreams and listened to her fears. And all the while fostering his own dreams, and making their shared environmentally-friendly vision for the park, a reality. Hannah had always admired a hard work ethic and Jackson had it tenfold. Perhaps they were more similar than she'd thought?

Not only had he project managed their own development, he'd opened and operated his own business: a development company specialising in eco-designs. Helped along with the finished pool complex at the Eco-Villa, he'd started slow and steady. The catch, of course, is that Jackson often had to leave the resort to work, but he always returned.

Her whole being lit up at having him next to her. He'd slunk back in the nick of time after being at a medical checkup in Brisbane. Her eyes questioned him and he nodded sombrely but curled his lips into a smile. She knew that was to reassure her. Jackson had to have his next open-heart surgery, soon, sooner than expected. The valve was deteriorating, but he was otherwise healthy and he'd pull through. They'd pull through together.

'You look different,' he whispered and Hannah play-punched him on his arm.

'It's called a dress. I do wear them you know,' she quipped in return, flashing him a cheeky grin.

He leaned down so only she could hear, 'You're stunning, it suits you.' Hannah's smile broadened and she fingered her necklace, the book trinket sitting at the nape of her throat.

Holding each other close, they turned as Rosie reached Davey and he embraced her long and hard. The celebrant touched their shoulders gently, reminding them that part would come later and the crowd tittered. But they need not worry, the formal part of the ceremony was very important to Davey, he'd agonised for hours over his personal vows and the promises he would make to his wife.

Hannah had always longed for more. For love. But she'd had it in abundance and had taken it for granted. Now, she had extra, an entire new family. All of the people she loved and who were important to her were here today, except her mother who was at rest, in peace. Hannah would always miss her.

Jackson leaned down again. 'What do you reckon, should we be next?' He tugged her arm towards the group assembled before the celebrant.

'What? No! Well, I don't mean no, I just mean, not today…' her words petered away as they arrived at the front and Davey gave Jackson a wink. Frantically she looked between the two and watched Davey and Rosie give her and Jackson the floor. The crowd erupted in cheers and Hannah searched for her father. He was there, behind her and offered a smile before Jackson clasped her hands in his and said, 'Let's do this.'

Hannah stepped into the arms of the man she loved. 'Yes, let's do this.'

ACKNOWLEDGMENTS

I have COVID-19 to thank for this book. For months my husband and I were training to hike the Milford Track in New Zealand. My husband had walked it multiple times before, but I wanted to experience it for an idea I had for a book. Months of training occurred and in February of 2020, we were almost set to depart. Except, the world had other plans. Our trip was cancelled as NZ closed its borders, like many countries did at the time.

We made a quick decision to divert our plans to Carnarvon Gorge in Outback Queensland. I had my doubts but as the story idea was one of nature versus modern development, it could still work. We left the kids behind in a blur of uncertainty but in the knowledge we weren't that far away (8 hours by car). Carnarvon Gorge turned out to be very special and the absolute perfect setting for the story that was developing in my head. It was such a wonderful thing to walk the track, gaze at its wonder and beauty and all the time taking notes, soaking up the atmosphere while forming my characters and the story in my head. So, thank you COVID-19 (for this one and only thing!)

And as always thanks to my writing tribe, my first readers, editors, cover designers and everyone else that has made this book possible. Special mention to Sue, Susan, Liana and Annie Seaton.

ABOUT THE AUTHOR

Leanne Lovegrove is a lawyer, wife and mother and a lover of romance and reading. Her law career created an addiction to coffee but provides countless story ideas. She is the author of four romance novels, now five, and three novellas. Leanne writes sweeping love stories with happily-ever-afters with strong female heroines and set in the beautiful landscape of Australia. She lives in Brisbane, Australia with her husband and three children.

To find out more about Leanne's books, you can find her here:

Web: www.leannelovegroveauthor.com
FaceBook: https://www.facebook.com/leanne.lovegrove.545/
Instagram: https://www.instagram.com/leannelovegroveauthor/
Bookbub: https://www.bookbub.com/profile/leanne-lovegrove

PRAISE FOR A GOOD LIFE

What reviewers are saying about *A Good Life:*

Lovegrove delivers another standout Australian romance
— Duffy the Writer, book reviewer

This was an amazing ride, amazing story and very creative throughout, very art oriented...loved the setting for the story, I bathed in a rural area of Australia, a little community where everyone helps out with each other, the dynamics and drama with characters I really enjoyed and kept me interested throughout, no way did I wonder at any point away from the story, the plot twists I loved, absolutely enjoyed reading the whole scenario, a bit sad near the ending but this story wouldn't be complete without it as the author weaves this as a well rounded balanced climax to the end. I feel I can't rave about this book enough, I'm overwhelmed by the exquisite talent of this author. Giving this a 5 plus star review/recommendation
— Pauline Reid book reviewer

I loved it! Such vivid images of the country side and the characters will stay with me. Great story too
— **Kate Hunter, Goodreads**

With a picturesque coastal feel as backdrop, A Good Life is a moving story about confronting fears, making amends, and forgiveness. It's about the most simplest of joys and loves, complicated by circumstances, missed opportunities, and the things left unsaid
— **aplace_inthesun, Instagram, book reviewer**

Wow! What a stunning story! A delightful surprise. Once I picked up A Good Life and began reading it, I was hooked! In fact, I had difficulty putting it down until turning the last page. And at that point my heart was bursting with such emotions and love for this story I was speechless. It is a stunning read and perfect on so many levels
— **Cindy L Spear, book reviewer**

ALSO BY LEANNE LOVEGROVE

NOVELS

Unexpected Delivery

mybook.to/unexpectedelivery

Illegal Love

mybook.to/illegallove

Keeper of the Light

mybook.to/KeeperoftheLight

A Good Life

mybook.to/AGoodLife

NOVELLAS

Escapades of a Personal Stylist

mybook.to/escapades

Love on the Sweeping Plains

mybook.to/SweepingPlains

ANTHOLOGIES

Love in a Sunburnt Land

Love in a Sunburnt Land Volume 2